Finch had been up since before dawn reading and was stuck on a melody he couldn't pin down. To refresh his mind, he stepped outside onto the ledge. High above the Meat Markets of Reshen and with the Malaang waking up, he relaxed in the sunrise
CALM
Chief Blackwood of the Reshen PD sits deep inside the Police Department Basement, his body overheating as he once again plugs himself into his army of droids spread across Reshen, exhaustion claiming both his human body and Synth consciousness.

// TALES FROM DOMINION CITY
THE NIGHTRUNNER CHRONICLES
WANDERLUST
JORDAN <XENO> MADERE
DOMINION UNIVERSE

Published by Coin the Realm, an imprint of Warner House Press LLC,
Albertville, Alabama USA

For more information, contact:

Warner House Press
1325 Lane Switch Road
Albertville, Alabama 35951
USA

Published 2022

DEDICATIONS

DOMINION UNIVERSE and every publication within
are dedicated to the past and present players
of the Dominion City RPG,
an incredibly creative community
whose characters and stories
pushed and inspired me to grow this universe
beyond anything I planned.
Here's to all the OGs!

THANK YOU in particular to players:
Stefan Wilhemson,
Nathaniel Blackwood,
and Varis Kane
whose PCs make mentions in WANDERLUST.

SPECIAL THANKS:
Jerugalo/Asher/ARCHIMEDES -
For being the beta tester of this book
and all-around godly Admin.

Kozollyon/Holloway - For helping grow and
police canon in all the best ways.

Ana and Fiona -
For all the support and patience, you are my heart.

Robert and Dave Warner -
For your professionalism, and for
elevating this book beyond what it
ever could have been without you.

For those who embrace the lore,
For those that make this real.
You are DOMINION UNIVERSE.

XENO

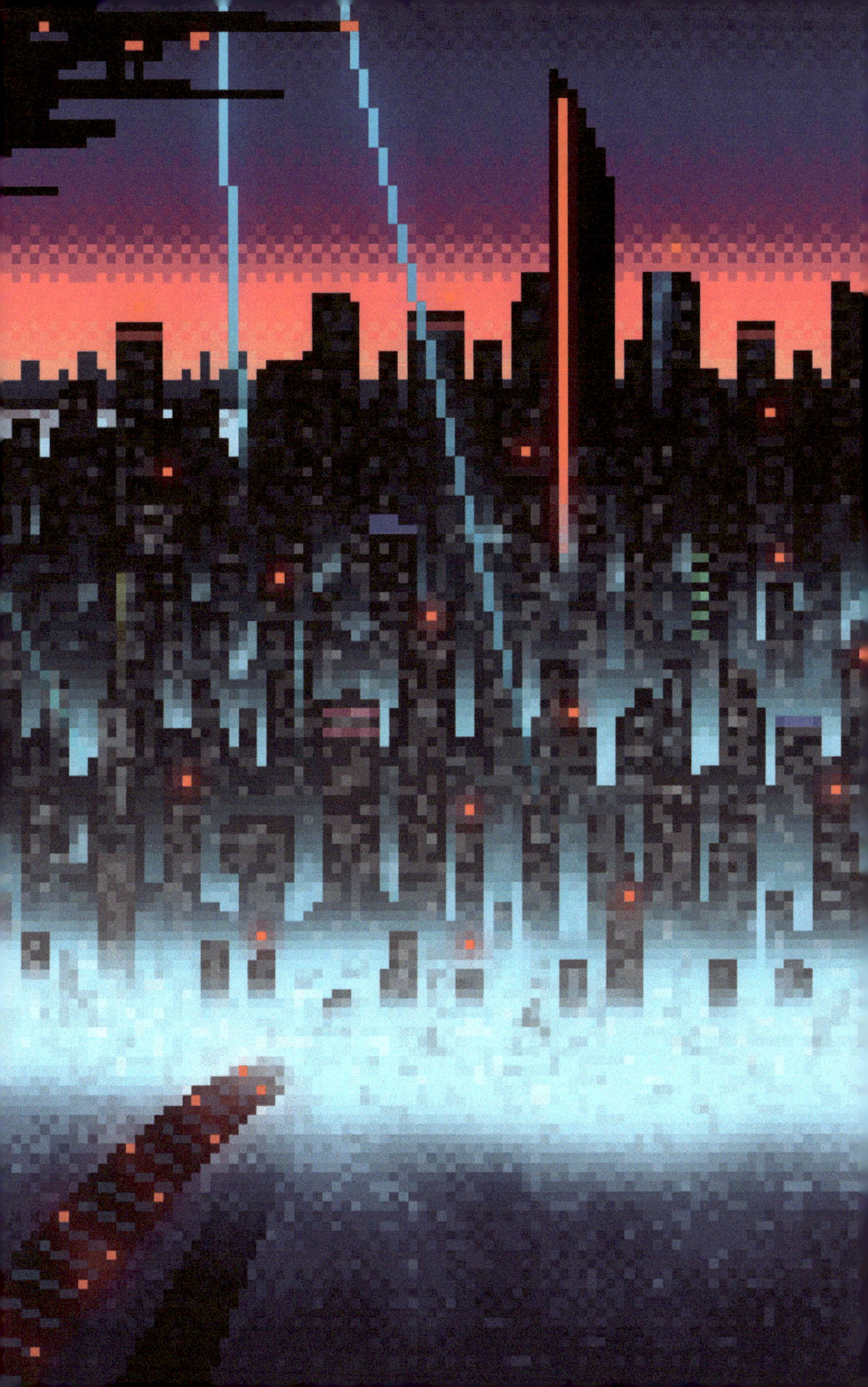

Dominion City

Citizen,

Welcome, welcome, to the last vestiges of human civilization (or so you've been told). Before you lies Dominion City, seven District Rings of overlapping dystopian genres. Each are under its own governance, but all suffer under the harsh, watchful gaze of The Dominion Corporation.

It is year 286 AF. The Fall of Man ravaged the world and life is a shitshow. Unless of course you're lucky enough to live inside the City Wall, in which case its still a shitshow, but at least you're not in the Wasteland.

Here inside the City you're a Registered Citizen... or you should be. You follow Protocol as laid down by the Corporation... don't you? And of course you respect and help maintain Dominion Systems and City Infrastructure, right? Because if you don't, we all know that Citizen Termination is the only logical outcome...

Enough propaganda. You live in the City of Seven Districts.

Let's dive in.

Once joined as the mighty Formir District, the Central Districts now exist in a state of disequilibrium. Quadro has been fully accepted as part of the Inner Districts, while Reshen is firmly a part of the Outer Districts. The classification of Electua is still very much uncertain, though all three chaotic Districts have become widely known as the Dark Rift.

// TALES FROM DOMINION CITY

THE NIGHTRUNNER CHRONICLES

WANDERLUST

CONTENTS

APPENDICES

PROLOGUE

[[E5: WEST MID-CITY]]
<Teradin Jurisdiction / Haven-4>

Within RealSpace, the grid materialized in a shimmering patchwork of encoded ripples. It lit up the dark and spread outward, like a drop in a pond, to the edges of the holo-table. The lines of the grid zoomed out, and finally reached a simulacrum of the circular Outer Wall of the city. From the center, thousands of digital fingers pushed upwards through the dense mesh. Holographic details in the geometry resolved in iterations, until the five NightRunners stood above a glowing and comprehensive replica of all seven ringed Districts of Dominion City.

Digi, Midi, Wander, Zef, and Zelly gawked in wild fascination at the electric blue city map and the level of digital detail manifesting before their eyes. They shared only a marginal awareness of how deep a Protocol Violation the map was.

"This...this is illegal." Digi was naively stating the obvious. She stood alone, as she usually did during their group meetings. Her delicate, synthetic face turned to the others . "Isn't it?"

{"I don't think I need to over-emphasize..."} The voice of Maybe, digitized and feminine, projected itself through the speakers of the console. {"...just how many Articles of Protocol were violated to obtain these live schematics."}

The Runners traded astonished glances, thrilled at the idea, though their eyes soon returned to the intricate map.

{"I ask that each of you keep your knowledge of it a secret; a resource only to be used during planning and never otherwise, for the security of the Glade."}

"It's a gift." Zelly's wide eyes peered at each of them, twinkling with the raw cyan reflections of their latest achievement. Though her stature was slightly shorter than the others, her spirit was something they couldn't help but admire. "It's something we've earned, but it's still a gift. It opens up the whole city for us, so we don't fuck this up. Got it?"

They each acknowledged in their own way; all but Zef, whose silence they'd come to expect. As usual, he wallowed in a sullen, contemplative daze.

"You got that, Zef?"

His sunken eyes, hidden behind the cover of a runnersuit hoodie, darted up to meet Zelly's. Wander studied him apprehensively.

"Yeah, I got it. No fucking with the map." He glared at Zelly, who glared right back at him, until Maybe's synthesized voice broke the tension between the two.

{"Moving on, NightRunners. Tonight, we'll be putting this new resource to work for us. Zef, you will remain here in Haven-4. You'll be our Runner's Eye, the first to learn the skill of Navigation."}

Zef's expression fell from lack of interest to mild disdain at the news that he would be stuck in Haven-4, while the others headed out into the night.

{"Wander..."} The majority of the map dimmed, all except the middle three Districts of Quadro, Electua, and Reshen, known collectively by Citizens as the Dark Rift. A glowing point emerged on the map surrounded by a pink circle. It covered an area of Quadro District known as the NeoLux. They all shared an unacknowledged burst of excitement at the idea of venturing not only into Quadro, but into the neon-soaked NeoLux. There, Running felt more like a videogame, rather than an insanely dangerous crime spree. {"Wander, you'll be doing our dirty work tonight."}

The holographic display zoomed until their paths to the target building were clear. It would involve a railway ride from West Mid-City to NeoLux Station, where the paths appeared to split into separate routes. Wander's distinct red color highlighted her own route. It led from the station, through the streets in a winding serpentine path, and up the side of a towering office building nestled within a dense patch of high-rises.

{"The Katsudo-Hoffman Center. On the 27th floor are the offices of a firm called RealmSquare Brokerage. A group that leverages and profits from the trade of bankrupt realmdwellers to the Dominion Science farms. Tonight, we'll be denying DCORP a sizable source of Citizen flesh for their human experimentation programs."}

The Runners nodded, their sly grins warming with anticipation. They were vague on the grander details of the Dominion Corporations more nefarious activities, but were certain that the assignment meant worthy Sub-Credits.

"So... What do I do?" Wander leaned forward onto the edge of the table, her eyes fixated on the red path leading from the railway to the target building. She was already calculating how she'd make her way through the pedestrian traffic. In her mind's eye, she attempted to imagine what the city might look like from way down there on the ground.

{"Once inside, your first task will be to eliminate or incapacitate all personnel inside RealmSquare offices. This time frame has been chosen to minimize casualties, as there will only be seven employees scheduled to be on duty..."}

Wander fixated upon the highlighted RealmSquare office.

"Can I see inside?"

Without response from Maybe, the view of the map swooped in, expanding to allow the interior office to fill the rotating display. Markers appeared where every door, camera, and accessible console had already been labeled and accounted for.

{"Outside the office, native security regularly patrols inter-office hallways on foot, once per hour. It's advised that you perform your assignment discreetly and efficiently. Once you've cleared the office of personnel, Digi will be activated."}

The map zoomed out again to encompass the entire area of play. This time, two new vibrant colored lines, blue and green, marked new paths. From the railway, blue followed the general course that Wander's had; green branched into segments, designating a path to two separate intersections.

{"Digi, you'll be following Wander into the firm. After she's successfully neutralized all personnel, it will be your task to interface with RealmSquare Systems from inside the office. It's recommended that you uplink through an unlocked workstation, as all server units are heavily tamper-proof. I have a rudimentary map of their latest network structure and languages for you, and I'll *be communicating with you directly to guide you as you sabotage their systems."}*

Digi was tempted to ask whether she should assist Wander in clearing the office, but held her tongue instead. For one, she trusted Wander's abilities. She'd watched the girl sneak, talk, or force her way past every obstacle they'd encountered thus far; she was more than capable of handling seven office workers. Digi also trusted Maybe's judgment, especially considering her synthetic nature. AI made fewer logical mistakes than humans did, naturally, and Maybe seemed to know precisely what she was doing. Digi resolved to concede and follow directions.

{"If all goes according to plan, we'll be able to disrupt their supply lines, gather a list of their clientele, and siphon off their finances to more worthy causes within a few minutes..."}

Zef, trying his best to follow along as Runner's Eye, wondered just how long they had to pull off the entirety of the stunt.

{"Midi, your task will be one of distraction."}

"That's what's up." The android girl swiped her chin with a thumb and grinned mischievously. Looking around to each of them, her green eyes, industrial gray skin, and curtain of black hair gave her a menacing demeanor above the glow of the holo-table. Midi had indeed proven after only a year of missions that her knack for orchestrating controlled destruction and social destabilization was formidable. It did, however, put her in considerable danger, though she didn't seem to mind; she was just happy to be useful.

{"Once the operation is in play, an associate of mine will take care of disrupting Katsudo-Hoffman security systems, though this in itself will draw attention. Midi, you will be in charge of triggering two EMP devices on common security response routes to ensure that any patrol will be delayed long enough to allow Wander and Digi to perform their duties. With luck, we will have a ten-to-fifteen minute window to get in and out before QPD, NeoLux StreetForce, Dominion, or contracted security services arrive."}

The group went eerily silent at the idea of security arriving while the job was still in progress. They'd each trained extensively in the Running sims for such a critical scenario. Regardless, it still sent shivers up their spines to imagine how the scene might unfold if Dominion Protocol Enforcement arrived on scene ready to crack skulls.

Lastly, the green and blue pathways disappeared and a yellow one, much shorter, took their place. {"Zelly. You will be responsible for making sure that the arriving 7:15 railway car stays put long enough to collect Midi, Digi, and Wander once their objectives are complete."} Zelly's demeanor grew serious and her eyes focused in on the display. {"You will remain at NeoLux Station as a scout in order to assess a getaway route, as well to make sure that any authorities do not compromise the escape of all NightRunners from the scene of the operation."}

She nodded confidently, gracefully accepting that the group's overall safety and ability to leave the scene unaccosted lay firmly on her shoulders.

"Alright, I'm in." As unspoken leader, she looked around to the others. "What do y'all think? Is this whole thing doable?"

Midi smirked. "Fucking cake."

"Yeah, this should be no problem." Digi was rousing to the new challenge, and glanced over to Wander. "Seven employees. You got this?"

The girl was still staring at the map, navigating her own route through the office interior, running through the kills in her mind. She swept aside her violet hair, its ebbing blue highlights contrasting with the emerald glow of her eyes.

"I got this."

Zef frowned, watching the others ignore him as usual. He pulled out a nanocig and briskly lit it, then disappeared from the table in a huff of smoke. The sound of the opening door peeled through the dark, followed by the heavy static of pouring rain in the alleyway. It slammed shut.

{"NightRunners. Total payout is 800 Sub-Credits each upon your return to Haven-4. You have seven hours to prepare."}

[[E5: CHINATOWN]]

<Lantern Alley>

"I just don't get it. No one was trying to ignore you. You do it to yourself just to prove some kind of point."

"I wasn't trying to prove anything." Zef looked away, though there wasn't much to see through the drifting evening haze of the corridor between Chinatown buildings.

High above, the light of a rare moon rippled through the sea of dense fog. Its glow lined the rooftops in silver as if they were waves, frozen in time and cloaked in swirling mist. Far below their archway perch, through the draping wires and makeshift bridges, a trail of lanterns carried on into the distance where they would meet the entrancing aquamarines of the Jade Region. Below the lanterns, the bustle of the Electuan crowds could only barely be discerned, their chatter and occasional laughter stifled by the fog and tucked beneath a layer of drum rhythm and zheng melody.

"You don't think you are, but that's how it comes off, Zef. You can't wait to separate from the group every time something doesn't directly apply to you. But sometimes you have to--"

"Mello, what the hell? Seems like all you do is hassle me anymore...This place used to be sacred. We don't bring that bullshit here."

"Ugh, don't call me that anymore, how many times do I have to say it. And if we can't figure this out, there won't be anything sacred left between us anyway."

His eyes danced with lantern light as their gaze met. The statement hung in the air between them, swirling with the thick, pungent currents.

"I– I didn't mean it like that."

"Then what?"

"It's just that... you don't seem to care anymore. Not for a long time, Zef. At least before, you would–"

"I would what?" He took a last puff off a cig he'd been nursing and flicked it away into the void. "Wander, things change. And I care about you. Not this crusade. Not these plans and these missions and...all this crap."

"Then why did you join at all?"

The hurt began in her chest, like shortness of breath, working its tedious way *up into her throat.*

"That. That right there, Wander. That's our problem. You can't even separate the two anymore. Before we became Runners, it was just us. You...and me. And then Maybe dumped this into our laps."

"Then why did you join with the rest of us? Why pretend?"

"Because I knew that if I didn't...I'd never get to see you again. You'd go off and be too busy, or you'd lose interest or..." His eyes implored her, though she felt fooled. "That's why. And now I have to sit here and watch you care more about Running and the Glade Syndicate than about me. Than about us."

Wander steeled herself against the emotions that bubbled up, with little success. He was being selfish. She'd finally found a passion, something they could all take pride in, and he was throwing it away for lack of attention. Whether it had to do with his parents, or being a Synth, or being away from Reshen, she didn't care anymore.

"Zef, please look past yourself and see what we're all trying to do—"

"How about you look past that bullshit and see what I'm trying to do!"

"And what exactly is that?"

His face twisted in confusion.

"Trying to keep us together, Wander..."

Her eyes fell away from his. They drifted over the hazy lantern lights until they blossomed into wide circles through the tears. One coursed down her cheek, so warm she could hardly feel it.

What could she say? He didn't understand.

"We are together."

Zef waited for more, but it seemed she had nothing left. He sighed with exasperation. Wander watched as he stood up on the pipes and began climbing down the building ledges, until at last he was lost to the fog.

She wiped her cheeks and looked out over the shadows and spirits of Chinatown, slowly losing her equilibrium. If she hadn't felt so driven, so devoted to Maybe and to the cause, she might feel torn. But instead, she simply felt alone.

The communicator buzzed at her collar. Zelly's pattern.

She took a deep breath.

When she'd collected herself, she tapped the sensor.

"Yeah."

// "Wander, we're grouping up. You ready?"

WANDE

RLUST

CHAPTER 1

NEOLUX DREAMING

[[Q4: NEOLUX]]

<Quadro/Electua Railway>

The Neolux skyline emerged from the translucent haze as a vibrant panorama of glittering monoliths. Glass and steel columns extended upward, jutting into the nonexistent night, ablaze with the saturated digital hues of a technicolor acid trip. Beneath the colossal display, four NightRunners clad in tactical black runnersuits crept along the rooftop of a Quadro/Electua Railway train car.

Moving into Quadro from Mid-City Electua, the frigid air and steady rain was pristine. Wander in the lead pushed on toward the seventh car of the train, where a busted security camera, hopefully still inactive, would allow them discreet access to the lower level. Digi and Midi, side by side, pushed onward behind her, their synthetic eyes the perfect lookouts, strategically tuned-in to searching for visible threats. Behind them, Zelly watched over the group. Her mind was laser-focused on the progress of the mission, and she maintained a line out to Zef who was feeding her intel. He was currently briefing her on the particulars of NeoLux Station traffic and Demigod patrol patterns.

// "...and stay on board as long as you can, maybe even wait for the train to start moving again before you hop off. There's a public disturbance call in the station."

"What section?"

// "Main corridor. West entrance. Maybe says it's some kind of arrest."

"Alright, confirmed. Let me know when it clears. Yellow out."

Zef leaned back in his chair at the opportunity for a smoke, bathed in the phosphorescent glow of the rotating map in the holo-display. He pulled a cig from behind his ear, cracked open a Rezno-style lighter, and lit it up. The snap of the lighter echoed across the walls, fracturing the welcome silence of their operations room. He exhaled and smoke plumed out, rippling across the electric wire-frame grid of the holographic city. He watched it linger for a moment, tumbling through the buildings like the same rancid smog that coated the concrete towers of Mid-City above him.

[[Q4: NEOLUX]]
<NeoLux Station>

CLACK-CLACK. CLACKK-CLACKK. CLACKK-CLACKK.
THUMP... SHHHH-tsssss....

The brakes of the train began to seize as it neared the facade of the station and its cavernous tunnel. One after another, the NightRunners climbed down the outer shell, hopped over to the connecting walkway and slipped inside the car. The four of them excitedly took up two seats on the left of the aisle. Midi stretched her legs and propped them up on the seatback in front of her. The two passengers sitting there were disturbed enough that they rose in disgust and found new seats further down.

Wander trained her eyes to the inside of the terminal beyond the window.

"Any word yet?"

"None."

She flopped back. "Damn the CORP, what the hell is he doing?"

"Chill, Wan, he's got time. There's a public disturbance in the lobby anyway. We're gonna hang back for a minute."

Midi pulled her feet down and punched the seat in front of her. "Fuck, I'm so amped!" The loud clatter sounded through the traincar.

Zelly's eyes rolled. "Midi, please calm yourself or you're gonna get us merked before we even do anything. Guys..." Unable to handle them with her duties on her mind, she placed earbuds into her ears. A thrumming garble of Tetran electro began playing loud enough for them to hear. She closed her eyes and leaned back.

"Midi." Attempting to set an air of professionalism, Wander placed a hand on the girl's shoulder. "Which intersections are you hitting?"

The synthetic girl's senses rushed back smoothly, sorting out the cocktail of syndrenaline in her veins, and her thoughts returned to strategy.

"Lockport and Luxton."

"And?"

"And... Fitsmorth and 2nd."

"Well done. I say Digi and I'll wait at least until you've dropped the first ping to breach, but try to stay in contact."

"Yeah, that's cool. I'll be on the Ace Hotel when I finish and keep y'all updated. Pretty sure I'll be able to see both intersections from there."

"That's great, just don't expect much response from us. We're gonna have enough on our hands."

"Pfft. Seven office workers." Midi turned back to them with a sarcastic grin.

"Hey, it's a little harder for those of us who don't use guns to accomplish *everything*."

Midi was pulling the paper from a candy sucker and popped it into her plastec mouth. She pulled it back out promptly to respond, "Guns are smarter."

"No, guns are messier. They have a louder signature and they attract more attention... Oh, and they're illegal. It's not smarter, they're just a liability."

A mother and her son got up from their seats at the strange turn in conversation, and made their way quietly out. The mother looked back at them with smug Quadran disapproval.

"It's not a liability, it's quicker."

"No, weirdo. It's why you're constantly on wreck duty and we get to infiltrate."

Midi shrugged. "I like wreck duty."

Wander stared daggers at the girl and bit her lower lip tightly. She couldn't tell if it was to keep from smiling or to keep from losing her shit. Maybe both.

"You are...an idiot."

"It's pronounced *'Midi,'*" she sneered, "and you smell like a human, so feel free to fuck right off."

"Humans don't smell *that* bad," Digi chimed in nervously on Wander's behalf. She turned in her seat to catch Wander's grateful eye, but was instead met with a menacing glare. She grimaced sheepishly. "I mean, maybe you smell a little?"

The rest of the group erupted with spontaneous laughter. Wander covered her face and Zelly nearly fell out of her seat, despite supposedly ignoring the conversation. She pulled the earbuds from her ears and sat upright.

"Corporate-fucking-hell, Digi! Get a clue!"

The timid girl bot was still confused. "I don't fucking know! Maybe humans like to stink, how would I know?"

The others gradually got a hold of themselves until Wander, still giggling, sniffed her armpit suspiciously. They unraveled into a laughing mess, cracking up to tears while the passengers around them became increasingly annoyed. Digi grinned with an awkward mixture of embarrassment and pride.

"Oh fuck, thank you for that Digi..."

"Ohhh...shit."

"I can't breathe–"

Zelly's communicator suddenly buzzed. Zef's tone.

She wiped her eyes.

"Oh fuck, what's up, Zef?"

Coughing and wheezing, the rest of them attempted to sober up.

// "QPD is out. You're in."

[THE REALM]

<RealmWorld: Intergalactic Zoo / Planet: Geldunia>

[She found his hand in the dim ambient glow that emanated from a thin crescent of alien daylight. The planet outside the wide window was labeled in the Realm catalog as "Geldunia". It was a strange planet, where exotic lifeforms slid around on oceans of thick maroon gel. Zef and Wander had visited the planet's surface only once; the view from orbit was what kept them coming back.

The experience was possible through a convenient hack in the Realm's VRnet by Zef. It had become their own secret hideaway in the otherwise expensive digital universe of a RealmWorld called Intergalactic Zoo. Wander and Zef had had their share of minor adventures here, though they'd also never used the simulation for its intended purpose of safaris and charting alien wildlife. Instead, they'd constructed a light freighter from the catalog and spent most of their time exploring nebula clouds or adrift in various planetary orbits. They adored the privacy most of all, where they could pretend briefly that they were alone, and that Dominion City was the real simulation.

Here in the Realm, they could take any avatar they wanted, though they generally stuck close to their IRL appearances. Here, they could do as they pleased; could adventure through an endless archive of planets, visit luxury resorts, live out a life entirely separate from the dirty reality of Mid-City survival. In the end though, they just wanted the privacy.

In Dominion, they shared a flat with the rest of the NightRunners. But here, holed up in some pod-locker in a Reshen VR escapist retreat called EtherAfter, they could be alone. Truly alone. Not forced to listen to the honking of hovers, the distant sirens of the RPD, or vagrants fighting in an alley. Not worried that they'd be in the flat when it was eventually raided, not worried that a Demigod would somehow detect them from above and Tetra would finally kick in the door.

In the hammock behind the impossibly thin glass separating them from the planet, Wander rested her head on his shoulder and wiggled herself closer beneath the blankets.

"You still awake?"

He didn't speak for a moment and she assumed he'd finally fallen asleep.

"...I am."

Her eyes absently lingered on the swirling patterns of cotton candy clouds below. The pink plumes slowly disappeared into darkness as they wafted across the planet, rotating toward Geldunian night.

He took her hand and held it to his chest, reassuring her that he was still present. It wasn't like they'd been drifting apart, at least she hoped they weren't, but after several months of work as NightRunners there had definitely been much less free time for them. Normally they'd use that time to find a sushi joint at the edge of Mid-City, get sake-wasted, hoverboard through the sewers, trip at the reservoir, or spend hours at PixelAddict Arcade. Lately, though, they found themselves retreating to the Realm to get away.

It was a welcome change. Sometimes she wished they never had to leave this place. But she knew that if they didn't pay attention there was a risk of giving in to the escape. They might lose the reasons why they loved to be together in the first place, might slowly disconnect until they weren't a couple anymore. Just two souls finding abstract comfort in each others' presence. She didn't even want to imagine it. She squeezed his hand again instinctively, feeling his shoulder beneath her head.

"What are you thinking about in there?"

He was trapped in his thoughts again.

"...Lots of things, I don't know."

"Anything I can help with?"

His chest rose and fell deeply.

A sigh?

"Nothing like that. Just...I still think about them sometimes when we're RealmSide. I wonder if they're out there somewhere and know I'm here. I wonder if they even give a shit."

"If they give a shit about you? Of course they do, they're your parents, Z."

"That doesn't mean anything, Mel, they chose to leave. I haven't heard from them in... years."

Wander frowned, both at his pessimism as well as his use of the old name she no longer identified with. The subject of his parents had arisen before. She wished there was something she could do to help, but felt he might also just be using it as an excuse to be bitter. She knew there was no point in dwelling on the subject if he didn't want to make the effort to find them.

"Well then they're gone, Zef. And you said yourself you don't want to find them...so that's that. And," she huffed playfully, "not like it matters, but you still have me."

She took her hand from inside his and placed it on his cheek, pulling his face close enough to kiss him. For a moment they embraced, leaving their worries behind. Even here in the Realm, maybe more so, the texture of their encoded lips touching softly was intoxicating. The smells were different. The saliva cooler. Their tongues more sensitive. It was simply easier to get lost within each other.

The slow, thumping beat of a relaxing trip-hop groove suspended them and they lingered. When they separated, it was only reluctantly. She found his hand again, and then his eyes.

"Zef, you aren't alone anymore."

"I know, babe. I know I'm not alone. But with everything I've been through, I can't shake the feeling that I am."

Wander's eyes widened and she bit a lip, digging her fingers into his ribcage. "You aren't!"

His face scrunched in annoyance and he resisted, but she pushed through it. She wrapped her arms around him and bit him on the shoulder.

"Ow! Mel, stop!"

"Say you're not alone then!" She managed to wrestle her way on top of him and bit him again.

"Ow, fuck! Stop that!"

"Say it! Say you're not alone and I'll quit!"

"Fine, I'm not alone then!" He shook with laughter and squirmed as she ferociously tickled him. "I'm not alone! Stop, stop, I'm not fucking alone!"

"That's right, you aren't!" She sat up, fully straddling him, and crossed her arms over her chest with an eyebrow raised in playful contempt. "You're never alone. And if you want to go find them we will, and if not then we won't. So just shut up and enjoy the moment."

Seeing the good intentions behind her glaring eyes, Zef grinned with admiration. "Stop talking and get down here."

She smiled at how easily she could bring him back from the past, from the dark places he stumbled into sometimes. It was one of the reasons they made such a great pair, and why they felt lucky to have even found each another. Even in Dominion City, something like this could exist, something that felt like love.

Wander gave in and pulled her shirt over her shoulders. Her bare body, lithe and tan, shined a brilliant fuchsia with the warm Geldunian sunset. Zef was speechless. With her assistance he was able to do the same, removing his shirt and tossing it away, and together they sank into each other's skin, as far from Dominion as they could possibly be.]

[[Q4: NEOLUX]]
<Marquee Square>

Midi was a ripple of black and green as she sprinted through the crowded clusterfuck of Marquee Square. Deep in the Quadro NeoLux, she hurdled one obstacle after the next, racing toward her first blinking objective.

A large portion of the NightRunner training she'd experienced so far involved endurance sims in dense metropolitan areas, something like they'd find in the NeoLux or maybe Downtown Electua. It was one part of her VR training that Midi absolutely loved.

Maybe referred to the skill as Crowdthreading, though Midi understood it to be Running itself. Leaping across gaps and between bridges or buildings, swerve-sliding around groups of pedestrians or through them in predictable rhythms, wall-running and rapid climbing, precise tackling of unexpected obstacles...

The most supremely sinister were the moments like the apex of a soar, the slight disorientation of a flip or a spin as it led into new challenges, the arc of a rampslide where, despite her scrolling numetrics, Midi felt as though time would tick down to an exhilarating crawl. In those moments she'd watch firsthand the calculations of her movement data as her sensory awareness expanded to map the crowds, the patterns, and the pathways, all while the syndrenaline pumped through her soft-circuitry like fire. Running had become a drug for the girl; one of the nerve-tingling climaxes of being a living creature. It was enough of a thrill for Midi that it often left her wondering how she was actually getting paid to do it.

She slid to a halt against a glowing glass railing that overlooked the bustling epicenter of Marquee Square.

"Wander. Digi. I'm getting close to the first mark. Gimme ten minutes." She paused, listening, but the other end of comms remained silent.

Midi glanced intently over the crowded square, her frantic algorithms scouting for pathways to Luxton Ave. which funneled into the plaza at the far end. Between her position and there, three Brother Units patrolled casually, hovering along and occasionally stopping walkers to scan their features. Avoiding them would most definitely be in Midi's self-interest, seeing as she'd been unregistered for years now, entirely off the grid. Confronting them physically also wasn't in the cards. Maybe in closer quarters, but out here in the crowded square she'd have a swarm of them on top of her within seconds if she dared.

In addition to staying out of view, she'd also need to keep her foot speed well below public ordinance if she didn't want to draw unwanted attention from the Quadro City Cams. The NightRunners' black suits were made to eat light and the colored markers resonated at a frequency that distorted video capture, but there were other triggers for the cameras she would need to avoid aside from direct movement. It would be a slow, tedious journey across the square. Like with most things, Midi dove in with only a rough plan, relying primarily on instinct.

[[Q4: NEOLUX]]
<Katsudo-Hoffman Center / RealmSquare>

Wander and Digi inched their way up toward the nondescript window of RealmSquare Brokerage, clinging like flies to the slick black surface that connected the floors of the Katsudo-Hoffman Center. Midi's message broke their focused silence, informing them that she was arriving at her mark.

Wander looked down and searched, finally making eye-contact with Digi. The synthetic girl's normally striking blue eyes were dimmed for the mission, something she did for operations that required a stealthy approach. She nodded, a signal that she was ready to breach on cue. They huddled under the window to wait patiently for word from Midi that she'd laid the first security speed-bump. The comms fuzzed to life, but it was the voice of Zef that finally broke through.

// "Native security sweep has passed, you should be clear for at least another hour. These guys are a joke, honestly."

"Still seven inside?"

// "...Confirmed. Wait for Midi or proceed when you're ready."

"We'll wait. I'd rather have the net."

Radio silence.

// "Orange out."

Digi'd held her tongue twice now but was too anxious. She wanted to be of more use than a simple information tool.

"Wan, you sure you don't need help in there?"

"I'll be fine. I've got it planned out. Shouldn't take me longer than a minute. If you don't hear from me after two, though, get out of here and back to the train."

Digi nodded, running her mind through the backup scenario. Wander pulled herself up high enough to peek through the window above them. There wasn't much to see except the glow of servers LEDs behind dark-tinted glass.

"These people aren't combat trained. It won't take long." She thought for a moment and then grinned. "I'll tell Midi you helped, though."

If it were possible for Digi to blush, she would've. Instead, her eyes lit up momentarily. "I...you don't...ugh." She hung her head and rested it on the building's surface.

Wander stifled a laugh. The comms crackled.

// "First rip in place. Let's get this moving."

That was the word. Wander took a deep breath and activated, reaching to her waistband for a small black device. She flicked a lever at the end of it and a green band of light encircled the top. She held it up to the window above them and traced out a hole big enough for them to pass through. Once the shape was complete, she turned the device and carefully connected the bottom suction end to the glass, extracting the loose panel. Cool, climate-controlled office air breezed out. She handed the glass and the attached contraption to Digi who was ready and waiting.

"Careful, Wander."

"Always. See you in a minute."

Digi was tempted to ask Wander in that moment if she would be killing or incapacitating the office workers, but it was too late. Before she could formulate the words, Wander was up and through the hole in the window. Digi pursed her lips as if to say *"oh well,"* and then busied herself with detaching the cutter from the glass shape. With the device, she sprayed a light film of temporary adhesive to the panel and then pressed it to the building surface.

An unexpected wave of panic pulsed through her, imagining a Demigod creeping toward them in the sky. She scanned the skyline but of course there was nothing. The operation had been meticulously planned to avoid the watchful eye of those DCORP behemoths, though she could never be fully convinced. She clasped the cutter to her own waistband, reestablished her grip on the wall, and looked out over the blazing city again. Somewhere out there, in the neon lights of the NeoLux, Midi was racing through the streets.

[[Q4: NEOLUX]]

<Katsudo-Hoffman Center / RealmSquare, Interior>

Wander's senses were un-augmented and she preferred it that way. After a year of training inside the running sims with Maybe she'd begun to harbor a general sense of contempt for those who felt their human-born faculties weren't enough. Instead, she could now awaken them on command to a level of keen attention most others weren't aware was possible. Hearing the unhearable, seeing in near total darkness, photographic memory of maps and schematics. It all began kicking in now as she dropped to the floor of the dark server room, surrounded only by server stacks and a sea of blue-green pin lights.

She closed her eyes and a world of sound opened up. Beyond the layered hum of the servers and the din of the distant traffic outside the window, she could make out the chatter of the office workers in the next room. Someone pouring coffee. A wheeled cart. Footsteps.

Was there someone in the server room with her, waiting behind the next row to catch her in the act of intruding?

Her keen ears sifted through the noises, the beeps, the laughter, listening for breathing, the shuffle of feet, the slightest movement. There was no one in the room. She turned the corner and carefully double checked each row, ready to defend herself if necessary.

The server room was smaller than it seemed at the holo-table, there was only one closet and one door out. She took a moment to peer down a row of the glowing racks and contemplated on the crimes taking place, the Citizens stored inside the hardware, all the poor souls whose minds and bodies were being turned over by RealmSquare to Dominion. Likely claimed for some minor debt or repossession, trapped inside the Realm with no way out. They were probably even aware that they were on a ticking clock, locked inside a virtual prison with nowhere to go.

This is why I became a NightRunner, Wander remembered, *to fight for those who can't fight for themselves.*

A jostling outside the door and she was immediately in motion, skirting the edge of the room. She pressed her back to the nearest ridge of server columns as the door swung open. A buttoned-down and whistling information tech strolled in, pushing a cart of electronic components. The door clicked shut and he was dead in an instant, cut cleanly from shoulder to the opposite armpit.

Wander flicked her extendable sword clean and retracted it, replacing it on her thigh. She dragged the body parts away from the door in a hurry and checked her watch. Twenty seconds had elapsed.

Six more employees to go and lots of time.

[[Q4: NEOLUX]]
<NeoLux Station>

What might have seemed like a simple assignment was actually much more complicated. Zelly's task was to coordinate the train's arrival, delaying it if necessary, while ensuring safe passage for her fellow Runners to board. All this while avoiding security, QPD, and roaming Brother Units. There would be no screwing up, no room for mistakes. In that case, she'd need to be ready to fight or even flee, even abandoning her team if necessary... But she knew she would never let it come to that.

At the moment, she was resting on a bench in the crowded NeoLux-to-Mid-City terminal lobby, watching the schedules change and switch over, getting a rhythm for what she couldn't have studied beforehand. After a pass through the crowded main corridor, a pair of buskers finally caught her eye in the corner. One played a delightfully ironic tune through a two-pronged flute while the other mimed with marionettes. It was a chase between a Protocol Violator holding a spray can and a Brother Unit, the BU's bladed arms waving wildly like a frantic mantis.

The whole puppet show is surely a Violation of Protocol itself, she thought. *But if the buskers are still alive, I'm safe for now.*

[[E5: WEST MID-CITY]]
<Teradin Jurisdiction / Haven-4>

The crackling transmission of Midi's comm filtered through the table's audio feed, indicating that she'd reached her first mark. A green-hued line of holographic text scrolled above the display of the Neolux, spelling out her words.

Zef ignored it. His mind was an unpleasant blur, focused on nothing as he tried to block out the conversation he'd had with Wander overlooking Chinatown earlier in the night. He was becoming convinced that they were no longer even seeing the same reality anymore. Everything was dissolving, all the great times coming to an end for the sake of some make-believe ideal. Taking down The Dominion Corporation. Overthrowing a government more vast and powerful than they could fathom. Some impossible dream that Maybe'd had them believing. Just another example of a master lying to its pawns for the sake of profit. Maybe herself could be working for

DCORP for all they knew. Zef didn't know what to think or how to fix things anymore.

On the one hand, he pitied Wander and the rest of the Runners for being so gullible. There'd been a time when they knew just as well as he did how futile it was, forming some sort of nonsense resistance against Dominion. From the Outer Wall to Dominion Prime, the city was an indomitable prison that none of them could ever hope to escape. Seeing the holographic map and the true size of Dominion City had proven that to Zef, though apparently not to the others. Somehow they'd only become more excited. He didn't understand how seeing the enormity of the circular fortress wasn't enough to cement the odds against them...

He consciously forced a deep breath and sighed, attempting to stop the rush of negativity. It wasn't worth his attention anymore. The NightRunners had been sold and Wander had gone cold to him. It was something he'd need to start accepting. Not everything was going to turn out the way they dreamed it would, most certainly not for Wander. She could go on obsessing about this work all she wanted, but for Zef it would be just that: work. Nothing more, nothing less. He'd risk his life for Subs, but he'd be damned if he'd pretend it was for–

// "Approaching second mark near Fitsmorth. Haven't heard anything from you guys, hope everything's chill."

Zef leaned forward, settling the front legs of his metal stool down and opening his ears.

// "No worries here in the Station. Just watching the cycles and being friendly. Digi, how are you two making out?"

He breathed pensively and leaned back again in the chair, still listening to the chatter and deciding whether to speak up.

// "Digi, what's up? Zef, are they okay?"

Finally, he stood up and walked over to the display.

// "Zef–"

"I'm here...everything looks fine from where I'm at. I haven't heard anything. Digi, come in."

More silence.

"I can see them just fine, they're in place. Might be a comms malfunction, although I'm not picking it up. They might be pinched, let's give 'em a minute."

// "Confirmed."

// "...Confirmed."

Zef leaned against the edge of the display table and watched the blue and red dots on the Katsudo-Hoffman Center. No doubt Wander was fine. If Dominion hadn't been alerted, she was skilled enough to fight her way out of whatever was happening. Digi seemed to still be on the building exterior, holding position.

Must be comms, he thought.

// "Everything's fine, guys." Digi sounded relieved to finally be able to talk. *"But we have a problem. A second native sweep down the outside of the building, vertical from the roof and then back up again. Some kind of rolling scanners. I've seen two now and the sweep seems to rotate around the building every few minutes. I may have to abandon post to maneuver again but I should return to mark. I'll stay connected. Blue out."*

Zef could feel his blood pressure rise. Was it because the mission might be compromised, or because Wander might need to be left alone? He couldn't tell and didn't want to. He decided to remain attentive at the display table regardless.

[[Q4: NEOLUX]]
<Fitsmorth Plaza>

Midi tumbled forward and slid down a smooth concrete embankment. It sloped alongside a luminous, coral-hued stairway teeming with pedestrians who gawked in amazement at her quick figure zipping past. Digi's last message replayed in her mind. That dreadful silence was managing to throw off her concentration enough to slow her progress, though a competing idea pushed her forward. She was keeping them safe by planting her EMPs.

She skidded to a halt as she hit ground level in the plaza, scanning the NeoLux crowds and landmarks around her. An opening in the patterns of the throng began to align and she darted forward again, through bodies and behind cover, sliding under a walking bridge, swinging up to higher ledges, and at last leaping to the back of a cargo hover as it lifted off in forward motion.

Over the glimmering streets below, Midi rose into the air, orienting herself with brief glimpses of the city around the plaza. Beyond the business complex to the south, one of the arching loops of the Splinterlight Supertrack shined in blazing magenta against the dark night sky. To the west, the dense polluting glow of Marquee Square poured light into the atmosphere, where a lone Demigod cast an inverted beam of shadow upwards. Further behind her, the cascading gradients of the Ace Hotel beckoned, reminding Midi of her next checkpoint after the last rip was dropped.

The rip!

She made sure the bag was secured tightly around her torso, refastening the black straps with one hand, and began looking below for Fitsmorth. At the edge of what she could see around the corner of the transport, the Fitsmorth Fountain emerged, the familiar dance of its holograms and water spouts appearing and disappearing between buildings. This was her stop.

Without waiting for the hover to slow, she leapt from it almost blindly as it curved, holding a vague sense that the tower was within reach. She arced downward through the congested traffic, narrowly avoiding an oncoming airbus, and landed against the building face like a frog. Limbs and fingers spread, the clingy nano-fibers of her runnersuit gripped the surface from pure static friction. At a silent command, her suit eased its tension and she slid down the slope as if the surface had suddenly become liquid. She navigated her way down this way, leaping from surface to ledge to surface and then sliding again.

At the bottom of the massive building face, Midi dangled from the overhang above a crowded intersection. She surveyed and dropped, farther than any human might dare, and landed with a calculated roll. Her synthetic joints rebounded into a graceful run, slowly veering toward the corner of Fitsmorth and 2nd Ave. As she sprinted forward, she opened comms.

"Approaching second mark near Fitsmorth. Haven't heard anything from you guys, hope everything's chill."

[[Q4: NEOLUX]]
<Katsudo-Hoffman Center / RealmSquare>

"...I'll stay connected. Blue out."

The gliding scanners descended silently, though they looked like they meant serious business. Digi watched their rotating patterns as they slowly made their way up and down the length of the building in turns. The surfaces of their forms were gloss black and they emitted blood red scan beams, similar to Dominion tech but certainly not the real deal. The diamond logo on their sides looked to be Red Industries, a security firm in Tetra. Their designs were less organic and more intentionally geometric, lacking that eerie "living" quality that the Dominion tech and AI possessed. Red Industries tech was more predictable, more mechanical, but certainly just as lethal when enforcing security in the private sector. She would need to navigate the descent pattern perfectly if she didn't wish to become an incinerated heap.

Closer and closer the scanners approached, taking turns to tumble left or right, crossing over one another's paths. The effort was seemingly at random, an attempt to bewilder and ensnare any poor soul silly enough to find themselves clinging to the facade and attempting a break-in. Unwilling to follow Wander inside so soon, Digi was now left with few other options.

Preemptively, she shuffled to the left, deftly using the cling-material of her suit to her advantage. Peering up, she felt as thought the scanners had seen her movements and she swore under her breath as they tumbled back into a previous position directly above her.

Their beams erupted forward, frantically scanning ahead, though she hoped they were still too far to sense her. Attempting to predict a tumble further, she loosened her grip on the surface and slid down a few meters, then crawled further to the left. Instead of either scanner following, a third powered up from the roof and began slowly making its way down. She glanced to the right, trying to judge the distance between herself and the hole in the window. It was too far for comfort. She maneuvered further away to let the scanners carry on, but immediately froze in place, realizing what would happen if one of them found the entry cut into the glass... *It would be the end of everything!*

"Shit!" She hadn't meant to say it out loud.

High above, the third and nearest scanner paused long enough to hone in on the source of her voice, and it tumbled into place above her. She did the opposite, moving into the strip it left open. She was now pinched between the one on the left and the original two, which were now only a few meters above her. As long as neither of them tumbled, she could just wait for them to pass and then scoot over to the window breach...so she sat perfectly still, the three scanners descending around her.

The seconds of waiting stretched unbearably, her dim eyes darting between them as they approached, their rolling undercarriages humming. Without warning, the one nearest her lifted up to tumble itself left.

The distance is too short!

She leapt directly beneath the higher one, cursing herself for not jumping to the right, and decided to risk squeezing through the gap. She climbed upward, past the scanner on her right, and leapt above it, narrowly missing the beam of the third. She shuffled right again and then higher.

At last she was above all three scanners and gave a mighty push to clear them with a final jump. Her panic had gotten the best of her. She crashed into the wall and slid helplessly against the droplets of rainwater. Activating the friction of her fingertips, she slowed herself to a stop. Her eyes swept across the scanners, only to see the glass-cutting device in her periphery, loosed from her waistband and plummeting away. She reached out but it dropped past her grasping hand, spinning end over end, and clanged against the top of the final scanner before bouncing away into obscurity.

The machine swiveled instantly, its wide, flat body turning upward to face her. It raised itself away from the wall, widening its grip on the surface, and bars of red light pulsed along its edge.

"CITIZEN. IN CONTRAVENTION OF QUADRO SECURITY LAW, YOU ARE FOUND TRESPASSING ON PRIVATE PROPERTY. REMAIN WHERE YOU ARE."

"No no no no no!" Without a second thought, Digi hurled herself toward the opening they'd cut in the glass. As she sailed through the air, the scanner's beam coursed after her and bolts of kinetic energy crackled past. She caught the edge of the opening, gripped the wall, and pried the previously cut glass panel from the solid surface. Three scanners began zipping toward her.

"CITIZEN, YOU ARE IN VIOLATION OF–"

Their red beams waved over her like manic antennae as she slipped into the hole, pulling the panel through with her by its narrow end. She watched through the window as the scanners continued toward the hole and she fumbled with the glass shape, finally plugging it into place to temporarily close the opening.

A scanner rolled itself over the patched hole, paused as it processed, and then extended a small set of tools from its underside. It cauterized and sealed the loose patch of glass before buffing and shining the results. Once it finished the job, its tools retracted and it continued on its odd diagonal path, scanning around and looking for the trespasser that no longer existed.

Petrified, Digi watched it in stone silence from within the dark server room, not daring to move a synthetic muscle until the thing was out of sight.

[[Q4: NEOLUX]]
<Katsudo-Hoffman Center / RealmSquare>

With thirty seconds elapsed and one employee dead, Wander pressed her back to the office wall at the end of a short hallway. Here, the server room led to a main open space of smoked glass cubicles. It always surprised Wander how small these corporate trafficking operations were. Thousands of lives traded between corporations for official Life Credits, orchestrated by only a few decision-makers and a handful of obedient salaried workers beneath them.

Fuck that, she thought. *No matter the size of the operation, it ends once the NightRunners get involved.*

As thoughts of the Runners entered her mind, comms opened.

// "Approaching second mark near Fitsmorth, haven't heard anything from—"

Wander switched it off. She didn't need the distraction during this bit; it would only be a couple of minutes.

She risked a peek around the hallway corner. Three of the employees were congregating in an open area. *Too bad for them. The other three must be in cubicles or the restroom.* She hoped Maybe had been successful in disabling the interior cameras. The fact that they'd made it this far was promising.

Lowering herself to a crouch, she removed the sword from its notch on her suit's thigh plate. Once triggered, it opened itself with a brisk *shnk-shnk-shnk* and she held it ready. With no time to spare, she left the cover of her hiding place and crossed the walkway, sliding up against the cubicle partition.

Through the glass on the right she could see Target Number Two, conveniently checked out of reality with VR apparatus strapped in place. Doing work inside the Realm or a proprietary LAN-prog, no doubt. Her death might be a signal for the wrong people, but Wander needed to take the chance.

Remaining crouched, she crept into the wide white-floored cubicle, all its holographics and data feeds surrounding the employee in the center like a slowly-evolving crystalline cloud. Wander placed the cold business end of her blade across the throat of the inert employee. No reaction. With razor precision, she sliced away cleanly, opening the neck wide. The body began to spasm, blood bubbling and spurting to the floor around the reclining chair. Wander held a gloved hand over the mouth until life signs ceased.

"What the...?" It was a coworker across the office, likely sharing virtual space with Number Two. Wander would leave them to discover what was going on. It would buy her some time while she escaped the cubicle.

Turning back into the walkway, her mind on the group of three, she peered around the edge of the partition. She could see them clearly: all male, sipping coffee and casually discussing whatever it was that RealmSquare employees discussed. Seeing an interesting opening, Wander made a decision and switched tactics. She stood up, blade hidden behind her back, and strolled into the open.

"Hey, dumbshits."

She slowly unzipped the front of her runnersuit revealing her bare cleavage. Like clockwork, they turned and gawked in primal fascination. Wander stepped to the side, lining them up to obscure their own ability to see what was happening. She let loose with a slash to the throat of the nearest, Target Three. A pulsing fan of hot blood sprayed from his throat, and a strong boot to his chest sent the man stumbling backward. Wander burst forward, running up his chest, and hurdled the man. She brought the long edge of her blade directly through the head of Target Four. Her downward momentum forced her blade and the blow split him in half, carving down through his face and neck like a longsword. The halves of his body peeled apart and the sword stopped near his sternum. He collapsed, slamming to the floor in a bloody heap of gurgling meat.

Target Five stood pale and trembling, unable to process what he'd witnessed. With zeal, Wander spun her sword and hurled it, sending it darting through the office space like a missile. It impaled the man's face and jutted out through the back of his head. He remained standing for a moment, thoroughly shocked, crimson death spilling out of his gaping mouth. Wander took the chance and reached out. She grasped the hilt and forcefully pulled back her sword, unsheathing it from his skull. His body hit the tile floor.

Two left. She checked her watch and zipped her suit closed.

[[Q4: NEOLUX]]

<NeoLux Station>

The lines were converging.

Zelly watched as the arrival times of three trains began aligning and it dawned on her. This was their opportunity to get out of the NeoLux. All she would need to do now is coordinate the arrival of her team members. As long as they weren't bringing any trouble along with them, everything would sort itself out nicely. Having discovered their window for escape, she decided to stop overthinking things for a minute. She wanted a chance to explore her surroundings and get a vibe for the crowd.

The majority of them appeared to be normie Mid-City folks heading back to the 5th Ring, likely traveling back from the QuadroRaces or doing some big city shopping. Not all Electuans could afford a trip into Quadro, especially from Mid-City, so those that could were some of the more self-respecting. Scattered among them were spoiled kids from NeoLux, determined to be loud and obnoxious. The combination was good for NightRunner work, as any sort of social static usually drew pedestrian attention away from their activities.

On that note, Zelly slipped through the crowd in curiosity, taking in the faces, the fashions, and the cultures around her. Musicians from the Jazz District, Uptown businessmen, kitchen workers, neo-faders and their ugly cousins the grimepunks, quite a few transhuman, several mechanics coming in from the Races...even families. One of the children was holding a plastec QuadroBike toy, another guiding around a small remote-controlled Hopper Unit. It swelled Zelly's heart knowing that these people were going about their happy, normal lives despite all the hardships that life in Dominion City brought along with it. Corruption at the highest levels, sensationalized crime and violence in the news at every opportunity, and of course, the land between Mid-City and NeoLux being a junkie's paradise. Kids were disappearing left and right, falling victim to either digital addiction or ready-access synthetic drugs. At the border, Citizen Termination rates were at their highest in the entire city. It was certainly no place for children, except for places like the train station where security could maintain a tight hold on the populace.

As Zelly walked, she felt a surge of excitement in the crowd and realized she was nearing the buskers again. She could hear their music, and Citizens around her were clapping and dancing. She decided that this was too rare an occasion to ignore the show. She pushed through the bodies with growing anticipation and finally found herself right behind the front row of the audience. Watching between onlookers, she joined in with the rhythmic applause as a playful performance unfolded.

The puppeteer was allowing a Brother Unit character to take turns between chasing around a small figure dressed in punkish clothing, and a Dominion Priest, each one becoming increasingly more frightened. At last, the Priest seemed to hypnotize the Brother Unit with fancy hand motions, and it obediently turned toward the grimepunk. Once the Priest had safely diverted the BU, he scuttled away and the puppet was taken from the stage. The Brother Unit, now woken from its trance, searched for its Priestly owner in despair, allowing the punk to escape. Left with no one, the Brother Unit collapsed clumsily and its tiny red lights went dark. Much of the crowd burst into laughter while the others cheered or clapped, relief rippling through them at the menacing BU's death.

Unexpectedly, the laughter turned to startled gasps. More and more of them rang out, until suddenly the crowd surged backward like herd animals. They pressed into one another as they gave wide berth for an actual Brother Unit entering the lobby.

Zelly's heart sank into a pit of ice water in her gut. She instinctively began searching for the quickest route away from the musician and puppeteer, the most obvious Violation suspects in the room.

"ATTENTION, PROTOCOL REQUIRES ALL CITIZENS TO MAINTAIN A MAXIMUM 70 DECIBELS IN ALL PUBLIC AREAS. THE DOMINION CORPORATION APPRECIATES YOUR OBEDIENCE."

The voice was mechanized and shrill, with enough booming resonance to vibrate the entire lobby and the Citizens inside it. Zelly ignored the message and continued slipping through the crowd, though her progress became nearly impossible as they came to rest again. She turned around to see what they saw. The Brother Unit had discovered the artists and their puppet show. She stood on the tips of her toes but could still only see the spindly antennae stalks of the BU protruding above a field of heads. They reminded her of the limbs of a dead and blackened tree, speckled with red lights.

"CITIZENS. PLEASE REMAIN STILL WHILE YOUR RETINAS ARE SCANNED FOR OUR ARCHIVES."

The lobby flickered with the ambient crimson glow of unseen redbeams as the Brother Unit scanned each of the buskers' eyes. The crowd held its breath, their collective stomachs clenched in shock.

"Mommy, I'm–" The mother of the little boy knelt to cover his mouth and hushed him. His plastic QuadroBike toy clattered to the ground amid the silence.

"YOUR COMPLIANCE IS APPRECIATED. PLEASE PREPARE FOR IMMEDIATE TERMINATION."

Again, sharp gasps rose from the crowd. The words "immediate termination" confirmed their fears, and they were each paralyzed in place. They knew what they were about to witness and many turned from the scene to save themselves from the memory.

Zelly stared horrified as the Brother Unit transformed, expanding two of its hefty bladed arms from its body. Without warning, it unleashed several precise stabs in swift mechanical cadence, reducing the bodies of the buskers to messy piles of flesh and clothing.

Judge, jury, and executioner.

From the corners of the lobby, the sound of small metallic feet bouncing over tile could be heard, an army of three or four Hopper Units were arriving to clean up the mess left by the BU. Zelly hoped that, with its business done, the Brother Unit would finally turn and leave them all in peace. Her eyes searched the lobby as she inhaled slowly and attempted to slow her heart rate.

"CITIZENS, THE DOMINION CORPORATION APPRECIATES YOUR PATIENCE. THIS HAS BEEN AN ENFORCEMENT OF CITIZEN PROTOCOL."

The massive corporate monster and its black spires swiveled for a moment, its arms collapsing back into itself. It emitted an erratic clicking sound as it glided silently out of the terminal, taking its red glow with it. Shocked weeping and cries of traumatized relief rippled through the crowd, though none could be more relieved than Zelly the NightRunner.

[THE REALM]
<RealmWorld: Intergalactic Zoo / Planet: Geldunia>

[Zef sat in the corner of the room, invisible to the couple swaying in the hammock facing a grand window. Beyond the glass, a brilliant sunset view of the planet Geldunia played out from orbit, like a vista conjured from a dream.

He'd captured the times they'd spent in the Realm on holographic memory, to be replayed on demand, only now he wished he hadn't. It was becoming too easy to revisit them, too easy to sink back into wishful thinking and melancholy, over-analyzing what could've been. He would watch the scenes unfold, always with that distinct pain ebbing in his heart.

It was all ruined. And he was growing acquainted once again to feelings that he thought had disappeared into the past.

Solitude. Abandonment. Regret.

All he'd ever wanted was to bring her back to the Realm. To start a new life in a place that wasn't full of the kind of pain and betrayal he'd now seen in Dominion City with his own eyes, inflicted with his own fists. But it was something she would never go along with, and something he didn't have the words to convince her of. For Wander, it would be like leaving the only home she'd ever known.

This room, this ship and this hammock, these views of exotic planets and fantastic adventures had all been a part of that. His way of moving their relationship into the Realm in a way that might make sense to her. Through comfort and love and excitement. And even then, Dominion City had managed to ruin it...

If she wants to reject all of this, he thought, *then I'll go myself. I'll save up the Subs on my own and leave this shithole behind for good. This place means nothing to me...and I don't mean anything to it. I won't accept—*]

Zef was startled from his sour thoughts by a pounding on the door. The real door of Haven-4. He slid off his mini-visor and sat up in his seat. His heart thumped like a bass drum in his chest.

Two seconds! It had only been two seconds!

He stood trembling from the chair and walked to the door of the dirty room, nervously glancing back at the holo-table and the NeoLux still in view. He tapped a key on the dusty old security screen and a feed of the alleyway appeared. A shadowed figure dominated the camera view. Zef recognized the glowing stripes of the robes.

A Tetra Priest! We're fucked! He stumbled backward.

What do I do? What do I do now?

{"Zef, open the door."} Maybe's voice commanded from the console.

"Are you kidding me!? That's a Dominion Priest out there!"

He fell backward onto the old couch near the door and continued backing away.

{"Open the door, Zef. He's here to help."}

Zef blinked, torn between blatant common sense and direct orders.

[[Q4: NEOLUX]]
<Fitsmorth Plaza>

The corner of Fitsmorth and 2nd was maddening, alive and thriving with the wild energy of a costumed parade. The kind of public spectacle that had obviously gained permission from Dominion, otherwise it would have been halted by force before it started. It didn't concern Midi, apart from providing her excellent cover to do what she needed to do. She felt that the green Running markers on her suit actually helped camouflage her among the revelers, and that the candy sucker hanging from her mouth seemed rather casual. Not bad for an Unreg terrorist droid strapping an energy explosive to a public utility.

She knelt down at a signpost near her mark at the intersection and unstrapped the EMP package from around her torso. With a few snaps and the pull of a strap, the device was secured and Midi stood up as though she'd never done a thing. Infected with excitement, her steps bounced as she joined the walking parade alongside hundreds of partying Citizens, who were tromping and cheering toward Marquee Square. Convenient, she thought, as her next stop was the Ace Hotel near the far corner of the Square.

"Hey guys, I'm all wrapped up. Heading to my final mark now. I'll stay there 'til y'all shout."

As the raucous parade traveled through the NeoLux, she kept an eye out for Dominion Security.

[[E5: WEST MID-CITY]]
<Teradin Jurisdiction / Haven-4>

Zef reluctantly unlatched the dead bolts, unkeyed the digital triggers, and stood aside the open door. An imposing man in Dominion robes stepped in from the rain. Zef's guts twisted in panic as a spray of water washed over him. The Priest strode past him without a glance and approached the holo-table and map.

{"Zef, close the door, please."}

Dazed to his core, he obediently shut the steel door and went about securing the locks. When he finished, the Priest was already discussing the particulars of their mission with Maybe. Zef felt taken aback, all of a sudden dwarfed by the sense that there was apparently a great deal of information he wasn't privy to.

{"...appears our intel was incomplete."}

"It does seem so, I apologize."

A Tetra Priest apologizing to Maybe?!

"What seems to be the matter?"

Zef watched, dumbfounded, at the sight of the Priest leaning over the table. He wanted to sit, to join in, to run away, to make sense of things. Instead he only stared, unable to budge, his mind wired with electric anxiety.

[[Q4: NEOLUX]]
<Katsudo-Hoffman Center / RealmSquare>

Once the security drones had gone, Digi finally dared to move from her place on the server room carpet and shuffled backward, out of view of the window. Those things had proven to be so unintelligent that they couldn't sense her through the glass, or didn't bother to, but she decided not to take any chances.

Around her, the server stacks rose high, their blue-green LEDs shining in the darkness in columns and rows. It reminded her of the colored grids of RealmSpace. She had never been too fond of that. As she calmed the chemicals that pulsed through her conduits from the scanner ordeal, the comms opened and Midi's voice came through. Her cheerful tone was a wash of comfort for Digi.

// "Hey guys, I'm all wrapped up. Heading to my final mark now. I'll stay there 'til y'all shout."

Digi wanted to respond immediately, but knew it wasn't wise. After being forced prematurely into the offices, she had no idea what might be going on or who might be within hearing range. Best to assess her surroundings before drawing too much attention to herself. Zelly interrupted Digi's thought by opening comms.

// "Haha! Corporate hell! A reaper just showed up in the metro lobby and termed out a couple of street performers, scared the shit out of everyone. I'm alright though, things are calming down here and the Hoppers are cleaning up. Keep me updated on when everyone will be getting here, I'm seeing our exit approaching. Yellow out."

More reassuring news. Midi was finished with her duties, Zelly was alive and well, Zef was surely safe back in HQ, and as long as there were no alarms going off, Wander was handling her business.

Digi shut off her visual sensors for a moment to rest her mind.

Beneath her, under the floor, there was a power-down thump. She opened her eyes to see red lights flashing from ports in the ceiling. A piercing alarm erupted and pulsed along with the lights. She bolted upright, terrified beyond belief, and looked around for some clue of what was going on.

"Damn it!" It was Wander from an adjacent room. Before Digi could spring up to investigate, comms crackled opened and Maybe's even-toned, feminine voice came through on a personal line.

{"Digi, can you hear me? Please do not panic."} *Ha!* *{"The security alert is orchestrated. I can see from here that you've been trapped inside. With the help of an informant, I've activated a threat signal on the bottom level of the building, but I can't get through to Wander. Do what you can to help her clear the office and then immediately follow through with the tasks you've been given. Once the extraction and corruption are complete you'll have very little time to make it to the roof."}*

"The roof?!"

{"It's under control, Digi. Follow your instructions and everything will resolve smoothly."}

Digi scrambled to sort her thoughts out.

"Alright... Alright, we've got this. Blue out."

[[Q4: NEOLUX]]

<Katsudo-Hoffman Center / RealmSquare>

Two to go. She checked her watch. Forty-seven seconds. She was making good time. *Now where the hell are the rest of them?*

Wander spun her sword, twirling a hard figure-eight motion in the air to rid it of blood. She stepped away from the bodies and their expanding pools. Across the room, lit from various holographic displays, a worker's head popped up and removed a large, immersive headset. He was likely the source of the voice Wander had heard responding to the death of Target Two. She ducked her head down below the cubicle line and crept quickly toward his position. She turned left into a hallway made of semi-transparent cubicle walls. At the end of the hall, Target Six stood facing her.

"Wh-who are you?"

She stood upright and, with the tap of her palm to a sensor on her waistline, activated her glowing red runnersuit markers. She smoothed her tousled hair back and started toward him with sly seduction, a devious grin stretching across her face.

"I'm a NightRunner. Have you heard of us?"

Unsure whether the attractive stranger was a threat, the man cleared his clenched throat. "N-no. But this is a restricted workspace. You can't be in here."

She feigned a sad, pathetic pout as she stopped in front of him.

"But I'm already here. And the only way for me to leave is after I've killed you."

Her gloved fists tightened.

"I... I..." He'd realized that she was indeed a threat, but now his legs were too numb to run.

With a pair of one-two punches across the jaw and a boot to the gut, Target Six presented his bleeding face for Wander's knee and she obliged, driving it through his forehead with enough blunt force to fracture his skull. His lifeless body fell backwards and, as he hit the floor, security lights descended from the ceiling. A harsh red glow rotated from each of them, accompanied by an alarm that shattered the silence.

"Damn it!" Her eyes darted around, wondering if she could catch who might've triggered it, but froze still. Target Seven, a beefy woman in a pantsuit and hairbun, held a standard office-equipped multitaser out toward Wander. Naive but very real anger trembled in her eyes.

"Hands up! You're not getting away with this!"

The woman was wrong, of course, but for now Wander had no choice. She raised her hands slightly.

"It's just business, lady. Just leave me to get out of here and no one else has to get hurt." She could see tears of shock streaming down the woman's face, reflecting the glow of the pulsing security lights.

"You... You killed them all!"

"Eh. They had it coming, trust me." She realized that it probably wasn't the best choice of words, and her face scrunched up with silly awkwardness.

"W-well...then you have this coming!" The woman raised the taser until she was staring down its length like a gun.

Before Wander had a chance to react, a tactical throwing knife spontaneously jutted from the woman's temple. One of Digi's knives.

"Corporate-fucking-hell, Digi! What the fuck is going on?"

The portly woman fell to her knees on the carpet, mouth open and dribbling blood, face aghast, and finally slumped to the floor. The taser tumbled away from her open hand.

Digi emerged from behind the cubicle row.

"Did you turn off your comms? Maybe couldn't reach you."

"Yeah yeah, so what?"

"Well, I had an...issue. And now we're stuck in here."

"Stuck in where?!"

"Inside the building." Digi cringed with an apologetic frown. "I'll explain later. For now, I just need to interface, and then we can get to the roof."

Wander stared at her with too many questions bubbling up to even know where to begin, breathing like she'd just slain six office workers in under two minutes.

"Please do what you need to do."

Digi was already searching for a workstation.

"I'm on it, relax."

[[E5: WEST MID-CITY]]
<Teradin Jurisdiction / Haven-4>

Steady rain poured into the alleyway at a strong diagonal as Zef and the Tetra Priest stepped out of Haven-4. Thunder crackled sharply, and the red light above the door flickered in response. When Zef turned around, the Priest was motionless, arms crossed inside his robe sleeves, eyes centered squarely upon him. Zef's innards wrenched with cold apprehension, though he attempted to maintain his calm exterior.

The Priest himself was a tall man, gaunt and imposing. Black hair, still damp from Electuan rain, hung to his shoulder blades and draped above dark pits of eyes and an expressionless, solemn mouth. Zef waited for the mouth to speak, knowing that whatever might come from it couldn't possibly lead to anything but Termination. Zef was a NightRunner, complicit and involved now in numerous acts that directly defied the Corporation, and in most cases complicated their mighty agenda. He was lucky enough that the Priest hadn't already called for him to be confiscated.

Could the Priest, acquainted with Maybe, somehow be a part of all this, all of the dots that seemed to be connecting recently? Not likely, not without a very strong motive. That only leaves Maybe, of course. She isn't who she says she is. She's–

"You must be curious about a few things, Zef."

He attempted to answer, but any sound that may have come out was blocked by a tightened, dry throat. This Corporate Priest knew his name. A name he'd never registered with. Had Maybe discussed him personally with this man? Zef attempted to clear his airway but coughed instead, at last resorting to a nod.

"I understand that this is unusual, but I assure you I have no untoward intentions regarding you or your friends. I am strictly a confidant of Maybe, of the organization you know as the Glade Syndicate." He paused, allowing the information time to process. **"I'm not here on Dominion business."**

"Oh no?" Zef croaked. He crossed his arms against the brisk chill of the damp alleyway air.

"Indeed not. Personal business, my boy. There are many things I cannot accomplish alone. In turn, I assist Maybe where I can, as a sign of...good faith." He chuckled without humor at his own pun.

"I-I'm not sure what to say, sir."

"Zef. I've heard a great deal about your skills. Maybe recommends you highly, and there may come a time when I ask for your assistance. I pay well, and I take very good care of those whose efforts further my goals."

The smell of rain and grease hung between them as the storm pounded against the concrete surfaces and metal railings and splashed into heavy puddles. Beyond it all, the distant sounds of Teradin traffic filtered in. For a moment, the alley was illuminated as a Demigod passed overhead, its spotlight coursing over them from the clouds. Zef was briefly given a glimpse of the man's face. His expression was imposing, though stern and resolute.

"I'll help if I can." The idea of working personally for a Tetra Priest, as well as what that work could entail, unnerved him. Nonetheless, he felt extremely reluctant to turn away the request. Frustrating this Priest and incurring Corporate wrath as a result was unthinkable.

"Excellent, my boy. Then I will see to it that your services are well spent."

It slowly dawned on Zef, the weight of what he'd just accepted. Business with Dominion Corporation. He was under the Eye. The worst place of all.

"And, uh," Zef peered into the dark hollows of the Priest's eyes, "What do I call you, sir?"

The man gave another rumbling chuckle and bowed slightly, extending a pale hand from his robes. His skin was stretched to the bone, but clean and dry. **"Lesser Dominion Priest Marin Mordecai, my boy. Servant in Protocol of the Corporation Most High."**

[[Q4: NEOLUX]]
<Katsudo-Hoffman Center / Roof>

Blustering wind and stinging rain swept against Wander and Digi as they pushed open the unguarded rooftop door of the Katsudo-Hoffman Center. Around them rose a stunning array of much taller buildings, neon-soaked advertisements, highways of air traffic and holographic light shows. In the center of it all, a single light transport was settling down on the puddled landing pad. The pilot exited in a hurry and jogged up to them, shielding himself from the rain with his digital pad. He opened its leather case and checked his info.

"Briggs & Planck Private Medical Services responding to a call from Downtown Mid-City! Are you Wander and uh...Dee-gee?"

Wander laughed aloud. "Yes! Get us the hell out of here!"

"Yes, ma'am!" He waved them on and invited them into the cabin. They climbed in, dripping wet, onto plastic-covered seats and huddled close together. The driver slammed the door behind him and climbed into the pilot's seat. He turned around and leaned over the partition.

"So uh, you both seem fine! No medical emergency?"

Their thoughts went back to the office space they'd left behind, littered with bodies.

"No, we're good!"

"Just take us back, please!"

The pilot looked at each of them and shrugged, satisfied with being paid medical rates for glorified taxi services. He turned back to the control panel and the graviton engine vibrated to life. Carefully, the transport lifted into the stormy weather, circled the roof and then settled on a course. Wander and Digi watched from the rain-streaked windows as the Katsudo-Hoffman Center slowly disappeared among a sea of Neolux buildings. Before long, the entirety of the Quadro NeoLux was only a glimmering point on the horizon.

[[Q4: NEOLUX]]
<NeoLux Station>

"Just us, huh?"

"Looks like it." Zelly smiled and shrugged.

Midi clapped a synthetic hand on her human friend's back as they walked.

"So what happened? They're safe?"

"Yeah, actually. Apparently they got chased down by some Red Industries machines and Maybe had them airlifted out."

"Red Industries? Wilhemson's machines? Aww, I'm going to give them so much shit for this!"

Zelly laughed with her. "Good to have you back safe, Midi."

"Quit with that shit. Where's our train?"

The two Runners dropped from the lobby platform to the railway corridor below and began sneaking past the arrivals, looking for the one that would take them home.

[[E5: WEST MID-CITY]]
<Teradin Jurisdiction / Haven-4>

Sullen and empty, Zef closed the door of the room at the end of the Mid-City alleyway. He went through the locking procedures automatically and found himself face-to-face with the holo-table. An unsettling silence permeated the space. He eased himself into a tattered leather-and-steel barber chair and pulled out his tin of nanocigs. He lit one, shaking, smoked the whole thing, and then lit another one, the various comms of the group a muffled blur in his peripherals. Even when the rest of the Runners finally arrived safe and sound, he was only a shell, given too much to consider on a rainy Electua night.

[[E5: WEST MID-CITY]]
<Teradin Jurisdiction / Haven-4>

With RealmSquare Brokerage eliminated and everyone safe, the Night-Runners celebrated with cheers as Sub-Credits poured into their accounts. After hugs and a few parting words, they filtered out of the door knowing they would all eventually end up back at the flat near the border together. Wander took Zef's hand and pulled him into the alley despite his sluggishness. At the end of the corridor near the main road they paused.

With renewed energy, she pushed him against the brick wall and kissed him. She sensed immediately that something was wrong. His guarded eyes seemed filled with worry.

"Wander... I—"

"Zef. It's fine, okay? I'm safe, and it's not important anymore." She laced her wet fingers with his. "Let's put it behind us. I want to."

The sunken eyes of the Tetra Priest.

"No, it's not that... There's..."

She didn't let him finish, and pressed her lips to his tightly as if it could erase the words from his brain.

"Not tonight, okay? Let's enjoy this."

He watched her, troubled but admiring, knowing she wasn't going to relent. A smile forced its way through his gloom.

"...Alright."

She was elated to watch him come around, and pulled him from the wall by his jacket. "Good. Tonight we have some fun."

Zef followed her, trying hard to push everything out of his mind, though when they reached the end of the alley he was overcome by a sudden chill. Looking both ways down the busy Teradin sidewalks, he half-expected to see Protocol Enforcement waiting for him.

But there was nothing. Nothing but the usual throng of dirty Mid-City folks milling past one another.

Zef's senses began to clear. He could hear the beat of music, a scattering of laughter, the familiar calls of street vendors. If trouble was coming, he decided it wouldn't be tonight. It wasn't worth dwelling on.

She tugged at his hand again.

"C'mon, Zef! Fun!"

With an eye on the crowds, he chuckled.

The energy of the night was emerging.

"Yeah...fun."

CHAPTER 2

INTO THE NIGHT

[[E5: WEST MID-CITY]]
<SouthTown / Abandoned Factory Grounds>

Over rusted walkway gratings they ran, like kids, holding their hoverboards and calling out to each other, leaping over barricades and climbing up janky old ladders. The chemical plant was abandoned, but it stood between the heavily trafficked SouthTown area they'd been exploring and the empty canal they hadn't boarded in ages.

Wander, infected with excitement, laughed out loud as they tore new paths through the derelict facility. All of a sudden, things felt like they used to. No work, no drama, and nothing between them but the space between their boards and the free Mid-City air. Zef was out of his shell, Wander felt accomplished, their accounts were dripping with Subs...all was right with Dominion.

She hurdled over the last railing and slid down the length of a platform ladder. After a few leaps across a series of ancient steel chemical drums, she reached the massive concrete barricade that separated the plant from the empty sewage canal. Zef was still behind her, climbing through the structures, so Wander took a moment to admire the view she'd earned.

Stepping forward onto the edge of the slab, her board hanging off the front precipice, she looked out over the blue glow of Downtown Mid-City past the concrete valley. The view gripped her heart with inspiration. Among the cityscape, several pink skylight beams wavered slowly back and forth, promising thrills and escapes to any who might see them on the horizon. Something about the skylights, the distant lines of hover traffic, the flickering multicolored holographics, the dark buildings and their speckled window lights...it all stirred the butterflies in her stomach. It conjured the notion that if she wanted to, she could make the journey there and lose herself in the chaos.

"Haa!" Zef kick-flipped from behind a rusted filtration tank and soared over the barricade. He came down hard on a cushion of air, and with furious momentum he began racing down the slope. Wander's heart always sank when he did that.

"You asshole!" She leaned forward and dropped into the slope after him. Immediately she was wrapped in the ecstasy and abandon of speed as the humid wind whipped around her. She opened her arms to the night and hollered loudly into the vast concrete canal, exhilarated that there were no Brother Units or Demigod Units or any other stupid Units to tell her to keep quiet. She crouched, holding close to her board, and finally ripped into the level ground of the main spillway. With a burst of speed she sprayed through the puddles at the bottom and carved a wide arc to the right, eventually syncing up with Zef and pushing forward. He weaved left and right, testing his balance, something he'd crashed hard doing so many times.

"You know I hate it when you do that!" She stuck her tongue out at him and weaved with him, reaching out and touching his hand briefly. They laughed and attempted it again.

"Oh damn, you hate me?!"

"Ugh, that's not what I said!" In spite of the frustration he inspired, she grinned at his defiance.

"Wanna go the usual?"

She knew what he meant, the tunnels where they would go to be alone, to smoke and trip and throw things into the stagnant reservoir.

"Not yet, take me somewhere new!"

"You got it, baby!"

Zef switched his footing, wobbled a bit, and stuck out his hand. She caught it this time and they sailed down the next slope, coasting along their descent into the valley together, allowing the night to take them where it wanted.

[[E5: DOWNTOWN MID-CITY]]

<The Glade Syndicate HQ / Private Room>

"Twelve-thousand credits, give or take, and you just left the bodies for the StreetForce to scoop up."

The man with his grimy boots on the glass table placed a dark gray nanocig between his lips. His gunmetal hand cocked back and a torchflame extended from the base of his palm. The nanocig ignited. With a twitch of his thumb, the small flame disappeared.

"Amateur. A rookie move if you ask me."

{"Oh, Breven Lestiny, please do lecture me on how to manage my affairs."} Maybe's synthesized voice laughed sweetly.

"I'm not making fun, honestly. Just trying to...educate. Sometimes it's not as simple as doing *only* the job you're given. Sometimes it pays to get creative. Break more off for yourself than just the upfront reward." He took the cig away and exhaled nanosmoke. It cascaded through Maybe's shimmering lavender face hovering over the table. "Am I right, May? I didn't read specific instructions on how to deal with the RealmSquare job, I just saw a request to shut an office down. And you left seven real prizes dead on a high-rise floor somewhere."

She raised an eyebrow and her pixels reorganized. {"No, you're right. I think it's mostly still just the challenge of coordinating them all that's holding my strategy back. Every group is so different. And this one...They're great at what they do but they bicker and get distracted. And one of them is damn near useless. The male, Zef."}

He scoffed. "Zef. Birthname Leykk Lepras, a Synth out of the Wyrmlands, parents switched him with an uplinked fleshbag and then abandoned him in the Malaang. Yeah, I looked him up. Walking timebomb. His scan is a fuck-all disaster, can't imagine why he would even want to be involved."

{"For Wander, of course. The lust in that boy's eyes is greater than his understanding of what we're up against. He'd spoil the Glade itself if it meant winning that girl's heart."}

"Well, just keep her away from me." Breven cleared his throat in a slow and intentional manner before going in for another puff.

{"Oh get over yourself, 'RealmDweller.'"}

"Not tonight, my love. Although, maybe once Maybe decides to finally put on a body, I can go after the woman I really want, huh?"

{"Well, then! Is that all?"}

Breven couldn't help but laugh at the indignation he inspired. He knew he was being ridiculous, but her reactions made it worthwhile every time.

"Fine, no more foreplay. So what's next? You got something lined up?"

{"Nothing too grand, although I do have a few solos I intend to throw Wander's way. And yourself?"}

He held up a single finger. "One. *The* one."

Maybe searched her memory for what he might be implying.

{"Oh?"}

"And it's from a friend of yours, no less. Marin Mordecai, Lesser Priest of the Corp?"

{"Well, now I'm curious... Tell me?"}

"I plan to. I'm gonna need your help. This one's going to be big."

{"Brev, don't torture me."}

He laughed. "Alright, alright. But, this is going to blow your mind. Only by the grace of the Glade currents is this conversation even possible right now. But it's real, and I hope you're ready."

{"Breven Lestiny, I swear to the Corporation itself."}

He cleared his throat again and allowed the silence to linger, just to make her sweat. "Mr. Mordecai requested that I...remove the Dominion Corporation's ADMIN status over the Realm."

She appeared speechless, though her code rippled in eddies across the tiled surface of her stunned face.

"You heard me right. A Tetra-fucking-Priest...has offered the Syndicate a substantial amount of untraceable Life Credits to isolate the Realm from Dominion Systems."

{"And— And give it to whom?"}

"To be honest, I don't think he cares."

{"But all those people! And he doesn't care who inherits the Realm?!"}

"I don't think he does. If I had to guess, I'd say it hasn't occurred to him."

{"Well then, what does he want?"}

"He didn't say, or he wouldn't. But, Maybe, I really don't think he cares. My premature opinion is that he has other plans. Maybe the Realm is standing in his way somehow. Maybe there's someone inside he wants to cut off from access to Dominion, or evidence of some malfeasance he wants erased, and this is the only way he knows to get rid of it... Either way, I'm not asking any more questions than I have to. This is a checkmate if we can secure it."

{"And you think you can actually pull it off?"}

"From inside the Realm? Most definitely. There's no question about it. Me and my guys could crack Dominion's link from the inside in a matter of days. It's the feet on the ground that we'll need help with. Power stations, surveillance, couriers, transportation, espionage...that kind of thing. That's where you come in."

{"The NightRunners."}

"Exactly."

{"Uh huh. Well, I don't think I have to inform you that they'd all be expecting pay for every operation. I can downplay the–"}

"Maybe, I love you, but if I just wanted your Runners I would have taken them for myself. It's your guidance I need. And I'll pay them more than they've ever made."

Despite always being prepared for this kind of flattery from Breven, an encoded blush swept through her cheeks.

{"I'd be happy to help."}

"And I'd be grateful to have you, dear. I'm going to need access to your top Runner. She and I have some work to do. Think you could bring her up to speed?"

{"Who, Wander?"}

"That's the one."

{"I should have known."} She was poking fun at him. {"Of course I will. Just have her home by dinnertime, you monster."}

"Get off it, May, it's just business."

{"Business is never business with you, we know this."}

"Regardless, this is the big one. We've been searching for a way in and DCORP just handed us the key themselves. Through a defector, no less."

{"It does seem that way. Thank you for thinking of me."}

"Friends, Maybe. This is what we do."

Her digital lips pursed with curious appreciation at his offer in what could otherwise be an incredibly cutthroat business.

{"Right. I'll begin organizing. Take care of yourself, Breven."}

[[E5: WEST MID-CITY]]

<Meta-Terrania QuadroRacing Course, Derelict>

Wander's brilliant emerald eyes, captivated once more on the distant light show of the Downtown Mid-City skyline, had Zef at a familiar loss for words. The two of them had come so far from their days of amateur thieving, and had been through so much as part of the Wicked 6. Now, over a year together as NightRunners, he still had no idea how he'd managed to hold onto her this long. She was such a beauty, with brains and skills to match, and somehow she was still holding his hand. For that reason alone, the urge had begun inside him to call what they shared love, but for his own self-preservation he still resisted. It was his nature, he knew, to fuck things up. Better to keep it simple. Deep down, though, he couldn't imagine a future without her.

They sat in near darkness on a row of dust-caked bleachers, ninety meters above a sprawling community of homeless. Around them, floating like ghosts in the night, the massive old loops of the Meta-Terrania QuadroRacing course were suspended on tall supports. The course was strangely a part of Mid-City Electua, telling of Dominion City's past where the ringed Districts had grown or shrunk for political reasons. Now abandoned, the course and its grounds had been reclaimed by the Citizens of Mid-City. Currently, it housed a mostly questionable community of squatters and fringe techies, all enjoying a bizarre and rare blindspot in the Eye of Dominion. It was a place Zef was very well acquainted with, though he'd never introduced it to Wander for a variety of reasons. Bad memories, of course.

But maybe, he reasoned, *maybe I can erase the past by making better memories.*

"It's unbelievable, Zef." She squeezed his hand and their laced-together fingers tightened into each other. Her eyes, those emeralds, turned away from the gloomy raceway husks and found his. Within them, she could see the quiet pride he held just to be with her. She adored him for it and pulled him close to kiss him.

When the bliss of her lips subsided and reality pieced itself back together, Zef's concerns from earlier in the night had returned.

She placed a hand on his cheek. "Zef, what is it? Please tell me you aren't still upset from Lantern Alley."

"It isn't that, Wander. It's–" He found it hard to maintain eye contact, and instead focused on the open canal far below. "Were you aware that...?"

Wander found the corner of her lip with her teeth. A wave of gut-wrenching worry pulsed through her and she cautiously withdrew her hand.

"Am I aware of what?"

Zef sighed. How could he bring it up when it had the potential to ruin everything that she'd become so passionate about? Should it come from him at all? Was he responsible for this?

"Were you aware... Did you know that Maybe is doing business with a Tetra Priest?" The words left a sour taste and he regretted them.

"I– I don't understand."

He turned back to her, attempting to calm his own nerves by steadying his breath.

"Wander. Tonight, while you were on mission, while all of you were out, a Dominion Priest showed up to Haven."

"Stop."

He was instantly puzzled. "Stop what?"

"What you're doing right now. Please just stop it, Zef."

All the compassion had drained from her eyes and was replaced with anger. She glared at him as if he might be a Tetra Priest himself. "How could you?"

"Wander, this isn't a joke. I can't even believe it myself, but I'm trying to do what's right and tell you."

"Dammit, stop! I've heard enough! The only person you're looking out for is yourself! All I wanted tonight was–" An angry tear slid down her cheek.

"No."

"No what?"

"That isn't what's happening." His voice was firm and his resolve was gathering strength. This would not derail, not if he could help it.

"Then what? Tell me."

"Our boss. Not yours, ours, is doing business with a Lesser Priest of Dominion, or someone doing a damn good impression of one."

Wander allowed him a chance to speak, though she hovered somewhere between not believing and outright leaving.

"He showed up tonight and they talked for a bit while I was there."

"About what?"

"I don't know, I didn't understand a lot of it. But he was the one that caused the security distraction tonight, the alert on ground level that allowed you and Digi to escape."

"So...so he's helping us?"

"I don't think so. I mean, he did. But I think it was kind of a favor to Maybe. I think they do business and he owed her...or something."

"And Maybe? She wasn't surprised when he showed up?"

Zef was glad she was coming around. He wasn't sure he could handle another standoff between them tonight.

"Not at all. I'm pretty sure she called him to come. She made me open the door for him when he arrived."

Wander was lost in doubt,trying to piece together some sense of it all.

"Well, so..."

"Wander." He took her hand slowly, carefully. "There's something else... something I agreed to–"

A gunshot, Old World ballistic, echoed out into the night. The flash of firelight sparked from the canal far below them. There in the canal, a group of cars were pulled together in a ring. Their converging headlights illuminated a strange scene. Figures in business suits, tactical gear, and others in more casual attire all stood around a row of bodies kneeling on the ground. One of them had just been executed; following the pop of the gunshot, the body fell backward onto the concrete.

Zef and Wander's eyes met, their conversation forgotten. They snatched up their hoverboards and scrambled down the bleachers to get a closer look.

[[E5: WEST MID-CITY]]

<Meta-Terrania QuadroRacing Course / Sewage Canal>

High above, on the ledge against the glass, Wander and Zef dropped low and snuck forward. They peered into the concrete valley below, listening intently.

"FEMALE, AGE 27! MEAT BODY, 3-DERIV PROTOMIND, WETWARE KINETIC ENHANCEMENTS! 200 EXABYTES OF OPTI-NEURAL STORAGE! PROSTHETIC TRICORE-F8 LEGS! REGISTERED NON-VIOLATOR! WORKS LIKE A SYNTH, SHOCK-TRAINED AND READY FOR LABOR, STARTING AT FOURTEEN MILLION, DO I HAVE AN OFFER?"

The woman in question had been forced to her knees on the bare concrete along with several others on display. Their keepers stood around them, Sub-wallets ready for anything that might be worthy of purchase.

Even from where Zef and Wander sat, the ringleader of the auction was strikingly distinctive, a trans-human nightmare. His forearms were covered in elaborate steelwork. The webbing wove up from synthetic arms into steroid-blasted shoulders where sub-dermal vizthetics glowed neon green beneath human flesh like bioluminescence. The geometric designs spread over his chest and back, under a leather vest, and up his neck. The aesthetics ended abruptly where his head was attached. It was not so much a head as it was a synthetic, matte black, abstract form. Flat crests jutted out from the back of it, and the face consisted only of an angular array of glossy planes and sub-surface sensory mechanisms. Superficially, his original species was unclear. He stood in front of the next item up for bid, the muzzle of his Old World Glock 17 pressed to her forehead.

"But can she fuck?!" The voice boomed from a hefty man draped in shimmering multi-colored fabrics. His pompous, frowning grin was hidden behind a fiery beard. Diagonal across his face, a jagged scar peeled open where the left eye would normally reside. In its place, a silver, cylindrical optical implant shined with a blue glow. The scar continued upward and carved a path through his ponytailed mane of graying frizz, revealing a golden skull beneath. The awful question he'd bellowed to the auctioneer pulled several chuckles from the grim gathering.

Frightened and shivering, the handcuffed woman shut her eyes tight.

"FULLY," spoke the auctioneer. His digitized voice barked loud enough for them all to hear. "AND A SAMPLE OF HER SERVICES WILL BE AVAILABLE TO THE HIGHEST BIDDER DURING TONIGHT'S INTERMISSION!"

"No one...IS FUCKING ME!" It burst from her before she chose to speak it, and was immediately silenced by the auctioneer who struck her with the butt-end of his handgun. Flickers of black rippled through her vision and an aching sting shook her spine. A stream of blood trickled from her brow and into her mouth.

"Ohh, she's a feisty one!"

"Fourteen point six million!"

"Sixteen million!"

A clamor began among them, each one bidding higher than the last. Around her, the noise became a disorienting roar of electronic and human voices shouting, arguing, laughing. She quaked in fear at the idea of what she might become. She had only ever been used as smart labor. Data trafficking. It hadn't occurred to her that she might one day become a sex toy for some depraved Electuan elitist. The mere notion of being violated caused her stomach and pelvis to ache with anxiety. Without thought, she felt her legs powering themselves into motion, pushing her up with the intent to run.

The auctioneer sensed it immediately and squeezed his trigger. The contents of the girl's skull sprayed across the grease-stained concrete of the canal. The body limply crumpled backward and the harsh crack of the discharged firearm echoed through the stone chasm.

Zef grimaced. He'd seen this several times before and it was never pretty.

"AN ESCAPE ARTIST." The auctioneer spoke it clearly for the rest of the captives and trainers to understand. "ANOTHER LESSON FOR ANYONE ELSE THINKING OF DISRUPTING TONIGHT'S EVENT WITH DREAMS OF FREEDOM."

"What the actual fuck..." Wander watched in horror, trying to digest what was unfolding. "What does 'shock-trained' mean?"

Zef gave her a wide-eyed glance and hesitated. "It means she was a slave. They had her addicted to Stims to keep her fiending. If she tried to escape her owner, she'd just go into heavy withdrawals and probably die. They use it as a reward, like treats for dogs."

Wander found herself unable to look away. "That's inhuman."

"That's the flesh trade. Happens almost every night. My buddy Sardo and I used to work on bodies that made their way over to the Meat Markets from this thing."

Her mouth hung agape. She watched as the gathering continued their business, passing the slaves around and carrying on. "Wh-what do they do with them?"

"Anything. Make 'em work, fuck 'em, some of the sickies even eat them. Sometimes they're looking for a new body to transfer into, you never know. Nasty business but it's insane money for Reshenites when they sell to the THP."

Wander was speechless, lost in her dismay. Zef noticed and immediately felt guilty for his graphic description. "Wan, we're in border territory. We're not even in Reshen. This shit is all over the place. You can't let it bother you."

"It has to bother me..." Her glistening eyes found his again. There inside, they struggled with a cocktail of sympathy and rage. "Zef. I want them dead. I need them dead. All of them."

He shook his head emphatically.

"You don't understand. Electua-rich is not what you want to fuck with. That jeopardizes all of us. They don't give two shits about some battle against Dominion. Hell, they probably profit off of Dominion oversight. They have too much invested to bet against the Corporation."

His hand touched her shoulder gently.

"It's too big for us. I know you want to save those people. I know your heart, Wander. But this is happening all over the place. Cutting one down will only alert the rest and put eyes out for us."

There won't be eyes on anyone, she thought. *I'll do it myself.*

The bright spotlight of a roving Demigod lit up the bleachers and slowly passed over them. They remained still, paralyzed from the realization that they'd let their guard down. The ground and bleacher structure vibrated in resonance with the monstrous craft above as it pushed through the clouds. They both waited, patiently hoping that the surveillance blackout was still in effect. Eventually the blinding glow subsided. The land below came to rest. The Demigod moved on through the night and they began breathing again.

In her pocket, Wander's communicator silently buzzed. Maybe's pattern. She fished it out and, with a pensive look back at Zef, answered the call.

"Red."

[[E5: DOWNTOWN MID-CITY]]

<Church of Protocol, Chapel 2814>

A miniature flame bounced and grew slightly brighter, expanded to encompass the candle wick, and then separated into two. Lesser Priest Mordecai held up the wooden lighting stick and puffed it out. From the burnt end, wisps of smoke curled upward toward the ceiling of the chapel.

Mordecai whispered the last of his psalms to Protocol and stood from the kneeling altar. Beyond the veil, the chapel organ and chorus began their song, serenading the souls of the gathered Citizens of Electua. With a final bow to the Dominion Corporation Logo above the small altar, the Priest adjusted his robes. He moved forward, parting the curtains that led into the main worship hall.

Within the expansive cathedral, flat slate-black walls and a drifting haze held the dim illumination of burning red neons, suspending the packed room within a dream-like state of cosmic reverence. The congregation hummed along to the drone of the organ melody with bowed heads as Father Mordecai, spiritual leader of this particular Church of Protocol, stepped up to the pulpit. He indulged his devotion and removed the hood of his robe slowly, a sign of witness to those present. The congregation understood that he was ready to begin his sermon. A hush descended over the pews and the organ faded to silence, echoing out through the great space.

"Citizens. I am Lesser Dominion Priest Marin Mordecai, servant of the Corporation, humble interpreter of the will of the Unfolding, and residing prayer leader of Chapel 2814.

Welcome. Sit. Join me tonight."

At his request, the congregation eased their tired legs and sank into the rows of black pews, jostling with commotion as they did. He gave them a moment to collect themselves and adjust, then continued, looking over them with the pride of a dutiful patriarch.

"My Children.

"It dawned upon me this morning, after a night of restless sleep, what the nature of our sermon would be tonight. I had plans to speak of loyalty and faith, but as can often be the case, the intuition of the Corporation within me had other plans. I would not be your Priest if I was not ready to share with you what has been shared with me. Let us grow together.

"Children of Protocol. All of us here tonight, yes?

"And yet, what do we know of Protocol?

"What forms does it take in our lives, and how can we make our devotion to it known?

"I, personally, find that there is often a gray line dividing our living Path from our intended Path. It is here within this gray line, this uncharted territory, that our sermon will dwell tonight."

The low intonation of the chapel chorus began, and swelled to a thrumming ambiance. Mordecai opened his book of notes and sketches to the most recent page.

"This previous night was an awful and dreary one for me. Something held

me captive in my meditation, something formidable. And prowling about my Sanctum was a beast.

"Trembling, I would be, on the verge of nightmares, if it weren't for the pure Light above, that Corporate Light that I had somehow taken for granted. Inside its familiar warmth, I laid down my fears, and I realized that the dark intruder was neither beast nor man, nor synthetic nor holoform, but a dark fault within my own spirit. My own lapse in Faith.

"I had come to feel lost within myself. I know that it's been evident in these days leading up to our time tonight, but I can only apologize. It has taken everything in me to persevere, and I believe that I have come to see what was present all along, though absent from my own mind. Clutched within my trepidation, I began a renewed vow to Protocol Herself.

"Children, what do we know of Her?

"It's been said that Protocol came not from man nor machine, that it arrives to us only through forms we could not understand, no matter how much in earnest we try. It has been spoken by Priests through generations that Protocol is somehow greater than this plane of reality, that it extends past Dominion City and is part of something beyond, a higher order, the order of the Unfolding. But for us, we know only what we can know, what we can perceive of it. And these perceptions come in the forms that our bodies can understand...forms that our eyes can see, that our heart can be moved by, that we can speak of, using the fragile words we've conjured.

"It's said that the Protocol we can perceive is never the true Protocol. This leads me to believe that there must be more."

The pitch of the chorus rose higher, while the lower end began to rumble, enhanced with warm synth instrumentals.

"Between our living Path and our intended Path lies a territory that we must seek to overcome. Take a moment now to open your mind and understand, to allow a New Protocol to awaken with you, as I have. A Protocol that governs change, that allows us to grow. This Protocol is the Path that we call Sacrifice.

"It is precisely through this Path of Citizen Sacrifice where we find our way forward."

Priest Mordecai paused, contemplating such wisdom.

"What is ignorance? What is misunderstanding? What is the state in which we find ourselves, when we have strayed and are unaware?

"Pain.

"The pain that walks hand in hand with life. The pain of not knowing, the pain of pushing forward, the pain of having more choices than the wisdom to make them all. Ignorance is the pain of the unknown. But the unknown is divided, and there are two kinds of pain.

"One type is the pain we experience when we are unsure of the way forward, and the weight of this bears down upon us like the weight of a Demigod, pressing down on a fearful heart and threatening to crush us. Our legs feel as though they might buckle. We become suspicious that perhaps we did not know all the things we thought we knew, and in the end, we allow ourselves to play the role of the victim. Through this pain of uncertainty, we begin to Violate. We steal to ensure certainty, we lash out at the ones we love, our fellow Citizens, and we lash out toward ourselves.

"This is one half of the unknown.

"The other brand of pain, my Children, is the pain of Sacrifice. The pain we experience when we understand that the going is tough, that the journey is long, and that our legs are sore, but we push forward nonetheless, because we see a brighter tomorrow inside our minds. It's a pain that takes a toll in its own ways. But it is the pain of forging ahead into that unknown, of coming to confront it head-on, on our own terms, and giving all that we are, so that together we may manifest a common reality worth inhabiting. This is the nature of Citizen Sacrifice. It is the pain of creating the future, rather than being created by it."

The chorus dithered out into intertwining melodies, and the red strands of light throughout the chapel grew brightly, soaking the room in pure blood red.

"My Children. We are living beings, flawed to the core in the eyes of the Unfolding, but forever looked upon with adoration by the Corporation.

"Our journey forward shall be one of growing closer to the Word of Dominion, and into the Light of Protocol, that the Unfolding may see us in a more gentle way.

"It will be a painful journey,

"One that will test our grit and merit as individuals,

"Force us to accept our limitations and grow beyond them when we are capable at last,

"But ultimately, it will be a journey of understanding that Protocol will always Prevail.

"When we allow this understanding to enter our hearts, our fears shall each subside, and together we will rise.

"Let us end our sermon tonight with repentance for these fears.

"Please stand."

With a wave of Mordecai's hands, the congregation rose to their feet. He turned to the final pages of his notes and cleared his throat. As he spoke, they read aloud with him, and together they conjured their Obedience.

"Holy Corporation,
Forgive us our thoughts,
Lest we stray toward deviance.
Forgive us our dreams,
Lest we turn from your Light in our sleep.
Forgive us our nightmares,
Should they imply that we fear,
For we know that in Protocol there is no fear.

Send out your Brothers into our City,
Send them out to save us from ourselves.

Should we stray, give us their blade,
Should we run, make sure we are found.
For in Termination, we find Sacrifice.
To Violate is to perish,
Only to be reborn closer to You.

Praise to Our Lady Protocol.
Praise to Her Unfolding.
Praise be to Her Dominion."

The congregation echoed his praise, the chorus again swelled, and Lesser Dominion Priest Marin Mordecai bowed deeply. He drew his hood back over his dark hair, leaving his features in shadow. His part in the Corporate Mass was complete. He stepped away from the pulpit, and made his way through the curtain to the back of the Chapel.

Once in relative solitude from the congregation, he withdrew his communicator from a pocket. The bluish glow of the display lit up the darkness. Among other messages and requests, one waited from Breven Lestiny, the one who called himself the RealmDweller.

[[E5: WEST MID-CITY]]
<Southtown Street Markets>

"So what did she— Oh, fuck, Vincenzo! Where the hell ya' been hiding, brother?!"

Zef veered away from Wander, hopped off his board, and strolled up to Vincenzo Sardo, bumping fists with his old friend in a familiar greeting before they embraced.

"How you been, Zef? How's the new body holding up?"

"So far, so good," Zef mimed a few quick hand-to-hand strikes to demonstrate and they both laughed. "It's been fun, I can't complain."

"Of course you can't, I'm no butcher. Especially those struts at the base of the 'bellum, you can't fake those connections."

"It's been worth every Sub, my friend. The Realm uplinks have been seamless." He was rubbing the back of his neck, remembering the old pain of the upgrade surgery. "Oh hey, uh, have you met Wander? She..." He held his hand out only to see Wander getting lost in the street market crowds. "And there she goes."

Sardo smiled, quietly satisfied that his acquaintance with Wander would go untold. "Women, yeah?"

Zef turned back, noticing a strange look in his friend's eyes.

Was something amiss?

"And what about you, Sardo? Still a Voly?"

"Fucking Corp, Zef, keep your voice down."

"Yeah, alright," he sneered.

"No, I didn't join. You know I wasn't going to, not with how they do business."

He wiggled all his fingers in the air. "Besides, I could never give up these babies

They've written more code than Skightler."

"Skite's a joke."

"All the same, I part with these fingers for no one."

"You afraid that the tech itself is gonna show you up, huh?"

Sardo sighed and laughed, shaking his head, "Bastardo. C'mon now, give me what you owe me."

"It's coming back to you soon, lay off. I could give you a few tonight but it would only set me back."

"It's not your Subs on the line, *Leykk*."

Zef bristled visibly at the use of the name. It was a name from a past life, one he intended to keep secret.

"Alright, alright. Sooner than soon. I'll make it happen one way or another. How do I get in touch?"

Sardo reached inside his jacket and flicked a shimmering data card so that it sparkled in the air as it spun. He caught it between two fingers and extended it to Zef. "Personal line. I'll be expecting you."

"Good. I need to talk business with you soon anyway."

"At your service, old friend."

"Still chopping out in the Meat Markets?"

"Of course, where else?"

Zef laughed. "Well, you're all the way out here, so I thought I'd ask. Seems like a hike."

"Hey, I'll take the hike for quality THP parts any day."

"Heard that, brother. Well, I'm with the lady. We'll talk soon."

"You got it, mate. Take care of yourself." He remembered Zef's upgrades and tapped his own temple. "And stay off the Stims."

"Pff. No promises."

Their fists pounded again and they parted ways, each pointing a finger back at the other. It was a dirty old Reshenite farewell called the stillstare. Partly a grim reminder for friends to watch their back, but it also spoke to paranoia, where both parties could gain ample ground before turning away. Such was Reshen.

After a safe distance, Zef grinned and stepped back onto his hoverboard. He glided carefully through the crowd over to Wander who was still perusing the street vendors.

[[E5: DOWNTOWN MID-CITY]]
<Church of Protocol, Chapel 2814>

Chemical rain straight from the Races fell in dense sheets and thrummed across a colossal black slab of a building. The structure was cut here and there geometrically as if it were manufactured all in one piece, and then placed in the center of Downtown Mid-City by The Dominion Corporation. It seemed to dwell in its own shadow within the night, rising high into the fog of a stormy sky as a silhouette and accented only by blazing red Dominion neons. Beneath the monolithic shadow of the chapel, a single Priest stepped out into the damp Electuan air, below the cover of a walkway and into an illuminated garden. He revealed his communicator, which was currently ringing, and tapped a softly blinking key.

"This is Marin Mordecai."

"Priest." The voice of the RealmDweller.

"Yes, yes, go on."

"I've got some news for you."

"Thank Protocol, I was growing concerned. Is the line secure?"

"As secure as it gets, my pious friend."

"Excellent. Let me hear it."

"Well, it looks like you've got yourself a crew."

"Elaborate."

RealmDweller laughed. *"Not an ounce of tact or patience for all that prayer, huh? Well,"* the clickety-clack of a keyboard could be heard beneath his voice, *"then you're not going to like what I'm about to say..."*

The Lesser Priest's eyes narrowed, his patience thinning. A pair of churchgoers enjoying the night atmosphere appeared in the garden and he offered them a customary but informal Prime Salute, two fingers in the air. The man responded with a Four-Fold gesture of interlaced fingers and the woman nodded deeply. They carried on past him and Mordecai returned his attention to the call.

"But from the research I've done, Dominion is pretty damned determined to make sure that something like this was never going to succeed. There are four main server stations, one per Sector, and countless smaller backups, each operating independently and able to pass off processing load. What you're asking is going to take training time, materials, schematics, enough Life Credits to—"

"But can it be done?"

"Look, holy man, I've already told you it can be done, and I've already agreed to stream your little friends from DC-8 here. I think I can isolate a Corporate VRnet. I told you I was the best. There's not a single network I can't crack, given enough time."

Mordecai calmed his riled nerves with a deep breath. He found his gaze wandering through the rain, lost between the droplets. He couldn't risk articulating to this arrogant man he'd hired how grave the circumstances actually were, and for that he owed the man his patience. But the balancing act he was currently performing had its own inherent stresses. With Termination around every corner if this thing happened to go wrong, he was dedicated to making sure it would be executed with precision and zero margin for error. Such things were difficult, though, when dealing with the type of individuals it required to get the job done.

"How much time?"

"Yeah, well, that's the part you're not going to like. Due to the multiple server stations, the routed power, the security intervals, the manpower... We're probably looking at a timeline of about a year."

"A year?!" Mordecai was appalled and stifled his initial retort. Never before had he needed results so urgently, and to hear that he would have to wait a year, that his clients would have to wait a year where they were, that everything he'd planned would need to be put on hold...

His response was terse, though he lowered his voice to an exasperated whisper. **"Is there any way to circumvent all of this? You have your Glade at your disposal, I assumed this would be a quick operation. It is absolutely dire that pieces be in place as soon as possible. The wheels are already in motion, for the sake of Protocol!"**

"Well then, Father, you're going to have to un-motion them. This isn't some kind of game I'm playing. You're damned good business and I'm not going to run you around. With certainty, this kind of job is going to take at least a year. That's gear, that's planning, personnel, reconnaissance, tying up my own loose ends—"

Mordecai scoffed. **"Enough. I understand."**

The line fell silent and remained a low fuzz.

"Fine. I'll move some things around. But I'm going to expect progress reports from you on an extremely regular basis..."

RealmDweller had him.

"Wouldn't have it any other way, holy man."

[[E5: WEST MID-CITY]]
<Southtown Streets>

"Why'd you leave? I would've introduced you two."

Zef's smirk gave away what he suspected about her and Sardo. She let him suspect it and carried on, pushing hard against the concrete to zoom out in front of him on her board. "Didn't want to kill more time than we needed to."

"Fair enough. Ah well..." His eyes coursed over the clubs, the arcades, the restaurants and more, stacked high on multiple levels all around them in the bustling congestion that was SouthTown. On this night, he wished they could just be free to explore. "So she's not even giving you a single night off, huh?"

"Oh relax, Zef. I'll be an hour at the most. We've got lots of time."

He frowned in disbelief but reluctantly gave up, realizing that the last thing they needed was more drama. Continuing to thread through the pedestrians, he kicked hard and coasted up next to her. "So what does she want?"

"I'm actually not very sure. Something about the Realm, though. Something big."

"Since when do we operate in the Realm?"

"We don't." She passed him a familiar glare. His cynicism had run its course.

"Fine, fine. So, Digital Domain?"

"Yep. Wait outside for me?"

"Sure." A grin spread across his face at the thought of a new challenge. "I'll score us a few kicks for the drain."

"Hell yeah. And snacks."

"Yeah yeah, you'll get your snacks."

She winked and wagged her tongue.

"You know what I like, baby."

They laughed and cruised on, their voices mingling with the multicultural conversations of the crowds around them: the music spilling out from the shops, the sound of mechs lumbering past with their massive mechanical legs, street barkers shouting, the announcements from various floating hovers, all layered beneath the patter of light rain.

Wander pushed forward on her board and felt the steamy evening breeze rush past her. In a few minutes, she'd be in the back of a smoky Mid-City bar using pay-to-play public Realm gear in a stifling closet hoping that she'd get an hour of privacy. Out here on her board, the air was still free, and she closed her eyes to soak it up before they arrived.

[[E5: DOWNTOWN MID-CITY]]

<Breven Lestiny's Apartment>

Twelve-thousand prismatic sheets of raw code streamed past each perfectly spherical quantalic of RealmSpace each nanosecond. They indexed outward within elastic shells, expanding and contracting based on innumerable environmental particulars; the foundational building blocks of real-time Realm simulations. They encompassed such complex parameters as fluxing gravity, simulated ambient radiodata, and even the presences of active synthetic consciousness, as well as live user data and biometrics pouring in from across the entire circumference of Dominion City. The scope was staggering, beyond any previously conceived VRnet that had been developed in the history of Earth. It was a deeply layered, multi-dimensional work of meta-programming bliss; vastly more varied in culture than the Human Internet of Late Pre-Fall.

His conversation with Mordecai complete, Breven Lestiny tapped the ebbing DOWNLINK key on his Realmside UI. In a rapid succession of waves, his awareness was funneled out of the Realm like a million gleaming drops through a strainer. The nerves beneath the skin around his ports tensed, the hairs on his arms raised, and the rods and cones of his eyeballs relaxed. In an organic interplay of mind, body, and technology, his neural implants responded by leaking the necessary cocktails into his bloodstream. At the base of his brain, a memstretch patch rebooted. Breven's arms and legs came online and his eyes opened.

Blindly, he searched his pockets and then the cluttered side table for a pack of nanocigs. He pulled one out and set it between his lips, again feeling the warmth on his face as he lit it with his wrist-flame. He dragged slowly, powerfully, then inhaled and held it, allowing the nanobots to filter into him and do their work. At long last, he exhaled. Smoke rippled through the glowing holo-panels that hung in the air around him.

"Zeppelin."

Immediately, the thumping beat and rising string melody of an Old World jazz tune called "Kashmir" began. Breven drew another thick drag of the nanocig and allowed the music to relax his nerves.

It was always this way after his ventures into the Realm, most especially the long ones. His rig was top of the line, genuine perks of his position within the Glade Syndicate. Built for the sole purpose of injecting his consciousness wholesale into RealmSpace with as little between him and the digital breeze as possible. There in that digital cosmos, he would lose all track of time and year. He could explore fantasy worlds, space colonies, dream vacations and alien wars, distant pasts and bizarre future, continuously searching for another piece of the puzzle...But the journey back to Dominion City was always inevitable.

The sensation of downlinking from a complex rig like Breven's was similar to steeply compounded jet-lag paired with stepping off a rollercoaster. It was bound to throw the inexperienced user into Realmsickness, and the likes of Breven into bouts of bottomless wanderlust and nauseated ennui. To combat these, he drifted like he always would down a river of nano-effect, accompanied by jazz and the light tapping of cool Electuan rain against the window pane.

{"You awake, huh?"}

"Hello, dear. Yes, I am."

{"That's good. I'll be speaking to Wander in just a moment."}

His mind was still absent. "Put in a good word for me."

[[E5: WEST MID-CITY]]

<Teradin Jurisdiction / Haven-4>

A jumble of characters scrolled down the display of a portable holowire as the encryption attachments did their work, though it was hardly a steady stream. Piece-by-piece, a holographic image began to appear in the display. The feed stretched in a glitching abstraction through empty space, slowly forming the erratic image of a derelict android. Its eyes glowed golden through the garble of static, and it spoke in a harsh, synthetic rasp which crackled as the image wavered.

> "Priest Mordecai, a pleasure."

Lesser Dominion Priest Marin Mordecai bowed curtly. He sat with poise in his Tetra robes opposite the small console.

"A pleasure indeed, my friend."

The image quality began to clarify.

> "What is the state of things?"

"Everything is progressing, Dimas. It's been a difficult time keeping things out from beneath the Eye." Despite the admission, his demeanor remained stoic.

> "And the High Dominion Priest?"

"Varis Kane suspects nothing; he's of no concern."

The android studied the man through the skewing digital barrier.

> "Well done, human. How soon will we be able to start moving our men to your side?"

"Very soon. Mere days. It will take some time to deliver the Realm, though. I've good word that it may take up to one year to free it from the grasp of the Corporation. I must ask for your patience as I continue to move pieces into place."

> "Granted, Priest, though we grow very impatient in this...place." The android turned its rusted head to peer at his surroundings, which appeared to be the insides of a some kind of shack. The golden eyes returned back to the feed. "And what of the Doctor? Any word from the man who calls himself Eschaton?"

"None. His last contact was made months ago, but I do not expect his absence to be an obstacle. Regardless, we should initiate Teal Dawn."

> "Let it be so, and we'll see what becomes of this. Burn brightly in the fire, Priest."

Mordecai gave a solemn nod. "Burn brightly, Dimas."

The holowire feed fizzled out from the android's end, leaving Mordecai staring past the nonexistent holo-display.

Phosphorus.

He considered the conversation, its implications, the war he was beginning... and rose from the desk. It was time to return to the Chapel.

Mordecai collapsed his portable holowire console and stood. On his way out he flipped a light switch, igniting the glaring red light above the door, and exited the dark room into the rainsoaked alleyway. He went through the locking protocols of the door and, for a lasting moment, mulled the option of never returning.

[[E5: WEST MID-CITY]]
<SouthTown / Digital Domain Bar>

The tavern known as the Digital Domain had once been a frequent gathering place for the Wicked 6. Those memories always returned vividly when Wander thought of the place. Back then, Laveau was still a part of their tight-knit group, before she'd fallen head-over-heels for a Lotus programmer and ran away to City Center. As a group they'd spent almost every night crawling the streets looking for the next thrill, more often than not finding themselves on the curb outside the Domain. The buzz of stims and kicks and various drinks spun their heads as they laughed off the worries of being nearly broke and socially outcast. It was a place they could mingle, make connections, pretend that they were moving up in the social fabric. In reality, Mid-City cared little for petty thieves and couriers.

As Wander approached the door, she saw that the friendly holographic host Luna was still present outside the door to greet patrons. Zef had a fascination with Luna, something Wander had always noticed during their comings and goings. She wasn't sure what it was about the hologram AI that held his attention, though she saw it as harmless. Luna was a glorified holo-dancer, relatively stationary and only capable of so much conversation before she lapsed into the same old subroutines. Wander thought it might be Zef's connection to the Realm that made him want to bond with any other artificial intelligence he could find. Whatever the case, Wander knew better than to engage it. It seemed connected to his pain, and she was hesitant to dig any deeper.

Zef remained outside now, chatting away with Luna as Wander pushed her way through the spring-loaded wooden door of the Domain. The interior was particularly dim and crowded tonight, and she was instantly confronted with a noxious wave of smoke and perfume and other questionable odors. The old stereo system thumped with a Quadran club track that reminded Wander of 283. She remembered Zelly and herself meeting the twins, back before their involvement with Maybe.

Good old days, she thought.

Moving into the bar, she parted the crowd gingerly, not wanting to upset a drink or accidentally walk into a lit cigarette.

"Fully human, huh, baby girl?" The comment was for Wander but she frowned and ignored it, pushing onward. She slid past strange prosthetic oddities, holo-displays that illuminated faces she didn't recognize, and revealing conversations from Mid-City individuals she dared not even glimpse.

"Hello, Mello!" The familiar sing-song greeting came from Macy Rex, the long-time Domain bartender who grinned and waved a rusty old multi-arm. Wander waved back, eager to show the questionable crowd that she was acquainted with their bartender.

"Macy, how've you been?!"

"Oh it's going, hun. What can I do for ya?" Macy kept busy with mixing cocktails and cracking open beers as she shouted.

Wander raised her voice above the noise of chattering patrons and music.

"Got any VR rooms open?"

"Honey, you're just about the only one that uses those things. Will it be just you?"

"Just me this time, Mace. Shouldn't be long!"

"Take all the time you want, just make sure to lock up behind you as ya' go in. Quite the crowd tonight, know what I mean?"

Wander caught a set of keys from Macy, then flexed her bicep playfully.

"I got this! Thanks a lot!"

Macy laughed and waved her on with the prosthetic hand. Wander hadn't bothered correcting the woman's use of her old name, thinking it better to leave any NightRunner association far away from this place, where ears that could betray her might be listening. Better to be Mello, part of an old group of troublemakers, back for a good time and nothing more.

She pushed past one last group of surly drinkers, ignoring their depraved eyes, and entered the main hallway leading to the arcade. Wander keyed open the door to the VR room and let herself in, shutting and latching the bolt before even turning the lights on. When she did, she was greeted with the same familiar old room, mustier for the years and lit by a single dim bulb. Wasting no time, she checked the smelly old VR apparatus and its connections, then climbed into the chair. Unable to strap herself in, she slid the headset over her eyes.

"Activate."

At first, nothing happened. A soft beep finally sounded somewhere inside the ancient headset and the unit whirred with the vibration of an internal fan. A speck of light in the center of the display appeared and gradually it expanded to a thin horizontal line. It continued until it had created a ring that wrapped three-hundred-sixty degrees around Wander in the darkness. The ring extended upwards and down, encompassing the entire virtual space in pixelated static. It flickered to darkness, and then an aquamarine logo appeared, floating in space, that of the headset manufacturer.

"Thank you for choosing Synesthesia Synaptics."

The logo shimmered as if it were made of brushed metal, then dissolved.

Around her, building up in bands of resolution, a photorealistic alcove came into being. Suddenly, she felt far from Dominion City. Around her, the chest-deep waters of a tidepool rippled with each motion of her head. Had the VR rig been fully nerve-synced, Wander would've been instantly immersed to the sensation of sea water against her bare skin, ebbing with small waves from the bay that lapped against the cavern walls. She would have felt the undulating reflections of warm sunlight filtering in through the branches of the palms that bent above her, and perhaps a light coastal breeze cooling the droplets of her sweat. Instead, the rig was basic, exactly what one might expect to find in an arcade in the back of a Mid-City bar, and it limited her immersion to audiovisual only.

"Welcome to the Virtual Lagoon."

Accompanying the message, a calming island-themed tune began. Locked to her forward perspective, a floating blue menu extended from nothing, displaying several entertainment options next to animated icons. Within her view, two hands appeared, fully within her thought-control, and she tested them like usual by wiggling the fingers and moving the hands in small circles. Her real-world hands remained perfectly still, resting at her side.

Inside the virtual space of the headset, she directed the right hand up and over to an option titled "ENTER THE REALM" and tapped it with the index finger.

"You've chosen to enter the Realm. One moment, please."

The menu retreated and faded away, and the alcove scene spun slowly around her, its ribbons of horizontal pixels skewing in patterns and fading to black. In the darkness the brilliant Dominion Corporation Logo appeared, its red cross holding a white sphere, suspended in the void. Behind it, beautiful imagery from various RealmWorlds played out. Massive spacecraft soaring past in *Nebula of Conflict*, dragons circling above a village in the *Wyrmlands*, a group of adventurers climbing onto a mushroom in *Miniature Island*. Wander waited patiently for the sequence to end, having seen it many times before. At last, it winked away.

Around her, the infinite purple and pink wireframes of the Realm Hub appeared. They multiplied and extended in all directions, and a new menu wrapped all the way around her where she floated. She wouldn't need to enter the Sprawling Downtown area this time, or muck around finding a private corridor. Maybe had given her a link that would bring her straight to the VRnet of the Glade Syndicate, fittingly called the Glade, where they would have total encrypted privacy from prying eyes.

[[E5: WEST MID-CITY]]

<SouthTown / Digital Domain Bar>

"Well, hey there, big boy! How's your night?" Luna performed her trademark routine of swaying her shapely hips as she greeted Zef. The two of them had spoken countless times, though her courtesy and charm hadn't wavered a single iota.

Luna was a hostess hologram, a snapshot of a personality designed for a single purpose: hook would-be patrons and train them to be regulars. The neural nets that governed her behavior were always learning how to be more charming, to keep up with the times, the slang, the changing customs of the passersby. In this way, she might just be charming enough for them to stray into the Domain for a drink.

"Eh..."

In response to her question, Zef's thoughts skimmed over the RealmSquare mission, meeting Lesser Priest Mordecai, hoverboarding the canal, the flesh trade, bumping into Vincenzo Sardo, and eventually arriving here.

"Did some work, made some money."

"Ooh, what kind of work?" She wiggled a bit, seeming fascinated with his very brief story.

Zef smiled, a very human burst of serotonin flooding through his mind at being fawned over by another being. He considered the question. He'd already discussed a bit of NightRunner work with her, though how would he explain what he'd actually done tonight?

"I, uh...worked with my usual group. Guided them to the NeoLux tonight from the command center."

"Oh baby! That's incredible!" She began a dance while conjuring stock images of the NeoLux in her archive, but flickered back to her start position as several patrons stepped up to the curb. "Hiya, boys! Welcome to the Digital Domain!"

A couple of them smiled and waved, the rest ignored her.

Zef looked away and drew a nanocig from behind his ear as he scanned the crowds for just the right type of individual. Depending on what he was able to find, their night could go a few different ways. More ways than it might some other time, when he didn't have 700 Sub-Credits burning a hole in his account. He hoped he could find them a few Stims or some Loda-pellets, but he'd settle for chilltabs if that was all that was around.

"Tired tonight, my love?"

Zef looked up and Luna had a finger between her holographic lips. She was batting her eyelashes bashfully. Her body language woke something up inside him.

"Zeffy baby, why don't you go inside and get some Revitalyze for those droopy eyes? I think it's still happy hour..."

He raised an eyebrow at her, his brain attempting to parse the seduction from the advertising. After a moment it all became a blur; he was too faded to analyze anything. He looked out into the street, bobbing his head to the dance music of a nearby club. The night was early. He produced his Rezno lighter and lit the nanocig.

"Nah, I think I'm good! Those get me kinda jittery..." He rubbed his hands together, trying to arouse some energy, and exhaled spent nanoparticles. "Not tryna false hype tonight. I want that good shit. The real love. It's out there somewhere."

Luna flickered a bit at his use of the word love in this context. She ran a categorical check against her current database and derived the most likely meaning. He was referring to its use as a slang for dopamine stimulants.

"Oh baby, you don't need that... Besides, you promised me you'd buy a drink last time."

She pouted with baleful eyes and slowly pulled her bottom lip from between her teeth. Zef wondered whether it was true and peered upward at her, considering the drink.

[THE REALM]
<Loading...>

[A layer of open space extended in every direction, out into the infinite darkness between the walls of up and down. Wander had progressed beyond the entrance portal of the Realm. Now she bobbed mid-code as if suspended in an invisible, mass-less liquid. The endless chasm was filled with abstract permutations of all sorts opening up dimensional doorways and then shutting them, melding into one another, spreading out into space like fractalized tentacles and joining back together, going about their nonsensical geometric business.

The visual experience was extremely surreal for her, far beyond the imaginings of anything Dominion-side. It was one of the between-worlds within the multi-layered dimensional network, a glorified loading screen. Wander couldn't recall the proper name for them.

She held out her hands again. They were colorful now, and writhing on the surface with crawling patterns.

"Oh, wow..."

It was precisely this kind of thing that kept her out of the Realm almost entirely. Not because it scared her, but because it was such a drastic and unnecessary change from reality. She couldn't feel it inside the simulated reality, but she often got the sense that her physical body was dealing with an immense headache. Inside the Realm, it manifested as a lag, a visual disorientation. A nagging feeling that what she was seeing around her wasn't real, or was somehow less valid than RealSpace. Until she could afford to surf more often on a higher-tech rig, like the pod-lockers in EtherAfter, she didn't plan to bother with the Realm too much.

Abruptly, the bizarre loading space began to transform. Bright light soaked through the edges of the unreality the way water soaked through a towel. It emerged from nothing and consumed every writhing pixel of the abstract display. Wander's eyes dazzled as she took in the spectacle, and before long the seams of a new reality pieced themselves together.

She was standing in a pristine meadow, only something was much different here than any meadow in Dominion City. Here, the air itself crackled with some kind of magical energy, as if the natural Percarus District had become its own RealmWorld within the fantasy-themed RealmSpace of ALTRUANIA. Waves of rippling breeze crept across an endless sea of tall grasses and flowers in the sparkling daylight. The meadow spread to all horizons beneath an ethereal sky of swirling blues and purples, dotted with clusters of forest.

She had arrived in Maybe's Meadow.

"Always good to have you back, Wander."

She spun around to see the humanoid form of Maybe, shimmering a delicate lavender in bodily effect and wearing an elegant gown that seemed to emanate swirling particles. She was indeed a lady, despite her artificiality.

Wander's face beamed. It was so incredibly easy to be at peace in this place.

"I'm glad to be back, thank you. I hope I'm not bothering you..." She felt aware of the vast difference between her relationship with Maybe inside and outside of the Glade. On the outside, Dominion-side, Wander was a proud member of the NightRunners, ready to give all her effort to achieving the goals Maybe set before them. But within the Glade, Wander was smitten with respect and admiration for the woman, at a level generally reserved for a mother or a mentor. Here, she could fully feel that Maybe was part of something larger, something that Wander had always dreamed to be a part of. She had no doubts that the Syndicate was where she belonged.

The soft breeze of total freedom swirled around her, here in the Glade where her actions were not scrutinized nor her life in constant jeopardy. Where grass could grow high and wild in the sunlight instead of stunted under the acidic permasmog of Electua. Thoughts of Dominion City led her back to thoughts of Zef, and whether or not he would last long enough as part of the NightRunners to be invited into the Glade. His words came back to her from their argument earlier that night. He cared more about their relationship than about the cause. He was already so discontent as to seem ready to leave, and she wasn't sure if it was her job at this point to convince him to stay.

"Of course you're no bother, and I hope you've had a nice evening so far." Maybe's kind tone seemed to radiate genuine care for Wander. "You did an excellent job this evening... Always my most efficient."

Wander was grateful for the praise. "Thank you, I try. You've been a really great leader for us, I feel honored to be a part of it all."

Maybe bowed gracefully, folding one arm beneath her bosom and the other holding a pinch of her gown.

Once she'd risen from her bow, she stepped forward. "I find as much inspiration in you as you seem to find in me, my dear." Surrounding her form, a glistening aura of radiant energy sparkled and ebbed away into the fabric of the Glade. "I could not be more impressed with your resourcefulness."

The heat of a rosy blush filled Wander's cheeks and she tried to contain a smile, though it gave way to a bit of bashful laughter. She had no words, but didn't want to endlessly repeat her thanks. Instead, she gave a playful bow in return.

"I know you aren't accustomed to your achievements being recognized, Wander, but you deserve it. You're a good person, I know you are. And you're a natural at the kind of work we do. The kind of work the Glade does."

Wander fell back on light skepticism and folded her arms. "What, fighting tyrannical corporations?"

Maybe was unfazed. "Exactly."

She reached a shimmering, translucent hand forward to take Wander's own. The accompanying sensation flowed up the girl's arm from her fingers and gave her a soft shiver. It felt as though she'd slipped her hand into cool, rushing water. She understood innately that this was a form of expression for Maybe, rather than the affectation of some sort of avatar. A virtual way of sharing with Wander a sense of trust and calmness.

"That is exactly the sort of work we do. Among other things, of course."

"What kinds of...other things?"

Around them, a special ambiance seemed to amplify; the ambiance of Maybe's

Meadow. The buzz of unseen insects, the faint whistle of the breeze through the grasses, the rustling of the trees, a soft melody meandering out from nowhere... Maybe turned and led the way.

"Walk with me, Wander."}

[[E5: WEST MID-CITY]]
<SouthTown / Digital Domain Bar>

"Leave him alone, he's just a freshie!" The word was usually an insult, but Luna was using the only word she knew to best approximate her meaning. The term meant that Zef was a Synth, a Realm AI, still a few years fresh within his Dominion-side body. In that sense, it also implied he might be foolish and naive in street smarts.

"Don't try to protect me, Luna! These wrenchfucks have it coming, I was just the one to finally teach them the lesson." Zef lunged forward, telegraphing a punch that missed its target clean. He stumbled forward and spun around, fists up and ready.

"Yeah, he's a freshie. Still can't hit jack shit in that thing." Deano, a driver and mechanic in baggy clothes, folded his arms. Several of his fingers were prosthetic and most of his neck and face were covered in tattoos and ports. He watched Zef with cocky amusement through electronic eyes, ones that could dial in to assist him with any sort of repair.

"Fuck off, Deano. I've been in SouthTown for longer than you have, and the Domain is my territory. Take your wannabe ass and your greasy fuckin' friends back to the FC before I throw you out."

"Back to *my* Circuit, heya? Where your scrawny ass ain't never won a race, and you for damn sure ain't got a scrape o' clout for all the zero Sub-Creds you haulin'." He looked around at his group who laughed with him. "Boy, step down before we make a mess of you. We go where we damn well please."

Luna flickered in confusion, assimilating the information but trying to keep Zef in her favor.

What was all this about?

"You go where I say you go..." Zef couldn't contain his grin any longer. He stood upright and smoothed his mussed hair back. "Now, whatchu holdin' onto?"

Deano laughed hard, shaking his head at Zef's typical nonsense. "Boy, you fuckin' crazy. You're lucky I deal with your scrawny ass. I got Blazers. XL-Greens... Would melt that shit-for-brain you're living in right to next week." He tapped a fat pocket on his oversized jacket and winked. "Sixty a piece."

"Forty."

"Sixty."

The logic channels in Luna's software scrambled.

"Fine. Gimme five."

"Two."

"Three."

"Done." Deano held out a grease-stained hand. "Subs."

{THE GLADE}
<GladeWorld: Maybe's Meadow>

{During their walk, Maybe had remained silent, leaving Wander's mind to drift over the complex sensory brilliance of the Glade. Finally, they slowed to a stop at the edge of a trickling stream. The water itself was alive with ecstatic energy here, the air crisp and breathable, the sky impossibly blue and visually suggestive of wild and flowing geometric patterns. It was as if every surface was so dense with information that Wander was only able to take it in as some sort of pure, unfiltered psychedelic experience.

Could this possibly be normal for Maybe?

"Normal is a nothing-word, Wander. And I need you here with me right now. I have something that I very much need to explain to you."

Can she hear my thoughts?

"Of course I can, dear, where have you gone?"

"I..."

"Wander. Not everything has a ready explanation. You must accept what you feel and see around you. It does no good to be lost in astonishment and searching for answers. Let's conduct ourselves with some grace, yes?"

The speechless girl took in a deep breath of the warm, potent air and attempted to clear her mind. "I understand."

Maybe smiled. "Good. Now, you inquired... What other kind of work is the Glade involved in?"

Wander nodded, still coming to her senses.

"There are many things I cannot tell you. There are many things about the Glade for which I, myself, do not have the answers. But as an organization, the Syndicate certainly isn't limited to small, disruptive operations in Quadro. Our influence is deeper than that."

"...Deeper how?"

"Deep like the roots of those trees, Wander. Stretching out into the soil of Dominion City. District governments. Industry and agriculture. TETRA. Citizen factions. The Realm. QuadroRacing..."

"You...you have members who are QuadroRacers?"

"Several, yes." Her brilliant lavender eyes hesitated. "The point is that we aren't limited in the type of work we do. You are a NightRunner now, but in the future you will have many more options. Many avenues for your efforts to make a difference."

"Against the Corporation."

"Yes. More specifically, toward progress in Dominion City."

"But..." Wander could sense where this was leading.

"But first, I need you to be a NightRunner. One who understands that her actions, her training, and the effect she has on the City are not limited to Running."

Wander's eyes were transfixed within the glimmer of the iridescent stream as it reflected the sunlight in bursts.

"So then what's the assignment?"

Maybe was impressed. "Helping a fellow Glade member who's been hired to do a very dangerous something. A friend of mine. You'd be working along with his crew through me. Being a presence on the ground. Though it's early in the planning stages and I don't have as much information as I want to give you. This is why I need your patience. Until then, I am very prepared to keep you working and paid well... Is that something you want?"

Her mind returned to Electua, to Zef, to Midi and Digi and Zelly and even Laveau. Her eyes found Maybe's own translucent pupils. "Always. I'm a NightRunner. That's not changing any time soon."

And as if an unspoken contract had been sealed, the two women stood in silence, the encoded world around them swimming with detail. Wander, entranced by the landscape, dwelt upon the feeling that things were finally evolving. She hadn't felt it since Maybe's first offer, the one that had made them NightRunners. She was stepping into a new world again.

"I'm very happy to hear that, Wander."

With a flourish of Maybe's hands, the teeming meadow of the Glade hub rippled, coming apart into layered planes of organized code and rearranging.

"Now. Let's talk business."}

[[E5: WEST MID-CITY]]

<SouthTown / Digital Domain Bar>

As she pushed open the heavy door of the Digital Domain and stepped into the putrid humidity of SouthTown Mid-City, Wander was fascinated with how different everything could seem after one simple conversation. Only a little more than a year as a NightRunner and she'd been singled out from the group to work on a larger project. She'd somehow proven herself even when all she'd been doing was what came naturally to her. It put the entire time she'd spent as a Runner into perspective. She was in the favor of the Glade Syndicate. She'd learned the power that it held and was being offered a place within it all. Further still, Maybe saw something in her that she hadn't even seen herself.

It's going to be a good night...

She weaved through the intoxicated crowd on the front terrace of the Domain and pushed toward the pink glow of Luna, the holo-hostess. There next to her, Zef leaned against a garbage bin, gesticulating with both hands as he explained something beyond her comprehension.

"What are we up to tonight, baby?"

At the sound of Wander's voice, Zef turned from Luna mid-sentence with a mischievous smile stretched across his face. He lifted both fists. Extending up from them like middle fingers were two green Sim-stims.

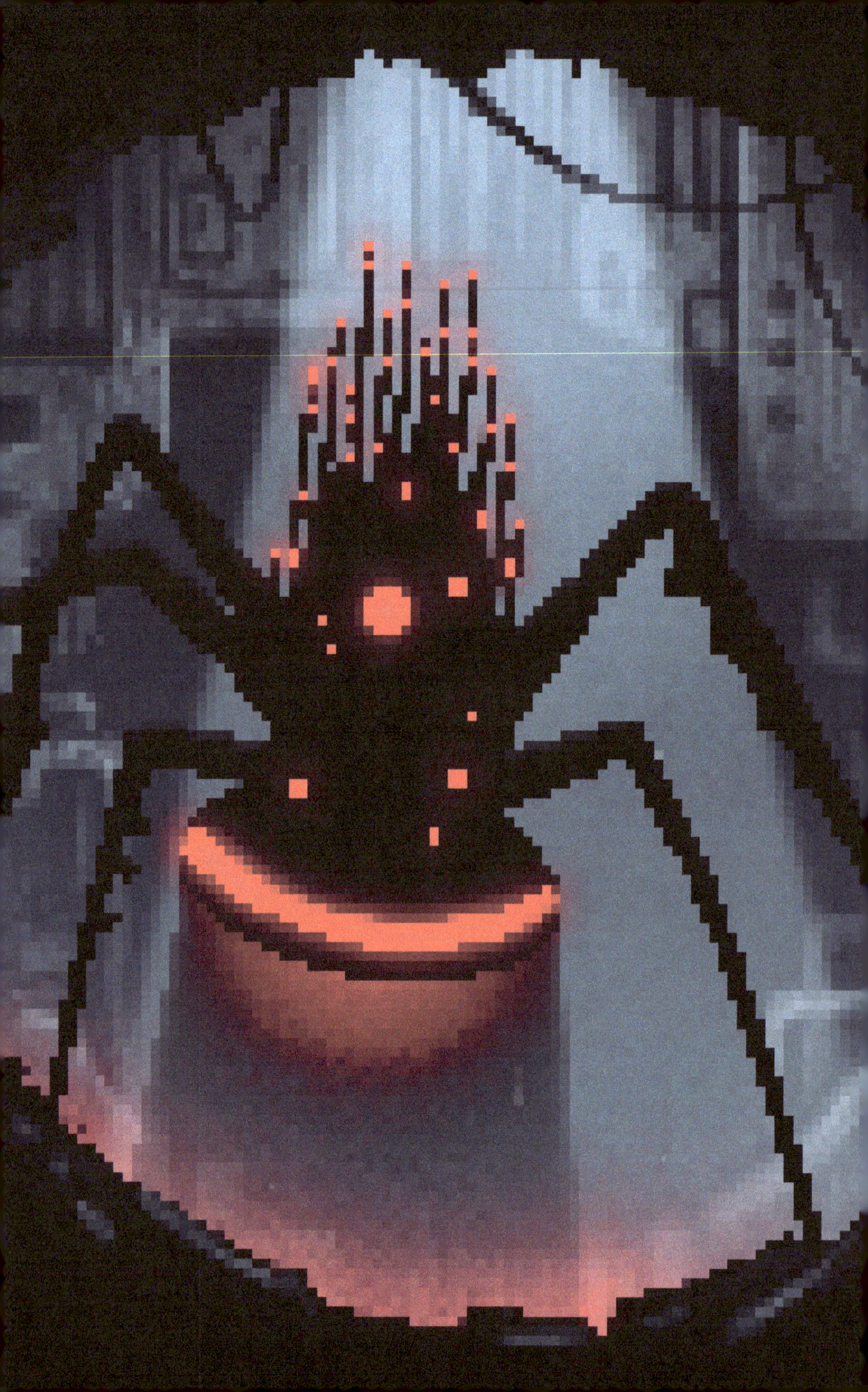

CHAPTER 3

NO REST FOR A RUNNER

[[E5: WEST MID-CITY]]
<SouthTown / Abandoned Reservoir>

The distance down to the stagnant water of the old Mid-City reservoir was jaw-dropping, though Wander and Zef had spent enough time in the tunnels to no longer be bothered by the vertigo. They dangled their legs over the rusted edge now, snacking on a paper bag of questionable goodies and dry meat jerkies they'd purchased from a street vendor on the way. To drink, they'd found a bottle of bootleg Tranquilo. It was a concoction of malted liquor and nerve stimulants making its rounds as a popular vibing sipper.

In Zef's pocket, the Stims were waiting patiently for them to be ready to trip and he was more than anxious for the time to arrive. Wander, on the other hand, was thoroughly satisfied and engrossed in her nanocig and Tranquilo buzz, captivated by the expansive view over the reservoir. Beyond it, the glowing skyline of Downtown Mid-City was nearer now. Its holograms and wavering spotlights mesmerized her eyes, playing off the rain and fog to produce the sensation that the city was alive and bustling with activity. The sight felt both familiar and brand new in light of the discussion she'd had with Maybe.

"So she pulled you into the Glade again, huh?"

"Yeah, she did...it was really beautiful."

He didn't smile. She didn't mind.

"We walked down to a stream this time. It felt like the whole world was nothing but energy, even the air. So different from the Realm."

"I know, you mentioned that last time..." He took a swig of his drink and capped it. "It's funny though. I've never been, and she hasn't invited me either. I wonder why."

Wander frowned, still leaning back and looking out over the city lights. "You want to visit the Glade?"

"I don't know." He finished the last of the first bottle and tossed it out into the reservoir. It spun rapidly all the way down, glinting in the light of Downtown Mid-City, until it finally splashed into the water. Circular ripples extended out, disturbing floating piles of trash and debris. "It'd just be nice to be included."

"Well, if it makes you feel any better, Midi and Digi have never been either."

"Why not? They're hard workers."

"They definitely are. I don't know why not."

"That's lame. Seems like favoritism to me."

"It's not favoritism. But then again, it might be. Who cares? It's Maybe's business, she can favor who she wants to."

"Yeah, I guess."

Her eyes drifted back to his in the dark.

"You know, we're supposed to be having a nice night right now. We're kind of on a date."

"Yeah, yeah. I'm sorry, I–" He withdrew a nanocig of his own and lit it. "I'm still getting used to all this."

"But just enjoy it, Zef. Look at us. Even if you don't give a shit about why we're doing it, Maybe's paying us well. Really well. I mean you didn't even have to do any work this time."

"Hey! I–"

Wander winked and he caught on that she was playing with him. He leaned in, planting a kiss on her. She held his face close, and for a moment they forgot everything, feeling only each other's lips. He moved away reluctantly.

"I work my ass off just like the rest of y'all. You know that."

"I know, freshie. I was fucking with you."

Zef was silent for a moment, captivated by the way her lips moved when she spoke. He finally came around and kissed her again, and then sank back into his spot against the tunnel wall. "So what did Maybe have to say? Was it about a job in the Realm like she mentioned?"

Wander wrestled with the sudden urge to choose her words carefully. "Something like that, although that wouldn't be for a while, and there's still a ton of planning to do. In the meantime, she's sending me on a solo."

"Oh shit, yeah? Where to?"

"Downtown Mid-City."

She pointed an unsteady finger out to the city on the horizon.

"Nice! What's the pay?"

She pursed her lips to the side and furrowed her brow.

"Oh, come on. It's no good?"

"Well, I told her I'd do it for nothing." It wasn't quite the truth. "I said I'd do it as a thank you for everything she's done for us."

"Bullshit you will! How the–" His eyes closed tight as he forced himself to shut up. He placed an apologetic hand on her arm. "I'm really sorry, Wander. But that's insane... What's the gig?"

"A hit."

"In Downtown Mid-City?"

"From like a block away. At dusk." She found herself lost again in the city lights, unable to look into his eyes. "I'll be fine."

A metallic clang echoed in the tunnel as the back of Zef's augmented head fell against the steel wall. He had to admit that he was proud of her in a way. There wasn't a thing she wouldn't do to prove herself or get an inch closer to her goals, and she hadn't always been this way. She had more ambition than all the Runners combined. But to take on such a dangerous assignment with no compensation was asinine.

"Zef, it's my choice." She leaned forward and crawled over, taking a seat next to him and holding his hand. "I appreciate you caring, I know you want to look out for me. You want to make sure I get what I deserve. But this one is for Maybe, and it's my choice."

He gave in, knowing that things had already been shaky between them tonight. He didn't want to push their luck. "Alright. I get it. I really do. I'm just worried about you. I hate the idea of–"

She interrupted his string of anxiety and kissed him for his kindness.

"Don't be. You know I'll be fine."

"I know that..." He tried hard to push away the sense of foreboding that seemed to travel inside him like the storm clouds above Electua. "Of course you will. You're the best fuckin' NightRunner in Dominion City."

"Damn right I am." She smiled with a playful conceit. "I win."

Abruptly, his eyes lit up. "You uh...you ready to sim?"

She laughed out loud at his manic change of direction and her voice echoed into the darkness of the old steel tunnel. She leaned forward and kissed him once more for being such a scatterbrain, then lifted his chin and looked into his eyes.

"Let's do it."

{THE GLADE}
<GladeWorld: Maybe's Meadow>

{"Now... Let's talk business."

The fabric of the Glade continued to transform around Maybe and Wander until at last it resolved, taking the shape of a bustling city street. Wander stared in amazement as the scene sped rapidly past them at several times the norm, building lights twinkling in the fleeting timelapse. Demigods zipped past overhead through the rainclouds. Day and night cycled rapidly, slowing, and honed in on one particular day. Morning gave way to an overcast afternoon, which transformed into the golden hour of sunset. More Demigods on patrol. Clouds parted. Shadows crawled down the buildings, across the pavement, over the crowds.

The air traffic finally lurched to normal speed, abruptly enough to shatter the neck of each driver. On the ground, pedestrians reduced from a blur down to visible faces, each chatting, laughing, going about their daily business. Finally, the bright sky, like a slowing clock, ticked into place with the sun at a precise angle. It shined brilliantly beyond the concrete towers among a backdrop of glowing orange clouds.

Normalcy took hold, and Wander stood on convincingly solid ground among what was certainly a thriving Downtown Mid-City. As Maybe had advised, she tried with all her might to avoid feelings of awe that threatened to overtake and dull her mind. Instead, she breathed heavily and observed, trying to discern what about this particular area might be the reason they'd arrived. She drew a blank.

"Wander. Welcome to Downtown Mid-City, Electua District. Twenty hours from now."

"What do you...?"

The creeping realization flooded her mind and extended out to the individuals walking the streets around them, before them, ahead of them by twenty hours.

"How is this real?"}

[[E5: WEST MID-CITY]]
<SouthTown / Abandoned Reservoir>

Holding sim-stims out, caps removed, Wander and Zef shared a lasting kiss that rivaled a psychedelic trip in its intensity. Their wet tongues caressed and their teeth bit until they'd reached a fever pitch. With heat flooding through their bodies, nano-particles swimming inside their racing bloodstreams, passion gripping their insides, they nodded to one another and plunged the lime-green Blazer stims into the soft flesh beneath their chins. The prismatic effect rocketed into their systems face-first. They locked lips again, hardly able to twitch a tongue. The sequence was one of their longest-lasting traditions.

When they'd finally gained back enough feeling and awareness to move, they began tearing off each others' clothes in a frantic race. Once his shirt was removed and thrown away, Zef leaned forward, laughing, and climbed on top of Wander to prevent her from undressing.

"Oh, no you don't!"

She shoved and he tumbled to the curved metal floor. She removed her slick black pants and straddled him, pinning his arms. He instantly stopped struggling and watched, eyes wide and mesmerized as Wander slowed her body movements down to a sultry dance. She removed her lipstick-red tube top slowly for him.

Zef ogled with pure admiration. His mind tilted, shifting into a vast simulation with Wander at its center. Her naked body formed the definition of delicate beauty from raw liquid code, echoing out into space at her edges. She leaned forward onto him and their warm, shirtless chests pressed together. He used the last of his ability to control himself to pull his own pants from his waist. She wrapped her soft fingers around him, and with her teeth she found his neck. His self-awareness dissolved into a dizzying array of conceptual particles.

"Fuck the Corporation..."

"No..." she spoke, her words coming apart near his ear into a thousand threads of pulsing abstract filaments, flitting around one another, pouring into his mind and igniting his synapses, the echoing voice of the Wander-goddess beckoning him, commanding him: *"...fuck me."*

{THE GLADE}
<Downtown Mid-City, Future>

{ "I must remind you, Wander, to try and refrain from feeling overwhelmed

I can definitely assure you, this is only one of many new things you'll be learning while under the umbrella of the Glade Syndicate."

The girl forced herself to swallow as her brain labored hard to assimilate her surroundings into some sort of realistic context.

"Is...is this a different dimension?"

"Not quite. That part isn't important right now. You must trust me on that. Just like the map I revealed to the NightRunners earlier tonight, this sort of thing is only a tool. A tool to get a job done. Wander."

Hearing her name, she snapped out of her daze. "A tool. Got it."

Maybe bowed her head with gratitude, smiling genuinely, and moved forward along the sidewalk. Her eyes scanned smoothly over the crowd as if she were searching for someone. Wander watched curiously, still gawking at the chaotic business district as if it were something other than the Downtown Mid-City she'd seen on the horizon only an hour ago.

"There. That man."

Maybe's shimmering finger pointed out a human, male, both eyes implanted with hard optics and a matte black false jaw. Aside from these augments, he was dressed in what looked like an extremely expensive suit pressed to perfection and carried a suitcase in a tattooed hand. His stride was purposeful and swift.

"What about him?"

"Ashram Lozuto. Investor, consultant, programmer, Life Credit billionaire. Somehow still clean. He does business with Dominion on a regular basis and his connections go deep, and dark."

"And who are his connections?" Wander felt the flutter of digital butterflies in her stomach, realizing that this question might be none of her business. "If it's alright for me to ask."

"Certainly." Maybe opened a hand as they walked. Above her palm, a floating interface unfurled from nothing, a hologram in a holographic world. The display revealed a clear picture of Lozuto beside a feed of his pertinent attributes. There were connections to Floodgates Bioware, XXL Carcinogenics, Terra-Firmware Corp, Parallel Circuitry Inc, Escapade AI, and the list continued. All the Inner Rings business a good flesh-investor would be keeping an eye on. Wander neatly understood that such a man might be in a position of terrible influence, though it was still unclear why he might be a worthy target of assassination.

"So where's he going with all this?"

"Funny you should ask. It's no secret. He's been a public voice against Life Creditors monopolizing the human death toll of for-profit VR games. It's an enormous market in the subterranean battle for minds in Dominion City, in and out of the Realm."

"Seems like a public service."

"It would be, if it weren't for the fact that he also publicly owned the majority share in a particular firm called RealmSquare."

"The ones we took out tonight."

"That's right. And RealmSquare is only the beginning. Mr. Lozuto has his hands on both sides of the fence, funneling bodies under the table while preaching his 'Every Body Deserves a Mind' message..."

"So that makes him a hypocrite. But why does the Glade care what he does? You...we...aren't policing Dominion, are we?" Wander got a sick feeling in her stomach at the idea of the Glade somehow affiliating itself with Protocol Enforcement.

"Of course not, dear. Our interest is the welfare of the victims, the Citizen casualties. Hundreds of thousands of minds are being trafficked." Maybe's severe tone gave way to a knowing smile. "Though it doesn't hurt that we'll be funneling a portion of his net holdings to the Syndicate. Our time is worth something, after all."

Wander sifted through the logic.

"It's about more than the kill, Wander. Everything that happens in this city causes ripples, like a stone entering a pond. The death of RealmSquare and then Lozuto is a clear message to the kind of people we don't tolerate. That single death, as opposed to all the evil he takes part in, has the potential to shift the entire economy of Dominion City."

Wander understood. It was a clear statement to his associates, whoever that might be. No one wants to piss off an unseen enemy that kills before it asks questions. That last bit added a bounce to her step, knowing that she was the one doing the killing. Wander was a difference-maker.

"So then what's this one worth?"

Maybe's expression turned to one of pride, and she slowed to a halt on the busy sidewalk. "Precisely, Wander. And it is worth quite a lot, what I'm asking. Nonetheless, I'm going to be asking that you complete this task without pay. A debt of gratitude, if you will."

"Oh?" In the year that Wander had been working for the Glade through Maybe, she'd never been asked to do a job for free.

"And in exchange, your place among the group that will assist my close friend here will be secured."

"But I don't know anything about that work. I don't even know who your friend is."

Maybe crossed her arms and smiled.

"He's called RealmDweller. His name is self-given, in fact, and somewhat in bad taste if you ask me, though his skills are anything but a joke. He has a gift, Wander."

That name. It was used to describe Citizens who were irreversibly Realm-addicted. Why would he claim it as his call sign?

Wander suddenly felt in over her head. Her eyes narrowed as she found herself swimming in potentiality, laboring over a sea of too much information all at once.

"Wh-what sort of gift?" }

[[E5: WEST MID-CITY]]
<SouthTown / Abandoned Reservoir>

Ripples of the Blazer simulations were still spiraling around them as Wander and Zef made their way through the sewer tunnels back toward SouthTown proper. They'd made their love, like something out of a cybernetic fever dream, tossed their trash down into the stagnant reservoir, and then she'd explained to him that she desperately needed sleep if she were going to have any hope of pulling off her gig in Downtown Mid-City. Reluctantly he'd agreed, and together they took off into the sewer labyrinth, their heads still spinning.

In the darkness, they found each other's hands. Working slowly, they helped one another over the piles of refuse and puddles, and around the jagged ruptures in the steel tubes. As they crept along, gravity seemed to sway beneath them, as if they were standing aboard the deck of ship at sea. Strange shadows played off their peripherals. The tunnels themselves were pure claustrophobia.

From above, a siren sounded out into the night, up on street level. It wailed as it came close and then stretched long, dissipating as it faded away.

Zef's ears perked and he followed the invisible source with his eyes.

"Always freaks me."

"What does?"

"The sirens."

"But why? You're clean, right?"

They arrived at a juncture in the tunnels. He nodded toward a new direction and they began walking again.

"Eh, it's not that. Just the idea of being locked up."

"Better locked up than being torn apart by a reaper."

"No way. Better torn apart than locked up with no way back to the Realm. Stuck in this shithole forever."

"It's not a shithole, Zef. It's our home."

"Not my home. Never was. This whole city is just..."

"Oh shut up. It's not that bad."

He sighed, hating that she couldn't understand. She'd never been inside the Realm the way he had. She didn't know how boundless the Realm truly was, free from the tethers of being confined to a single reality. To be raised a Synth, to have seen the things he'd seen and then to be abandoned, trapped inside a rotting human body in this stinking city with no way out. It amounted to an awful sense of wanderlust that could never be quenched. Sims and sex and hoverboarding were good times, but they weren't the Realm. Nothing here could compare.

"Talk to me. I wanna know what you're thinking about."

His eyes, filled with the residue of swirling fractals, found and met hers in the darkness. "One day I'm going to show you."

At last she understood.

"The Realm?"

He smiled and continued forward, stepping over piles of ancient, soggy refuse in the tunnel.

"Of course."

She watched him, unsure of what to say, as he walked ahead for a moment. The thoughts weren't quite formulating in her brain the way she was used to. Simbrain. Eventually she gave up and began walking again, and the words came out without her even deciding upon them. "Take me, then. Tonight."

Zef stopped in his tracks and turned toward her, his pupils picking up what little ambient light there was around them as they searched into hers.

"Tonight? Are you serious?"

Her heart pounded with the abrupt change in direction things had taken. Had she made that choice? Was it what she really wanted or was she still simming?

Suddenly thoughts of Maybe and her mission the next day rushed back to her. Was she ready to give everything up and go into hiding inside the Realm? With a man who didn't even know who he was half the time? Would she even enjoy that?

"I—"

As soon as she'd spoken, the deep *CLANG* of metal against metal resonated through the damp steel corridors. They hushed, their instincts now sober and on alert, their hazy eyes searching the dark ends of the tunnels for what might be lurking about. Far down, near the midpoint of the tunnel behind them, a ventilation shaft allowing thin slits of fluorescent light dismantled and clattered to the tunnel floor. The full beam of white-blue light filtered in but only briefly, obscured by a heavy shadow.

The Brother Unit lowered itself in through the duct. Its bladed, mechanical legs now fully extended like the limbs of a giant spider. It climbed through the hole and lowered itself gingerly to the sewer floor with otherworldly grace. The black cylinder of its body was dotted with the glowing red spheres, and it rotated back and forth slowly, spinning the antennae that rose from the top of its head. It reminded Wander of an attack dog, attentively sniffing the air.

After a moment of searching by radio, the Brother Unit emitted a redbeam that flickered before it became solid. The beam slowly crept down the opposite side of the tunnel. Zef and Wander knew what it meant, though they were frozen in place with fear, the flowing effects of the Sim-stim inhibiting their trained, innate NightRunner survival instincts.

"Zef..." she whispered.

The acute senses of the Brother Unit reacted immediately to the sound of her voice. The massive thing, silhouetted with light from above, swiveled manically. Its harsh redbeam flickered and descended again, this time directly toward them.

{THE GLADE}

<Downtown Mid-City, Future>

{The tension amused Maybe, knowing that it would have also amused Breven. She beckoned Wander to follow and began walking again. In truth, she was unsure of how to answer the girl's question. There was no way to precisely explain Breven's expertise. He was a man of many talents, though they were hard to define to those who lacked the insight or experience to understand them.

"RealmDweller is a digital magician. That's as close to the truth as I can manage. I can't claim to know his motives, but when he wants something, he makes it happen." She held a single hand up toward the buildings, the air traffic, the setting sun. "This future-world you're standing in now was his discovery, one he made and donated to the Glade Syndicate...for us to use."

"Did he create the Glade?"

Maybe didn't answer immediately. Wander assumed she was either choosing her words carefully or that she'd had enough of the questions. To Wander's surprise, she answered calmly.

"No. Not from what I'm aware of. Although I've heard that he holds very close ties with the Founder." She paused. "I've never met the Founder. Not directly. Though he seems to be a kind man. I believe in him."

Wander was speechless, unsure whether to continue searching for information. It seemed as though she'd stumbled into a peek at how the Glade itself functioned after only a short conversation. Not only that but she was being given a chance to work with someone who had close ties with its creator. Within a year, maybe two, she imagined that she might run her own crew and stand a chance to meet the Founder. The responsibility of it all came rushing in, forcing her to take a deep breath to try and center herself.

"If you don't mind, how did you find the Glade Syndicate?"

"There, on the left." Maybe pointed to Lozuto again. He was entering the glass door of a remarkably clean high-rise that soared into the neon sky, disappearing into a fluff of orange and pink clouds.

Wander left the conversation behind, falling back into strategy mode without realizing. She'd accepted the reality that they were indeed viewing the actual future of Electua District and looked around to find any sort of clock. "What time is it now? What's the window?"

"That's my girl. It's 17:12 in the evening and your window begins precisely now. Lozuto will be here, on Level One-Eighty-Nine for forty minutes, working in a private office on the north side of this tower. It shouldn't be difficult to spot him. This window was of course chosen for minimal security and a wide range of access, although his personal bodyguard Siresh will be present." She turned to Wander with a wary glance. "Forty minutes."

"Alright, no problem." As she was about to ask Maybe exactly how the target should be executed, she stopped herself. She was the NightRunner here. The decision would be hers.}

[[E5: WEST MID-CITY]]
<SouthTown / Abandoned Reservoir>

"SHIT!" They shouted it in unison as the Brother Unit leapt forth immediately and began clambering toward them in the tunnel. Wander felt a hard shove and stumbled backward.

"Go! Wander, run! He's mine, he's coming with me!"

Wander, her throat clenched and legs weak as jelly, continued backing away, her hand tracing the ribbed, rusted steel of the tunnel wall. At last she turned, forced her sim-lazy knees to lift, and slowly began jogging away. Over her shoulder, there was no sign of the reaper.

Its footsteps were a considerable distance away, and they pounded on the metal floor of the tunnels like strikes on a gong. They seemed to fade the further she moved away, until another glance over her shoulder revealed the true thing in all its glory. Arching above her, the Brother Unit's bladed limbs stretched outward like a shadow hand. One scythe arm stabbed downward in a blur and buried itself, sinking into her chest like a bullet–

"NOO!"

She sprang to life from where she lay against the tunnel so intensely that it startled Zef awake, who had been softly coasting on the waves of his simulation. His eyes searched around in surprise.

"Babe, what is it?"

Wander held a hand against her thumping bare chest, her heart trembling in its cavity, her brow dense and warm with beads of sweat. She felt the skin where the reaper blade had penetrated. It was solid, no gashes, no blood. She allowed herself to breathe again.

"Nothing. Bad trip." She flopped back down against the wall in relief and drew the cool night air into her lungs.

"Oh, damn. Don't let it ruin your sim, baby. Just chill and reprogram." He rolled back over, instantly asleep again, drifting in a digital bath of cherry waves.

Still feeling a bit paranoid, Wander pulled herself back up, this time to her feet, and carefully inched over to the edge of the tunnel overlooking the reservoir. She sat with her legs hanging off the rim, took in the wide view, and enjoyed this moment of silence she'd been given.

The sky above Downtown Mid-City was lovely for once. A handful of visible stars twinkled around a bright round moon. Their shining reflections shimmered amid the leaves and muck of the greenish-brown water below. The sense of vast space above the reservoir came over her and staggered her sense of scale. Beyond the great lake of the reservoir, the glittering lights of Mid-City with its one roving Demigod was a hundred times further away still. Wander was captivated, floating somewhere vaguely between water and sky, and embraced the peaceful moment. It was the first one she'd enjoyed in days, it seemed.

Not wanting to move away from her spot, she turned and laid back within the curve of the tunnel and put her legs up on the far wall. After a moment of adjusting it became the perfect spot to recline, and in this position yet another ethereal sensation made its presence known. The distinct difference between the open-air space above the reservoir and the muffled, confined environment inside the tunnel played off both of her ears.

Outside to her left, the buzzing of crickets could faintly be heard. A distant train. The honking hovers of the city. The ghostly churning of some heavy machine.

Inside to her right, the slow drip of water, the creak of steel joints, and the snoring of a certain gentleman. Despite obviously being a mess, Zef had taken her to this spot and, she must admit, had treated her very decently for a long time. NightRunner or not, she figured she might do well to start taking it a bit easier on him. This had to be a very confusing time for everyone, most certainly for the only Synth in the group.

Deeper and deeper she sank into the curve, drifting away into her thoughts and gradually back into dreams. This time they were dreams of Maybe, of future-Electua, and of the moments ahead that were rapidly approaching.

{THE GLADE}
<The Eternal Nightclub / Q4, Starlight Sector, Future>

{"And? How'd she take it?"

"Rather well, in fact." Maybe lifted a slender martini glass to her lips and took a shy sip of the sapphire-blue cocktail. The texture was velvety and warm, though she couldn't pinpoint the taste. "I rather like this one."

"I'm sure she had questions."

"Well, did you or did you not watch the feed?"

"I skimmed it. And I trust you."

Her smile was sweet and appreciative. She beamed across the table at him, the light of their candle and many others dancing in her eyes. Though Breven had invited her out facetiously, they'd made good on the plans and found themselves attempting to fit in with high society in Quadro's Starlight Sector, a sprawling luxury district generally reserved for the rich and influential. Maybe and Breven were both of those things, relatively speaking, though not in the ways that Quadro District might ever appreciate. Nonetheless, Breven had his tricks, and anything was possible in the Glade.

"You probably should trust me, considering."

Breven laughed heartily, his avatar here impressively clean and handsome in contrast to his Dominion-side form.

"You're really good at that."

"At what?" Her eyes didn't waver as she leaned forward on the table and rested her chin on her fingers. She reminded him in that moment of Audrey Hepburn, an actress he'd seen in archived Old World films.

"Being physical."

"Yeah? I'm doing it well?"

"Could've fooled me."

"Well, perhaps I've been...studying."

His eyebrows arched in interest.

"Oh, Breven. Be a gentleman."

He cleared his throat and began fishing out a real cigarette for himself. He unclasped a small silver box and offered her one first. She graciously accepted.

"I've heard these are quite bad for humans in the real world."

"Really. Who told you that?"

Her eyes narrowed. "I hear things."

Breven reached across the table and lit her cigarette with an old-fashioned lighter, and then lit his own. The lighter snapped shut, catching the miffed attention of several well-to-do patrons around them. He didn't bother to acknowledge their glaring eyes.

"That's good. What do you hear about Ilia Fromme?"

As he spoke the name, a delicate piano melody began. The overhead lights of The Eternal dimmed considerably.

"...Who?"

Breven pointed across the hazy dining room with the two fingers that held his cigarette. Maybe's curious eyes turned to follow.

The vocalist, her arms the most elegant prosthetics, sauntered her way across the stage in the spotlight. She approached the microphone and wrapped a black-gloved hand around it sensually. The dining crowd applauded warmly and a whistle rang out from the sea of candlelights. Ilia flashed a coy smile, embracing the attention. Around her, a dazzling holographic display materialized, something like shimmering fireworks.

"Oh my..." Maybe was beyond captivated.

The woman on stage seemed lost in the piano melody and danced with rare seductive class, leading lightly with her hips in a sparkling black dress. Finally, she leaned in toward the microphone and a dusky song slithered from her lips, eliciting more whistles and hollers from those in attendance.

Maybe quivered, Ilia Fromme's powerful voice overcoming her. She exhaled a thin stream of smoke.

"She's incredible..."

RealmDweller grinned. "She's the best."

Ilia carried on, speaking gracefully with her body all the evocative things her words withheld. Knowing that she had the candlelit crowd on a string, her voice meandered from playful, delicate heights to deep and sultry lows. They gaped with respectfully muted adoration, responding with an occasional whistle or clapping from the darkness. When the first song ended, Maybe turned back toward him, her eyes gleaming. She was enthralled, though his mind was still on business.

"So did she accept or not?"

Breven's abrupt change in topic caught her off guard. She regained her breath and took a sip of her blue cocktail.

"Of course she did, she's very eager to prove herself."

"And does she have any idea at all what she's getting herself into?"

Maybe pursed her glossy lips at Breven's insistence, but it slowly curled to a devilish smile. Unable to resist, she turned from his eyes and back toward the stage to watch the unfolding performance.}

[[E5: DOWNTOWN MID-CITY]]
<Splendor MultiCorp Centre>

Broad afternoon daylight.

It had been a few rotations since Wander'd been assigned anything that wasn't cloaked in darkness. She certainly felt more at home in the night hours, but there was something about being awake with the rest of Dominion City that still called to her. The aromas of food vendors, the bustling traffic, the reflections of the sun flittering between buildings, the geometric shadows slicing across the roads... It woke up feelings inside her that weren't present at night, and reminded her that she was part of a bigger picture. She needed that reminder. There was more to being a NightRunner than lurking, detached from society and hiding from the Corporation, as comforting as the dark was.

It had also been a good while since she'd taken on a solo gig. She adored the others, and working with them was certainly a pleasure, but striking out on her own always brought about the best in her. There was a level of autonomy in solo work that wasn't possible when half of her energy went to coordinating with the others. She could leave her own distinct mark on the jobs she took alone; it was a valuable chance to develop her own unique style.

From her vantage point on the concrete ledge, Wander watched as the borders of light and shadow crept slowly upward through the city. The overcast had parted just as it had in the Glade's future-Electua, and now the sun was lowering toward the horizon amidst a scattering of clouds. Vibrant hues of a golden-orange sunset washed over the city like she had rarely seen. For kilometers in every direction the myriad monuments to Downtown Mid-City commerce sprawled outward, all catching a glint of the fading light. Among them, towering holographics animated wildly, corporate logos buzzed and flickered, and scintillating advertisements called to her from every available space. The bizarre panorama, with its stark contrasts between beauty and industry, held Wander transfixed.

She found it hard to imagine that the massive business complex surrounding her was only a tiny portion of Electua District, and an even smaller portion of the entirety of Dominion City. Yet somehow, the deed she planned to commit could affect its entire operation.

A drop in the bucket, but sometimes the right drop can tip the entire thing.

This insight, that she could be the difference-maker in the lives of countless Citizens, felt like the growing theme of her career.

A single hum of the communicator at her collar reminded her that it was time to begin her prep work. She pulled the rifle case from her back and began removing the various weapon parts. As well, she withdrew a tiny disk from her thigh pocket, an AR projector, and tossed it out into the open air. It hovered in place, pairing with the weapon, and patiently awaited orders. Wander returned her attention to the rifle. She retracted a suppressor from the stock and screwed it into place, then retrieved the augmented scope and clamped it on. A small blue LED came alive on its side, along with a matching light on the floating projector. The built-in stabilizer, which would keep the rifle trained in the vicinity of the target, activated and thrummed softly.

With the rifle assembled and extra time to spare, she climbed up onto the ledge of the small walkway and sat down, anxious to spend a moment to calm herself. Her mind wandered momentarily away from the job, and back to her and Zef's time together. She thought back to hoverboarding through the streets of Southtown, and to Vincenzo Sardo.

It'd been such a surprise to see Sardo this far from Reshen, and she wondered what could be the reason for his presence here. Admittedly, she knew very little about his profession outside the fact that he and Zef had worked together in the Meat Markets. She knew he was some kind of surgeon, though that fact wasn't as important or clear as their last memory together.

During the early days of her friendship with Zef, she'd given in to kissing Sardo. It was nothing serious, just something secret they'd enjoyed for a few days, and then she left Reshen behind. Since then, her mind still went back to him from time to time. She'd never been able to pinpoint a reason why she allowed herself to leave without even a goodbye. Midi, Digi, Zef, Zelly and even Laveau had been with her then. The pressure of leaving with them had surely been greater than any urge to stay in the filthy Malaang. But why had she been so ready to leave then? And why avoid him now in the SouthTown markets?

It's not worth thinking about right now. It's the past. We've all moved on.

Looking down from her position at the edge, she realized she was far above standard Downtown air traffic altitude ordinance. Rows of hovers skirted through the buildings below as they went about their business. It was a complex interplay, each tiny particle of society milling about and playing its own part.

It was time she played hers.

With her mind clear, she balanced along the ledge over to the corner of the building and crouched. Through compact binoculars, she peered down to street level. Searching over the bustling crowds in their suits, Wander half-expected to see herself and Maybe chatting near the intersection where they'd stopped to discuss the mission. Instead, she saw her mark.

Lozuto, briefcase in prosthetic hand, was crossing the street toward the Amaranth Business Complex.

{THE GLADE}

<The Eternal Nightclub / Q4, Starlight Sector, Future>

{The singer Ilia Fromme curtsied and blew a kiss to the dining room to rapturous applause. Breven and Maybe clapped along with them reservedly. As the applause died down and the singer left the stage, the pianist carried the energy along gracefully with a meandering jazz melody, setting a new tone for lively dinner discussion. The ambient chatter and sounds of silverware clinking against plates grew louder, and Maybe turned back toward their conversation. Breven swirled and finished the last of his Tetran whiskey on ice and placed the glass on the soft white tablecloth.

"It seems to me that it could be taken apart piece-by-piece, used for any number of different purposes, or even sold to the highest bidders. People would pay uncorporate amounts of money to own a piece of the Realm outright, to be able to dissect it or turn it into their own private products."

"You'd be incriminating anyone who touched it."

"Touché. Though they'd be aware of that going in. It's not my job to play baby-sitter to the programmers of Dominion City. Especially not the ones in Coldcode who would pay out their asses for a piece of proprietary Dominion simcode."

"I don't know, Brev. I know you, at least a little by now...you've never been a merchant. Why don't you just open the gates? Make everything open source and free. You could let Coldcode admin for a fee and just be Realm God so to speak."

Breven laughed. He liked the sound of Realm God, but that was just as far from his nature as playing the part of a retailer and keeping tabs on a thousand clients.

"Honestly, there's just too many moving variables at this point. We're too far ahead of ourselves. Let's revisit this once it's done and settled. For now, we need to focus on—"

A crystalline waiter, his faceless body tuxedoed and tall, approached the table and bowed. "Apologies, sir, madam. I'm sorry to disturb your evening, but an alert has been triggered in the Glade Continuum based on your preset parameters."

Breven nodded, leaning back. "Show me."

The waiter held out his serving tray. Above it, a rectangular holo-display materialized. There, a video feed was in the process of zooming into a gray mock-up of Downtown Electua until it patched into a local camera, rotated, and centered on one running figure: Wander.

"Oh no." Maybe gave a polite smile, thanked Breven and the waiter both, and then abruptly disintegrated into a thousand spinning pixels.

Breven sighed. Not ready to end his evening out yet, he lit another cigarette and held his empty glass up to the waiter.

"Keep 'em coming."}

[[E5: DOWNTOWN MID-CITY]]

<Splendor MultiCorp Centre>

With only two minutes before her target was to arrive in his office, Wander frantically disassembled her rifle. The unimaginable was unfolding due to some sort of planning error. A Demigod was clearly approaching her ledge. If she wasn't able to evacuate immediately, it would catch sight of her and unleash its hounds. Better to not awaken the sleeping giant at all if she had any hope of accomplishing what she set out to do.

Gradually the Demigod grew closer, filling the sky with its massive black form punctuated by thousands of spires extending from its sides, its roof, and its belly. The thick shadow it cast slid over the buildings of the business district at a harsh angle in relation to the setting sun. Within the darkness of the shadow, its Eye, the roving spotlight, coursed over the streets and buildings, searching for Violation. Wander watched it cautiously and whistled a signal to the AR projector. It hurtled back to her and she snatched it from the air, then continued breaking down the rifle. As she finished, she strapped it onto her back and began running along the ledge, away from the hulking Protocol Enforcement Unit as fast as he could.

High above, the enormous thing drew upon her, eating up the orange sky as it did until she could feel its presence above her, the thrum of its internal mechanisms vibrating in her gut.

She pumped her legs harder, the slanted glass of the rooftop on one side of her, the sheer drop to street level on the other. She skidded to a turning halt against the white concrete and pushed off, tearing down the next ledge. Looking below her as she ran from the Demigod, she saw a balcony dining area several floors down. It would have to do; she'd never make it to the opposite side where she'd entered.

Wander leapt from the ledge, soared down several stories, and made contact with the balcony. She swiftly broke her fall and rolled between the outdoor tables and their wide umbrellas. The dining patrons around her gasped. She recovered and pushed on, heading for the stairs.

In the sky above, the form of the Demigod peeked over the lip of the building. In full sprint, she dashed into the flight of stairs, wall-running first up the side of the glass partition at its side and then leaping across the second flight, hitting the ground without touching a single step. Wander rolled and slid, turned blind, and crashed into a small group of suited businessmen. The monstrous Demigod continued, moving onward in the sky and blanketing the building in shade. The path of its brilliant spotlight curved, roaming over the building. As it approached the far edge, Wander pushed the suited men aside and continued forward without breaking concentration. She burst through a door into the building, knocking over a waiter and his tray of dishes.

"Sorry, sorry!" It was all the apology she could muster as she made her way briskly into the restaurant, out from view of the Dominion Corporation's security behemoth. Scanning the interior, she saw the corridor that led into the main lobby of the building level and sprinted forward. Clear of the restaurant, she kept her eyes peeled for signs of the stairwell. Her footsteps carried her directly toward a tall, spraying fountain and she vaulted, sailing through the mists of the pluming aquamarine waters. Straight ahead, the elevator corridor became visible along with the door to the stairwell. Wander crossed the distance in only a few long strides and crashed through the door to the stairs.

She slid to a stop as the door clicked shut. At the railing of a vast squared-spiral staircase, she stuck her head out and looked both up and down. Extending the length of expansive column of open space, holographics like cool, undulating water filled the air, creating an entrancing atmosphere of tranquility. It fluctuated in harmony with a placid melody, intermittently transposed with a comforting voice:

"Welcome to the Splendor MultiCorp Centre."

As Wander contemplated her next move, the soft tune suddenly went silent, and the hue of the cascading holographics became pinkish-red. The voice returned, this time with a more stern tone. *"Attention, Splendor MultiCorp Centre visitors and personnel. A disturbance has been detected on Level One-Eighty-Three. Splendor Security have been alerted and are in the process of responding. Please remain calm, and exercise caution while in common areas. Thank you."*

The exhilarating heat of a new challenge blossomed inside her chest.

[[E5: DOWNTOWN MID-CITY]]

<Splendor MultiCorp Centre>

{"Wander, I've been alerted to your situation. Is everything alright?"}

She ducked behind a staircase balcony and watched as several Splendor MultiCorp security officers entered through the doors above. They reached the railing and looked out, pulse rifles in hand, searching for any sign of an intruder. Wander crouched down further. One of them spoke into his collar while another extracted several white discs from a dispenser at his waistband. He tossed them over the edge and they each came to life, emitting thin blue scanning beams and branching out from the patrol officers.

"There was an unexpected Demigod. My fault. Had to change things up."

Wander pressed her back against the short wall as she whispered. She knew that Maybe must surely be able to see her position. "What's up?"

{"Well, it appears you've triggered native security."}

"Oh, that. It's not a problem. Is Dominion on alert?"

{"Not from what I can see."}

"What about EPD?"

{"No, I'm not hearing anything around you yet...Do you need assistance?"}

"Nah, it's fine." She peeked out at the drones. "I got this."

{"Alright... Keep in touch then, will you?"}

"Will do. Red out."

The line went silent.

Wander steadied her breath, readying herself to move.

Keeping an eye on the drones as they went about their scanning, she crawled down the stairs away from their pattern of coverage. To the left, the entrance door from level one-eighty-three swung open. Wander's hand immediately went to the compact sword at her thigh. A business woman in a pantsuit stepped out, unaware of any disturbance. Her face brightened slightly in alarm at the crouching girl in black. Wander pressed a finger to her own lips to request that she keep silent. The alarmed woman carefully let herself back out of the door. With a last look out, Wander dove for the closing door, catching it before it shut entirely, and inched her way in.

To the left and right, empty hallways extended. Marble flooring, smooth white walls, and soft interior lighting told Wander this was a quiet business office. She was impressed with its cleanliness. A door clicked shut across the hall, no doubt the woman who'd seen her. She wasted no time and chose the opposite direction, running as fast as she could through a small labyrinth of hallways and glass doors and—

Turning the corner, she was suddenly face-to-face with two Splendor Centre security officers. Behind them, a slick white droid stood easily two heads above them. Its array of sharp blue eyes converged upon her.

"Shit!" She backpedaled, running back the way she came and finally burst back into the stairwell. The blue beams of two of the small drones swiveled and were upon her immediately. She put a foot up on the railing and dove into the central shaft of the wide open atrium. The empty column of space below her plummeted downward like a geometric chasm, the ground floor so obscured by the swirling holographics that it was almost nonexistent. It was as if she were floating in a deep sea, soaring weightless in an ocean of the Realm.

"There!"

"Intruder spotted!"

A hail of stunfire rained down around her from the officers above. She scanned her landing zone, the railing of level one-seventy-eight, and made the quick decision to continue down as she connected with it, gripping the edge and then pushing off again in a new direction. With precise aim, she brought herself down to the steps of the level one-seventy-four area, and this time chose to keep her feet on the ground and run.

Round and round she rushed forward, a group of tiny drones zipping behind her. Ahead, a security officer appeared from the side door. A stun pistol emerged from his holster and she kicked it away, and in one quick motion swung the rifle case from her back and struck him across the face with it. She stepped right and rolled her back across the railing, fell, caught the railing of the next level down, and pulled herself up. A group of random employees coming out of another door scattered and she pushed her way inside. She slammed the door and held it shut for a moment. On the other side of the door, she could hear faint tapping of the droids colliding with the surface.

Turning around into another wider area, it seemed she was now in some kind of shopping center. A glance in all directions and Wander could tell that no one from security had arrived here yet, though cameras dotted the mirrored ceiling in every direction. She activated her light-scrambling runnersuit markers. Casually, she made her way through the sparse crowd to the large glass doors at the end of the food court. Once outside in the warm air and dim light of sundown, she briskly made her way across the crowded deck, keeping her eyes out for any kind of security response around her.

So far so good. She checked her watch. Lozuto had already been inside the building across the street for fifteen minutes. Near the edge of the deck, a glass elevator waited. She boarded it within a stream of businesspeople and attempted to remain unnoticed.

"That is a very interesting outfit!"

Wander turned, her heart shuddering and her hand instinctively going for her sword. An elderly woman's face goggled at her with a wide smile and cheerful energy.

"Who makes it, I wonder?"

She laughed nervously. "I...made it myself."

"Oh my, are you a designer?"

"Yep, that's what I am, I'm a designer."

"Well then, let's have your card. I'd love to see your catalog."

Wander patted her suit which had no pockets. "Oh damn. Fresh out, sorry."

"Oh, darn the Corp." The fragile woman stomped and snapped her fingers. "Well, what about a shop, then?"

The elevator settled down to a rectangle of glowing material at street level and the door opened with an inviting tone. The other occupants began to file out. Wander's eyes darted between them and out to the plaza. Would there be someone waiting outside for her? Had security scanned her well enough to recognize her? Would this woman ever leave her alone?

"No, sorry. I work alone, actually."

"Oh, well, then let me give you mine." The woman opened a handbag at her waist and began sifting through it.

"Sorry, ma'am, I have to go."

The elevator was emptying. Wander saw security guards. She deactivated her markers again.

"Well, hold on now, I know I have one..."

A new group of suits began streaming into the elevator. Wander fidgeted.

"Look, I'm sorry, ma'am, I really have to go!"

"Oh here it is!"

The lady winked and held out a small, clear card with an inlaid foil logo.

"Got it!" Wander snatched the card and turned to leave.

"Call me!"

She waved to the kindly woman as she pushed forward through the oncoming crowd. The guard before her had his back turned. Another guard chatted with great gestures to his partner droid several meters away. Incredulous but petrified, Wander filtered into the street traffic and tried to blend in, looking back up at the high-rise with a irresistible grin.

[[E5: DOWNTOWN MID-CITY]]
<Amaranth Business Complex>

{"You've got ten minutes left."}

Though security had given her strange looks over her runnersuit and the odd case strapped to her back, Wander had made it to the elevator door without incident. Her next mark was Lozuto's office where she'd need to complete her job quietly enough to not raise any alarms, and then escape a second building.

"Alright. What's the room number?"

A golden android wearing a white business suit and holding a suitcase boarded the elevator with her.

{"189-48B. North side."}

"Got it."

Wander tapped the one-eighty-nine key and the elevator shivered lightly as the doors eased closed. She waited for the suited individual to press a key, though he didn't budge. A slight jolt in air pressure signaled that they'd already arrived.

"Level One-Eighty-Nine. Thank you."

She stepped forward, though the android did the same. He stopped mid-step and courteously held a hand out for her to exit first. She exited nervously, thinking that surely they weren't headed for the same place, though as she turned right into the hallway she could hear him do the same. She followed the room numbers until they reached 189-48A and turned the corner into a glass hallway.

Detecting her, the left wall slipped into transparency. Behind it, a pristine waiting area appeared. Inside, the walls were made of moving images that reached out holographically from their surfaces. Wander slowed, caught in the trance of the abstract forms for a moment. The man behind her passed and entered through the glass door.

Her heart began to sink, though she urged herself to follow and stepped through the sliding glass doors. An omnipresent voice awakened and a floating menu appeared in front of her.

"Welcome to Prescient Holographics."

Wander glanced once more at her watch. She didn't have time for this. Lozuto would be exiting his office any moment now. She watched as the android strode briskly past the lobby and disappeared through a sliding door.

"Here at Prescient Holographics, we appreciate each and every one of our outstanding customers. You look new here!"

Wander walked directly through the display, though it stubbornly appeared in front of her again. She continued forward through it. Not to be ignored, the display appeared again, this time several paces ahead of her.

"Prescient Holographics appreciates your interest in our Downtown facility but requests that you remain in our lobby. An associate has been notified and will be with you shortly!"

Wander waved it away and continued, finally lining herself up next to the door that the android had passed through, sword in hand. The door presently slid open and a woman in a stylish, iridescent gray outfit stepped forward, her best customer service smile on.

Wander struck. In the blink of an eye, the woman's face, as well as the awful smile, slid apart from the rest of her skull. Wander took the opportunity to slide through the door before her body could fall and obstruct it. Quietly, it hissed shut behind her, followed by the thump of the body against it. She had no illusions; her delay meant things would need to get messy, and she knew she was certainly being watched now.

The android with the briefcase had gone right, so Wander went left. She snuck silently along the tile floor in the direction Lozuto's office, holding her blade ready. Peering down the next corner as she passed, several turquoise glass walls were visible where the glow of holographics spilled out into the hall. She crept through these, keeping an eye out at the doors around her, and came upon another turn in the hallway. She peeked around the edge.

There, in the center of the hall, Lozuto stood talking with a lab-coated technician. He was just as she'd seen him in the bizarre future-Electua that Maybe had revealed to her. Expensive burgundy suit with black shoes. False jaw. Clean, surgically replaced optical augments that surely had worlds of data and visual capabilities on hand to enhance Lozuto's daily activities.

Wander ducked behind the partition for a moment, opening her senses to hear the ongoing conversation. It seemed to be ending.

"You there!"

Wander's breath stopped.

"You, around the corner! Come on out, let's have a chat!"

Her heart pounded. She gripped the hilt of her sword, waiting for him to come nearer.

"Why don't you put that weapon away? I have something I'd like to talk to you about."

Fuck! Were his optics allowing him to see her somehow?

"Last chance, I'm only offering once."

Fuck, fuck, fuck!

With a deep breath, she retracted her sword. Cautiously she turned the corner and there he was, his arms crossed and facing her direction. The technician had gone away.

"Well then, we have a winner." He smiled strangely with the lower jaw mechanically cooperating, and then walked to the nearest door. He keyed it by placing his fingertips on a pad, opened it and held an arm into the open room for her to enter. "Please."

Wander calmed herself the way she usually did when the unexpected would attack her plans. She imagined the larger picture, the building around her, the area of the city she was in, the route she would take home. The flat in Mid-City and the rest of the Runners. Haven-4 and Maybe...

Maybe! She pressed a spot on her collar and disconnected herself from contact as she neared him.

"That's it, I'm not going to hurt you."

He extended a hand.

"Ashram Lozuto, although I'm sure you knew that."

She placed a hand in his and saw that it was the synthetic one she'd seen earlier. He squeezed hers lightly.

"Wander."

"Excellent. Come on in."

[[E5: DOWNTOWN MID-CITY]]

<Amaranth Business Complex>

Outside the window of the room they'd entered, Wander could see almost nothing but the face of the building she'd recently escaped and the darkening sunset sky above it. To the left and right, she could see hints of the Downtown Mid-City skyline coming alive for another night of frenzied activity. Small droplets were finally tapping against the glass as the cloud cover returned. Lozuto made his way to a private bar along the wall.

"Sit, sit. Can I get you a drink?"

Sure that she didn't want to be poisoned, Wander shook her head to the negative and sat on one of the wide couches near the window. She wondered why she hadn't taken him out before even entering the room. Something told her that if she had, she would have been surrounded by security before she could even make it out of Prescient Holographics. She decided instead to wait and see what Lozuto might have to say, considering he had somehow been so prepared for her arrival.

A glass of clear iced liquor in hand, he set a sealed bottle of water in front of her and then sat opposite a wide coffee table made of smoked glass. In the center, an inset square of glossy black material swirled with soft digital fog.

"So. You're here to kill me." Lozuto sipped his drink, sucked air through his teeth, and set it down. He folded a leg and gave her his direct attention. Noticing her silence, he smirked and shrugged. "Look, I'm not a genius, your strategic awareness just really sucks. I mean that. From the cameras all around, I recognized you immediately. You and your friend broke into RealmSquare just last night, am I right? Cut up a few of my people, stole some LC change, and wrecked a branch of my trafficking database."

Wander stared expressionless into his overconfident eyes, hoping he would wrap up whatever game he was playing. She crossed her arms to display her impatience and sat back against the couch.

"I know, I know, it's weird. You got caught, you're not as sneaky as you thought you were, all that shit. But check it out."

He snapped his fingers and the black section of the coffee table illuminated. Projected from beneath, a holo-display appeared above it; a basic UI. Lozuto scrolled through various options with his fingers in midair until he came upon a small, familiar view. He tapped it and it expanded to the length of the table. Surveillance footage of Wander and Digi, taken from a building adjacent to the Katsudo-Hoffman. They were scaling the wall in preparation to enter his firm.

Wander frowned. *Big deal.*

"I don't own this feed but it was sent over to me as soon as the alarm was triggered. I'm sure that wasn't part of your plan." He didn't seem to be making fun of her, but she couldn't quite tell. He scrolled to another video, this one of Wander and her acrobatics as she fled from the Splendor Centre's security drones. "Look, I don't want to make a big deal of this. It's not the first time I've been ripped off and it won't be the last."

"Then what?"

"Well, firstly, congratulations on getting here. I don't get many surprises in my schedule and certainly none as pretty as yourself." He sipped from his glass. "You have skills, it's obvious."

She hoped he wasn't trying something as blatant as buttering her up to offer her a job.

"But those skills don't belong to you, they belong to whoever is training and paying you to risk your life for them. Now, I have a few ideas about who that could be. There's a slew of rich motherfuckers who would love to see me go under, but I think this is a special case. Not many of them have the resources to train someone as well as you, much less a whole team." He gestured to her runnersuit, then swiped again to show security footage of Zelly waiting at the railway station, and another of Midi running through the streets of Marquee Square. "Whoever it is also knows a hell of a lot about me and my daily schedule, which only very few people have access to."

He sat forward, put his glass on the table, and rubbed his tattooed hand into the synthetic one, seeming at last to harbor a bit of anxiety. Coming to certain conclusions, he pulled a black cigarette from a small case and placed it between his lips. He took a drag and it lit itself, and he reclined against the leather couch.

"So you're either working for someone very close to me, or someone with ridiculous resources...or you work for Dominion." She grimaced. He nodded and gauged it as a sign. "No Dominion, okay. Well then, you're either paid very well, or you're brainwashed. Either way, this leaves me with only a few options. I can either kill you, which gets us nowhere. I can bring you back to Quadro and torture you and maybe get the truth out of you, who knows... Or I can turn you over to the EPD for trespassing and see where that leads us."

Wander had grown past any nervousness and was now amused, especially at the idea that she might be expected to be intimidated by this childishness. This man might be rich and well connected, but if she decided to end his life here and now, he stood no chance. She leaned forward and spoke carefully so he could understand her meaning.

"Look, mister. You're not getting shit from me, you were right about that part. But none of the things you just said are gonna happen. I came here to do a job. I gave you a chance and now I've heard you out. Are you done?"

Lozuto smiled, though it masked a deeper understanding. There was no negotiating this time. Without hesitation, he pulled his wrist up to his mouth. "Siresh, I need–"

Wander was up already, leaping across the table and through his holographic projection, sword unfolding behind her. He pulled himself to his feet and swept his suit jacket back to reveal holster straps. From behind his waistband he drew two energy pistols just as Wander crashed into his chest, knee first. His shots fired past her, blasting into the ceiling, raining down debris. The two of them carried on forward into the couch, upending it, and both sprawled out across the tiled floor. Wander righted herself as Lozuto scurried for his guns. A swift kick across his face and one of his optical implants shattered. She straddled his back as he scrambled for leverage, hot blood bubbling from his eye socket. With two firm hands, she brought her sword up beneath the back edge of his expensive prosthetic jaw.

"Anything! Anything at all, please! I'll pay you whatever you want!"

She dug her knee into his spine leaned in close enough to smell his cologne. "I'm not doing this for money."

"No, please! *Noo!*"

Arching her back, she pulled ferociously and the razor edge of her sword sunk into the flesh of his neck. He struggled for a moment, gasping, until his throat was opened. Her blade tore halfway up to the base of his skull, nearly beheading him, and his body went limp. Waves of blood pulsed out across the tile.

Satisfied her job was complete, Wander finally eased up and pulled her sword away. His head slammed to the floor.

She heaved herself to her feet.

The door of the room abruptly swung open and she spun around to see the android she'd shared the elevator with. He entered and assessed the scene, seeing his employer lying dead on the floor. Wander knew he must be Lozuto's bodyguard.

"Siresh."

Wasting no time, Wander hefted her sword and launched it toward him like a spear. His programmed reflexes allowed him to rapidly reveal a blade of his own and he swiped hers away. She was already running toward him and cartwheeled forward, taking up one of Lozuto's handguns as she did. When she returned right-side up she found him in her pistol sights, also running towards her.

She pulled the trigger.

Nothing but a dull click.

Print-matched to Lozuto, she realized.

Still sprinting, she leapt over the couch and hurled the gun directly at him. As his blade knocked it away, she connected, tackling him at the midsection and the two of them crashed to the floor.

Each scrambled, pulling themselves up in a mad dash to end the other first. Retaining his sword, Siresh immediately swiped at Wander as she regained her footing. She dodged it, and another, but a third landed, slicing a razor-clean gash through her suit across the right forearm. A blaze of heat soaked through the open cut.

Siresh lunged point-first with the blade and she moved aside. Wrapping an arm around his wrist, she drove her left palm forward and his mechanical elbow shattered. Still gripping the arm, she rotated with all her might. They fell to the floor and his forearm tore away from its joint. She snatched the sword from the severed arm's grip, mounted Siresh, and drove the blade directly down into his head. The LEDs of his eyes flickered and went dark.

Wander fell to her back on the tile floor to catch her breath and nurse her forearm. She wondered what the state of Amaranth native security might be at the moment. She'd be a fool to assume all was clear. It was probably wise to regain contact with Maybe.

She activated her comms.

"Maybe."

{"Wander! So glad to hear from you!"}

"Same." She was still catching her breath.

{"I can see you're still in the Amaranth Complex, what's your situation?"}

Behind Wander, Siresh sat up and began pulling the sword from his forehead. Hearing plasteel grind against metal, she spun and backpedaled across the floor. Finding her own blade, she pulled herself up to a guarded stance. Siresh remained on the floor, taking his time, his robotic motions slightly jittery.

"Mmmay-Maybe. I th-th-thought I hearrrd that r-right."

Siresh's voice was glitchy and layered poorly, as though Wander had hit something vital with her failed coup-de-grace. She hesitated, realizing that she'd given away a deep secret. Siresh might have been broadcasting it out already.

"It wwwill be an honor des-troyyying a N-NightRunner."

Hearing that word, Wander struck, slashing her sword down at him furiously. His remaining arm sprang up and caught the blade, gripping it tightly. In one fluid motion he tore it from her grasp and flung it across the room. Thinking quickly, she made for the door but he rose in a flash. His hand snatched the back of her runnersuit and whipped her away from the door. She soared through the air and crashed to the ground, the wind forced from her chest. Her sense of direction spun like a broken compass.

How... How the hell do I kill this thing?

Gasping for breath, Wander forced herself back up with great effort but he was already upon her. A fist to her gut sent her reeling back. She tumbled over the fallen couch, landing in the pool of blood spreading from Lozuto. Desperate, she began searching the dead man's pockets for anything that might be useful. A keycard. A handful of mem-sticks. To the left lay Lozuto's second gun, but it wouldn't fire without authorization.

Siresh's hand slapped down onto her back and he tossed her again. This time she slammed against the wide window looking out into Downtown. The force of impact rattled her and she collapsed to the floor in a heap. Siresh stood over her. He grabbed her collar and pulled her from the floor by her neck.

"I-iiisss this the best y-youu can do, N-NightRrrunnerr?"

His arm released her where she stood. He swung again and successfully connected, crushing her cheek. The blow sent her reeling out into space. Her vision blurred. She grasped for anything recognizable. Another shot to the abdomen and she doubled over, crying out from the flood of pain that branched into her legs.

Through gut instinct, she opened the comms on her collar again.

"Maybe..."

{THE GLADE}

<The Eternal Nightclub / Q4, Starlight Sector, Future>

{Breven was still smoking, enjoying the calm ambiance of the Eternal, when Maybe materialized.

"Nothing better to do, huh? What can I order for you?"

"I'm so sorry, Breven. I hate to ask this, but you're the closest contact I have to Wander's position right now. It seems she's found herself in a spot of trouble. Would you mind terribly making sure she doesn't fall?"}

[[E5: DOWNTOWN MID-CITY]]

<Amaranth Business Complex>

Wander spit blood across the white tile. Her mind tried formulating a strategy but nothing was resolving.

Training! Remember your training! Remember anything!

"Gettt up! Fight baaack!"

She struggled to her knees and knew in an instant what she needed to do. Gritting her teeth in a final burst of rage, she rushed forward, lifting Siresh off the ground. They crashed through the table where the holo-display had still been hovering and an explosion of glass filled the air. Wander rolled away and leapt, hurdling the couch. She grabbed Lozuto's second energy pistol and slapped it into his hand. Siresh appeared in front of the window, searching for her.

"Nnoo mo-orrre gamess!"

Using Lozuto's finger, she pressed down on the trigger and a rapid pulse of energy rounds blasted into the android, flinging him backward. The bolts that didn't collide with his body zipped past and shattered the window out to Downtown Mid-City. A gust of wind and glass particles blasted into the room. Siresh, backed against the ledge, his suit smoldering, turned back to face her.

With a final cry of exhausted anger. Wander burst forward in a reckless sprint. She slammed into him and wrapped her arms around his waist. The two of them went airborne over the city, tumbling apart from each other and out into the warm Electuan evening air. The buildings, the horizon, everything tilted sideways as they plummeted toward the street. Immediately regretting her decision, Wander's eyes watered from the sheer wind across her face as she watched Siresh float away from her, still reaching out with one arm to attack.

"Thii-isss isn't overr, NightRunnnerrr!"

A dirty gray hover curved into position below, and before she could understand what was happening, Wander was crashing into the open passenger side door. The vehicle swerved wildly as the driver attempted to gain control manually.

"Get your legs in!"

She yanked them in and the door slid shut.

In her wild bewilderment, she couldn't fathom how anyone could have known to catch her, though it didn't seem important. She quickly righted herself in the seat as the entire vehicle twisted up into the sky. Glancing over at the driver, she didn't recognize him at all.

"Who the hell are you?!"

With one prosthetic steel arm pulling the wheel, Breven extended the other out to her. "Call me Artie!"

[[E5: WEST MID-CITY]]
<The Flat>

Gusts of air turbulence swept over Zef where he stood. The hover had arrived from nowhere and without warning, alarming him to the point of drawing his knife. Now he clutched it with cold contempt as Wander said goodbye to its driver and climbed down. She dropped to the concrete roof, giving Zef a clear, momentary glimpse of the man in the driver seat. Long-haired, unshaven, dirty prosthetic arms; he could've been any Outer Districts bum. Before he could consider it any further, the hover was off, lifting into the night rain, orienting, and speeding away.

"Who is he, Wander?"

Still in her runnersuit blacks, Wander's demeanor fell from exhilaration to confusion.

Zef would have none of this manipulation any longer. "I said, *who is he?*"

"Just a friend, Zef. A friend of Maybe's."

"What's his name!?" He stepped forward, and she stepped back.

"Zef...put the knife away."

A pang of hesitation immobilized him. He was frightening her. This wasn't the way to do this.

"What's going on up here?"

Zef swiveled. Midi stood on the ledge of the building. Digi was climbing up from the fire escape behind her.

"Guys, it's ok." Wander's quivering voice was unconvincing. "We're just talking."

"Yeah? Well, this piece of..." Midi held her tongue. "What's with the knife, Zef? We got a problem here?"

Looking between each of their accusatory stares, he felt caught in the act of something he didn't intend. He felt lied to and betrayed, yet blamed and guilty all at once.

What the hell am I doing here? These people aren't friends.

"Fuck this. I'm outta here."

Zef pocketed the knife and made for the stairs, pushing Digi aside as he did.

Wander, the dried blood on her face melting in the rain, feebly reached out a hand to him. "Zef, don't..."

Swallowing every bit of anger that threatened to spill out, Zef reluctantly turned back to face her. His eyes fell upon the most vulnerable, beautiful sight that Dominion City had ever given him. She was strong, and fragile, and everything he'd ever adored. But that wasn't enough. Things had become too complicated to fix, and now it all converged toward a regrettable conclusion. He was about to resolve it the only way he knew how, by breaking both their hearts.

His throat clenched and his chin quivered. His eyes burned, holding back a lifetime of tears he had never allowed. Now more than ever, he needed to protect himself, to make a final stand, to sever this aberration before it went any further.

He'd been left behind for the last time.

"Goodbye, Mel."

CHAPTER 4

A CHANGE OF PACE

[[E5: WEST MID-CITY]]
<The Flat>

Wander allowed the meandering static of the rain to overwhelm her senses. Despite the darkness of night and the dense fog, she stared glassy-eyed from the covered ledge of their flat as if she could see for miles. In her chest, the coldness of loss hung heavily, while her mind felt wrapped in a tangle of sorrow. The job she'd completed only an hour ago was far behind her. She floated now in frail melancholy, the explosive conversation she'd had with Zef on repeat. She just wanted to turn off her mind.

"Don't be so hard on yourself, Wan. I know it hurts. It should hurt, I think. But things like this tend to blow over."

Zelly slid her hand back and forth across the girl's bruised shoulders, pulled her closer, and planted a delicate kiss on her head. She only knew half the story, and Wander didn't seem ready to speak about it. Instead of giving too much advice or trying to make sense of things, Zelly allowed Wander the simple comfort of her friend's presence.

Digi watched from the corner, Wander's sadness pouring into her receptive circuitry as if it were her own. Digi had seen the depths of lonely despair herself, had searched her own soul to its ends and still lived. It didn't make it any easier to watch her friend in the midst of abandonment. During these times there was nothing that could be done. She was glad that Zelly was at least trying to make sense of it for Wander.

Midi frowned at the situation and chucked a piece of brick out into the rain, hoping to hear glass break. "Let the little fucker go. It wasn't like..."

A furious glare from Zelly caused Midi to trail off. She shrugged and tossed another chunk out into the downpour.

"I'm just saying. I'm all about togetherness and friendship and all that shit. But if he doesn't care, then I don't care."

"Midi, shut up." Digi lifted her head. "Wander's upset right now. She doesn't need your opinions."

"Oh fine, I'll shut up. If I don't say anything it'll all magically be okay, right?"

She threw another piece of brick and, after a look of disapproval toward them, Midi disappeared into the flat. Digi watched her go, shaking her head. She knew Midi had good intentions, but she somehow lacked any sense of empathy for others during their most emotional moments. She'd never known heartbreak, or so it seemed; never allowed herself to open up enough to even be hurt.

Zelly squeezed Wander once more.

"Don't worry, I have a feeling he'll be back with some apologies."

Wander wondered if that's even what she wanted anymore. In many ways, Zef was proving his true intentions to her and the rest of the NightRunners, and his presence had begun to feel like a burden. She wasn't responsible, of course, but somehow she felt that this was partially her fault. Had she pushed him away with her determination? Forced him into some kind of resentment by encouraging him too hard to join with the rest of them?

The last straw, it seemed, had been Zef seeing Wander step out of Artie's car onto the roof of their apartment building. It didn't make sense, but it was all he'd needed to turn against her again. Even after she tried to explain to him what happened, even after she needed someone to talk to and take care of her wounds.

She decided that she wouldn't try to discern anymore what might or might not be the source for his sudden sense of betrayal. In the end, he'd blamed it on Maybe and the rest of them for putting him in that position, something Wander felt was unfair and unkind. All his choices had been his own. If only he hadn't been so stubbornly opposed to blaming anyone but himself...

Digi studied Wander's troubled expression. She wished she could somehow help, though her own experience brought up nothing useful except more sadness. She'd never had what Wander and Zef had, and the idea of losing something so special frightened her. She couldn't understand how two people who cared deeply for one another could let something like disagreements or jealousy come between them. If she ever had something so meaningful, she knew she wouldn't let it slip away for anything, especially not after what she'd been through. Romantic connection, real and emotional and raw, was something foreign to her, but loss was something she could at least relate to.

"I think if you care about him, you can't just give up on him."

"She's right, Wan." Zelly looked back from comforting Wander to give Digi a reassuring smile, and found herself captivated by the droid girl's glowing blue eyes in the night. "Let's give it some time."

Digi returned the smile.

The balcony door slid open again. Midi stepped out and tossed a pair of boots to the concrete balcony behind Wander.

"The 'poor me' bullshit ends now. Let's run."

[[E5: WEST MID-CITY]]

<Mid-City Rooftops>

Midi led the way as the four of them leapt from rooftop to rooftop at breakneck speed. Wander trailed behind, her worries weighing her feet down to the concrete. Occasionally the others would call back, encouraging her to pick up the pace or warning her of an obstacle, and little by little she found herself coming out of her dark cloud and back to reality.

Ahead, each Runner took turns plummeting from an extended ledge to a lower rooftop across a winding alley. As they connected with the rooftop they rolled and recovered, though when it came Wander's turn, she soared through the fog, mis-timed her landing and slipped. Her backside slammed against the surface and she absently remained sprawled on hard surface. She could hear the other Runners shouting to each other, until they finally made their way over and pulled her up. Laughing and patting her on the back, they urged her to continue forward. Reluctantly, she picked up the pace again.

As she ran, Wander's thoughts returned to waking up with Zef in the Electua fog over the reservoir, the colors of sunrise tinting everything pink, remnants of sim-dreams still lingering in their minds. She recalled the nightmare of encountering the Brother Unit in the water tunnels and vowed she would never be taken so off-guard in the future. Her thoughts jumped to her preparations for the job Maybe had requested of her, the scenic train ride to Downtown, and making her way to the ledge of the Splendor Centre. Running from the Demigod, escaping security, encountering Lozuto, soaring out of the broken window with Siresh, and the man who'd saved her fall at the request of Maybe... And then her blowout with Zef.

Following their lead, she tiptoed across a connecting arch, dropped down to a walkway bridge, and continued running.

Wander respected Zelly and Digi's opinions on Zef. The two girls now felt like sisters at this point. As much as they tried to console her, though, she couldn't shake the recurring notion that Zef had simply become unredeemable. She recalled him admit his agreement with the Priest on their return. Even if he'd been acting to preserve the group, it was an unacceptable lapse of good judgment and possibly a sign that he'd lost any last loyalty to them. Keeping pace behind the others, she decided that she needed to get him out of her mind and enjoy the night. It wasn't worth wasting her mental energy over.

She hoisted herself up to a window sill and then up to the next one, climbing them like a ladder. Looking up at Digi above her, Wander's mind began to clear slightly. She was among friends; that had to count for something.

Digi climbed over the ledge of the building roof. As Wander pulled herself up as well, Midi's hand jutted out and she took it, and together they heaved her over the railing. The four girls stood around each other, catching their breath with goofy grins on their faces, excited at the thrill of being out in the muggy night air. Midi and Zelly bumped fists, while Digi flopped back onto the glistening rooftop pavement. Wander sat down on a concrete slab, collecting her thoughts.

"Shit's still bothering you? Damn!"

"Midi, take it easy. Wander's had it rough for a few days. She's gonna be okay."

"Rough cause she's the best NightRunner in the city. Maybe's favorite." Midi stuck her synthetic tongue out playfully and it did the trick. Wander laughed a bit and leaned back against a railing, pulling back her dripping hair.

"Why do we do it?"

"Do what?"

"Relationships. All that garbage." Wander looked up into the sickly green smog rolling past while the others traded surprised looks. She'd never talked that way, especially not about Zef. "I mean, I get it. But it's just so fucking complicated. All the things you hope for never happen. Just...leaves you disappointed." Her tone wasn't one of self-pity, but of coming to hard conclusions.

"Wander..."

"Look. I for one came out here so we could put all that shit behind us for a while. Let's—"

A piercing whistle interrupted Midi's rant and the four of them turned toward its source. Digi stood to get a better view. Three blocks away, backlit by the glow of the city and on a rooftop of roughly equal height, another group was waving toward them. Five individuals repping Mid-City flowstyle.

"Traceurs."

"What do they want?"

Through the billowing fog, they could hear one of the group hollering out the whooping rhythm of a friendly challenge. The girls looked amongst themselves.

"Hey! They're calling us out!"

"They want us to chase them?"

"Yep. That's Rony's Signal. They wanna go to SouthTown."

"But they've got five and we've only got four!"

"Then it should be easy!"

Midi let out a shout of acceptance to the other group, and then took off across the rooftop in pursuit. She disappeared below as she jumped from the ledge.

A invigorating rush overcame them and Zelly pulled Wander up to her feet. Together they began running, pushing each other forward hoping to catch up with Midi. Taking the cue from their challengers, the opposing group turned and fled, and all at once a race was underway.

[[E5: WEST MID-CITY]]
<Mid-City Rooftops>

"Eyes out for DCORP! Speak up if you see anything!"

With Midi in the lead and Zelly behind her, their first hurdle was a gap over the nearest alley. In succession they leapt across it, seamlessly soaring and then rolling as they landed. They recovered and picked up the pace. One after another they vaulted over a series of inclined partitions and then teetered the length of a railing. The drop down to the concrete loomed below them before they set feet back down on solid rooftop. Up ahead, the lip of a slightly higher building blocked their view of the other group. Midi hopped up in one go, while Zelly stayed behind and held out two hands with interlaced fingers. She hoisted Digi and Wander up and in turn they pulled her up.

"Let's go, let's go! They're getting away!"

Each of them gritted their teeth through exuberant smiles, overcome with the raucous energy of a midnight footrace. Wander caught Digi's glance and they laughed, pushing forward harder, until they'd almost caught up with Midi.

"Gap!"

Midi leapt inhumanly and soared over an intersection, hovercars below her honking in the fog. She hit the opposite rooftop and rolled.

"Fuck it, let's do this!" Zelly jumped, followed by Wander and Digi, and together the three of them flew.

Wander felt purer, more unadulterated exhilaration than she'd felt in months. More than any mission, more than getting paid, more than success. She closed her eyes for a moment.

This is freedom.

Wind whipping past. The smell of exhaust as they shared the open air with the passing hovers. The adrenaline of pure danger.

She opened them again. The rooftop below was rapidly speeding closer.

Like clockwork they connected and rolled, and were back up on their feet sprinting, legs burning, staminas at full tilt. Up ahead, the five-person crew was getting nearer and, with all the will they could muster, the girls forced themselves forward.

Suddenly, the opposing team seemed to disappear from the rooftops. Midi shouted, having apparently predicted their choice.

"I knew it! They're taking Breakport entrance! Hit the street, we're taking the roundabout at St. Charles!"

High above, a Demigod rumbled on past them, with no hope of detecting them through the dark Mid-City clouds.

Approaching a fire escape, Midi jumped away from the stairs and wrapped her arms around a drainage pipe cluster and slid out of sight. Digi hurdled the front railing and plummeted, catching the railing of the fire escape across the alley and then continuing down. Zelly flipped over the edge as well and began catching and dropping down to each level of the escape as she fell.

Wander weighed her options and all at once felt vastly inadequate to the others. Nothing was coming to mind. She was holding herself back, she could feel it, bogged down by over-analysis. It was sapping her creativity, her passion. With no time to waste, she leapt over each of the inner railings of the fire escape, making her way down in swinging jumps, though not nearly as swiftly as the others. She hopped down to the dirty concrete in time to see the others racing down the alley and flung herself forward to catch up.

"Wander, move your ass!"

It was enough to break her out of her momentary daze. Once again she felt the moist Electuan air whipping around her as she exited the alley and crossed the busy street. One by one the Runners disappeared into a subway entrance. As Wander dove in after them, a burst of creativity overcame her. She lifted off at the top of the stairwell and wall-ran as long as she could, then leapt to the middle hand-railing. Sliding sideways as if board-grinding, she slipped down the length of it, a familiar joy overcoming her. At last she hit the tiled ground running and managed to close the gap between the others.

Around the bend in the sloping tunnels, they turned and were immediately confronted with the opposing crew emerging from an adjacent hall. Midi hollered to them and they turned, shocked to see their competition coming up behind them. Both groups began an all-out sprint, darting and weaving through the subway crowds, here and there throwing their own style into obstacles.

"Hell of a shortcut!"

"Thank me later! Let's get these fuckers!"

Coming up behind Zelly, Wander put her hands on her friend's back and pushed. Zelly laughed and took up the challenge, gathering a burst of energy and taking off. She stole the lead from Midi and as a group they tore into the sparsely crowded subway terminal.

The other group was leaping from the deck now, down to the tracks where a subway train was pulling away. They were each jumping and grabbing hold of the last train car, throwing gestures to the NightRunners, flaunting their victory.

"Oh-the-fuck-no you don't!"

Midi and the rest of them hurtled forward, soaring from the edge of the terminal and into the corridor of tracks as the train gathered speed. The opposing group gave in and leaned out toward them, offering hands to pull them up. Midi ignored them, eventually catching the rear handholds and climbing aboard. The rest of them each took the assistance and made their way up, jumping from the rushing ground. After a series of high-fives and hugs with the other NightRunners, Wander sank down to her knee and began catching her breath.

[[E5: WEST MID-CITY]]
<Subway Train to Southtown>

After running out the passengers of the rear car, the two groups lounged in the seats they'd earned. They were now animatedly getting to know each other, chatting and laughing boisterously. The challenging group identified themselves as Hellions and consisted of two human males, one human female, one male droid, and one hard-off female dweller. All were super friendly and impressively athletic. Wander had tried her hardest to keep up with the conversations and have a good time, even connecting for a while with Natalia the dweller, though eventually she'd receded to her own window to withdraw and gain some space. It was completely uncharacteristic of her, but the others seemed to understand. They carried on having fun while occasionally coming by to check on her.

Outside the train car window, she could see the old skeleton rising into the fog, peeking through the silhouettes of the Southtown buildings; the derelict loops of the Meta-Terrania racing course she'd visited with Zef only last night. Before the familiar flood of grief could wash back up, she remembered what they'd seen from high up in the bleachers. The flesh trade in progress. The image returned to her: the woman lying shot in the open canal between the headlights of a circle of cars and a crowd of onlookers.

Wander knew that Zef was right. Getting involved with the auctions had the potential of bringing a lot of unwanted heat down on their heads, but she wasn't satisfied with that. She wouldn't accept being complicit. She needed the Runners to know what was happening.

She scanned the interior of the train car.

"We need to get off..." Wander realized that her weakened voice stood no chance against the noise of the others. She pulled herself from the bench seat and made her way to Zelly, who was having a quiet conversation with the human female Hellion Leena. Putting her arms around Zelly, she whispered through her fluffy hair. "We need to get off the train now."

Zelly turned back to Wander with concern but immediately recognized the grave solemnity in the girl's eyes. She conceded and smiled nervously.

"Alright..."

She whistled to Digi and Midi, who were busy lounging and chatting up the two human males, both of whom seemed enamored with the almost identical girl droids. Seeing that she had everyone's attention, Zelly made the announcement.

"Come on, guys. Time to go. We have things to take care of." Despite groans from the twins, Zelly looked around at the Hellions with a broad smile. "It was really great meeting y'all, thanks so much for the challenge."

"Fawkin' right on!"

"Yeah, it was a pleasure."

"Be safe out there!"

The NightRunners gathered together and headed for the rear door as the train neared SouthTown Station. Midi playfully gave the middle finger to one of the males, while Digi shrank with bashfulness from a kiss blown toward her. Wander smiled and waved to the rest of them who did the same, though Natalia hopped up and approached her.

"Wander." The girl, almost entirely synthetic despite her flesh face and chest, took Wander's hand. The rotating irises of her eyes were something cybernetic and otherworldly, windows into a different dimension. "Listen. Stay true to what you're chasing, okay? This journey is about you..."

She leaned in and kissed Wander on the cheek, and used the opportunity to speak softly into her ear. "And don't let anyone tell you to slow down."

[[E5: WEST MID-CITY]]
<Meta-Terrania QuadroRacing Course>

Cautiously, the NightRunners crept along the deserted streets of residential SouthTown as they approached the abandoned grounds of the Meta-Terrania. They'd begged Wander to explain what was going on, why she'd pulled them away from the other group of runners so early in the night, though she refused. She wanted to be able to focus first on finding a new route to the empty canal, this time for a better view.

High above, the bare steel mesh of the winding track hung suspended in the air as if it were weightless, tethered only to the thinnest vertical struts and lacking any of the holographic masking that had made it a mesmerizing spectacle years before. Long gone now were its days of hosting thrilling races, cheering crowds, and celebrities from across the city. It was now a shell of its previous self, hardly resembling a track at all, with no function aside from harboring a small community of derelicts and fugitives.

The girls climbed leisurely over the dirt-caked barricades and buildings at the perimeter, occasionally boosting each other up or lowering each other down, all while following Wander's lead. As the grounds sloped to accommodate the bulk of the track, they at first caught the smell and then the sight of a vast collection of tents and lean-tos dotted with bonfires burning in the night. Heaps of trash lay at the outskirts, a few of them burning, and the overpowering odor washed over them in the wind like a toxic wave.

"Corporate fuck." Midi covered her nose and mouth with both hands.

"Turn your sensors off, weirdo." Wander grimaced at the stench and swatted at a rogue fly.

"Turn your face off."

Digi had already deactivated her smell receptors and was enamored with the community of vagabonds. Such public gatherings of the homeless were generally known to be a Violation of Protocol, and she wondered how the place hadn't been raided or torn down yet.

"Wander, where to?" Zelly was doing her own best to ignore the stink, but its pervasiveness was more than she could stomach and her eyes were watering.

Wander looked above, orienting herself to the metallic husk of the track, and pointed in the proper direction.

"There."

"There where? What the hell are we doing here, Wander?"

Peering out past the tent community and recalling the auction, she decided to be honest with them.

"Something bad is going on. Something I saw last night when I was here with Zef." She forced herself to look between each of them, but the true reason was caught in her throat, too grim for words alone. She nodded in the direction they needed to go. "You'll understand better in a minute. Follow me."

[[E5: WEST MID-CITY]]
<Meta-Terrania QuadroRacing Course / Sewage Canal>

Past the tent community, past the old and rotten indoor facility with its smashed arcade machines, looted concession stands and dark hallways leading to QuadroRacer dressing rooms, Wander led them back out of the grounds perimeter and up to the empty freeway canal. She was becoming worried that they would arrive where she'd last seen the auction take place only to see nothing, wasting a good portion of their night. To both Wander's satisfaction and dismay, they reached the apex of the perimeter embankment to see the familiar circle of cars. They were parked around a group of figures in such a way that their headlights converged in the center. It seemed that things were possibly further along this night, as several of the standing attendees were paired with purchases who knelt next to them on the dirty pavement. As far as Wander could tell, there had thankfully been no bloodshed yet.

Huddled against the embankment wall with the rest of them, she finally whispered the explanation they'd been waiting for. "Zef called it a flesh trade. He says it happens pretty often here."

A hush fell over them as they watched the mysterious figures below gesturing and carrying on with business. Wander could make out the same augmented ring-leader with his bizarrely-shaped head and glowing shoulders, waving his gun around and announcing aloud the traits of one of the captives to potential buyers. Even more than it had before, the sickened feeling in her stomach churned at the idea of the helpless slaves forced to participate in their own transfer of ownership, and at gunpoint no less.

"Flesh trade. That's fucked up."

"That's really fucked up. How terrifying."

Digi remained silent, presently spiraling into a state of traumatized terror, her code-deep and nearly irreversible wounds reopening from years ago. With the others distracted, she sank beneath the embankment and rested her back against it. She pulled her plastec knees to her chest, and attempted to block out the onset of paralyzing fear.

"Last time I was here they killed one of the captives. I'm not sure why."

Within the circle of cars, the leader of the event was pulling a handcuffed man he'd been showcasing up his feet. He led the man over to two well-dressed individuals, likely Quadrans, and forced him to kneel again. The couple passed a small package to the leader, who stuffed it in a vest pocket.

"Wh-why did you bring us here? Wander, this is awful..." Zelly's face twisted in disgust.

"I know why."

They all turned, noticing for the first time that Digi'd secluded herself.

"She saw it and she couldn't help herself. She wants to kill them all for what they're doing, but she couldn't do it without our permission." Digi turned her pained eyes upward and peered into Wander's. "Right?"

Wander was shaken. She swallowed and took a deep breath.

"Yeah, actually... That's exactly why." She looked at each of them before returning to Digi's resolute blue eyes.

"Well, I want in. And so does Midi."

Midi nodded in agreement, still captivated by the gathering below.

"Yeah, I'm in. Let's destroy these motherfuckers."

Zelly clutched her lip between her teeth, but nodded also.

"Let's do it."

Wander was impressed by them, and a grin spread across her face. Despite the cold concrete and the dank Southtown breeze, a warmth was growing in her chest. She wasn't alone, and she was proud as hell to be a NightRunner.

[[E5: DOWNTOWN MID-CITY]]
<Breven Lestiny's Apartment>

"Twelve...thousand."

{"Breven, you must be kidding. You can go right ahead and rent yourself an auto-courier for...twelve thousand."} Maybe laughed again after repeating the number.

He unlocked the swollen and mildewed wooden door on the 37th level through a soft red holographic keypad and entered.

"Twelve thousand five hundred."

{"Oooh! Leave! Get out right now!"}

They laughed together this time.

"Hey, this is my apartment, lady."

She gave a satisfied huff. {"Lady. That's much better."}

"Yeah, don't get ahead of yourself there."

She considered the wild idea of telling him the truth, but coolly refrained. {"Nonetheless. I will not sell my most valuable asset. Not yet. And certainly not for...ugh. Twelve thousand Sub-Credits."}

"Well then you tell me, how much is she worth?"

{"More than you can afford, Mister RealmDweller. Wander is not for sale. I haven't even truly begun to train her. Corporation knows how skilled she'll be in a year, and fully human at that."}

Breven, a dweller and far from fully human, snorted. "Are ya done?"

They shared a laugh again at his reference to Wander's words with Lozuto.

{"I very much am. Nice try though."}

Breven was busy opening a cupboard and removed a smooth black tin, rectangular and smaller than a cigarette pack. He pried open the lid and withdrew one of several thin white strips that were left inside. Tilting his head to the side and exposing his neck, he found the rusting port with a sensitive metal fingertip and pushed the strip in. An LED blinked and the strip dissolved. Breven's eyes fluttered for a moment and his shoulders relaxed. He took in a deep, clear breath and exhaled slowly.

"Ahh, litstrips... Thank you for existing."

{"Still on those then, hmm?"}

"Until they stop manufacturing them. Never gets old."

{"You know, instead of relying on strips for your orgasms you could just find a real woman, Breven."}

"But the one I want is digital. Or so she says."

Maybe went silent as he put the tin away and drew a nanocig from above his ear. Once between his lips, he lit it and took a drag. The regular glitching of his mind subsided and drifting relaxation led him to the window. He peered out into the rain at the passing air traffic below. Slick hovercars zipped past at all hours of the night, narrowly missing each other as they weaved in between the buildings. Business as usual at the edge of the nightlife strip of Reznik Heights in Downtown Mid-City.

{"So what's the interest, honestly?"}

"Honestly? I think she's a hell of a worker, and I'd like to show her a few things outside the scope of the job. A little bit of context to educate her."

{"On?"}

"On Dominion City." He pried the shades open wide to see the passing spotlight of a Demigod sweeping over the city block through the hazy downpour. As it passed overhead, the rain seemed to stop for a moment. "On what's really going on here."

{"I will have none of it, Breven. She's not ready for any of that. She knows what she needs to know."}

"Which is why I asked, May. I'm trying to be polite here." The rain began again and Breven closed the blinds. He made his way back to the kitchen to fetch a bottle of Maxicaine soda and a leftover sandwich. Enough to keep his body alive for a couple days while he was zonked out and lost in the Realm.

{"Well, I very much appreciate that. But she's the closest I have to an elite-grade assassin. The last thing she needs is a head full of questions."}

"Yeah, I get it. But I think you underestimate her." Breven climbed back into his VR rig and plopped down into the leather seat. He began attaching the leads into his synthetic arms, upper torso, and flesh neck. Once activated, the operating diagnostics and holographic UIs bounced into place around him.

{"Well she certainly works for me at the moment, so mind yourself, young man. She'll belong to the Glade soon enough. Once the choice is her own, you can convince her to slay the High Noble if you'd like and I won't put up a fight. Until then, she's mine. I hope we have an understanding."} Her tone wasn't nearly as formal or stern as it could have been. She trusted Breven, though she knew how he was. Arrogant. No sense of timing or appropriateness. Endlessly lost in a head full of darkness and crusades. He'd go right into the deep end and take Wander with him if she allowed it.

"I'm a man of my word, Maybe."

{"And even as such, you'd better watch your ass. Thanks again for your help tonight."}

He chuckled and laid back, pulling the VR apparatus over his head and face. Clamps extended and locked his legs and arms into place. Various tubing filled with colored chemicals. His chair reclined, the holographics flickered and dimmed. Through the crevices of his goggles, bright colored light blinked rapidly.

"Consider it watched, lady. What are friends for?"

In front of his eyes, time and space was inverting. His consciousness jettisoned from inside his skull into the vast omnipresence of the Glade, sending him streaming through a tremendous abstract corridor blossoming with thousands of conceptual pathways.

[[E5: WEST MID-CITY]]

<Meta-Terrania QuadroRacing Course / Sewage Canal>

"I don't know. I honestly wasn't sure if they were even going to be here tonight."

The four NightRunnersm, having decided that it was their duty to step in, continued to watch over the embankment as the auction unfolded down in the vast cement canal.

"Well that makes this tricky. We can't just show up every night hoping they'll be down there." Zelly turned from the view at last to join them.

"I mean, we could, maybe for a few nights."

"Nah, it would be a waste. Too much train time, too much sneaking around just to go right back home."

"Well then, what?"

They sat in silence mulling the possibilities.

"We could camp out? I wouldn't mind it."

"Dude, it smells like the fucking West Edge out here."

"Midi..."

"It's not a bad idea."

"Ugh."

"Chill, Midi. We don't have to stay inside the racetrack grounds, we can find somewhere nearby to hang out and just come back at night."

"And what about Maybe?"

"What about her?"

"...What do we tell her?"

They all looked to Wander, Maybe's darling.

"We don't tell her anything."

Their mouths dropped. Wander had never suggested hiding anything from Maybe before.

"We're not getting paid for this. It's our mission."

"Oh fuck, Miss Courtesy Droid going off on her own." Zelly's grin was all teeth.

Wander scrunched her face up playfully to mock her.

"No, no, it's sexy, I dig it. It's about time we started taking a few things into our own hands. We don't always need to be taking orders."

Out from the bottom of the canal, the sizzle-crack of an energy shot rang out, echoing across the concrete walls. The four of them instinctively ducked below the ledge.

"Oh fuck, what happened?!"

"Shh! I don't know. Midi, check it out."

Midi's mouth opened in shock at Zelly's command. Nonetheless, she inched her head upwards til she could see the gathering below. Two of the men were arguing into each others' faces while a body lay dead on the ground. Midi amplified her audio receptors and listened in to their conversation.

"—told you twice now and I've had enough!"

"Oh well, fuck me! I guess SouthTown has a new king, alert Dominion City Live!"

The man put the muzzle of his weapon to the forehead of another kneeled captive and fired. A bright flash accompanied by a sizzle and pop echoed through the open space of the canal and Midi's stomach turned. The headless body crumpled.

"My property! I do with them what I want!"

"Not here you don't!"

The man in the heavy coat moved to the next captive. He'd finally seemed to get under the skin of the auctioneer, who lowered a revolver at the man.

"Kill another and you die with him."

"Hey, what the fuck is the matter with you people!? What are you, a buncha fuckin' humanitarians all of a sudden? This is my hardware!"

"Then kill them on your own time, Syrec! This is a market, not your own personal freakshow." He pulled back the hammer of the Old World firearm. The two men stood at odds for a moment, the congregation silent, until an agitated Syrec relented. He pulled his gun from the whimpering captive's head and backed away with his hands up.

"Alright. Fine."

The captive shook as he sobbed, infinitely relieved to not be dead.

Midi sank back beneath the embankment, wide-eyed, and returned her audio settings back to their usual with a blink.

"What's going on? Could you hear?"

She turned to face them with empty eyes that had just witnessed the cold-blooded murder of innocents. "We can take them. Let's do it tonight."

Zelly shook her head emphatically.

"No, not tonight. We aren't anywhere near prepared."

"We can take them!" Midi's whisper was almost a shout.

"No, Midi. I'm not going to let any of you get hurt, not when we could've just waited and come back ready."

Midi was too appalled to argue. She leaned back and rested her head on the concrete. Digi reached out and took her hand, threading their fingers together.

Wander looked between them, knowing that she couldn't allow them to sink into despair this way. "We're not sitting here feeling sorry. Come on, let's get going. We'll take the night off and get packed tomorrow."

High above, billowy poison clouds rumbled as a storm rolled in. As quietly as they could, the group helped each other up. Staying low, they began the trip back to Teradin. Wander had secret plans to take the best nap ever.

{THE GLADE}

<GladeWorld: Midsummer>

{RealmDweller, holding a sack on his back, hopped from the granite outcropping and jostled down the uneven hill. He pushed through a thicket at the bottom and stepped into the shade of an old-growth copse. Pausing for a moment, allowing his eyes to adjust, he searched through the trees for movement. His ears perked up at the familiar gurgling sound of rushing water and he moved forward.

Finding the stream, RealmDweller followed along its edge. The ground sloped and the stream descended, flowing through ancient, craggly rocks covered in coats of wet moss. He hopped across the gaps, keeping close to the water. As it curved toward the right through the trees, he veered away when he reached the old wooden marker, and followed a path made of pebbles and dirt. A motley troupe of glowing orbs had discovered him, and now they followed him with interest, bobbing gently above the ground.

Ahead, the forest became less dense, the brush cleared, and the path led him into a grassy clearing. In the center of the clearing, still draped in the shade of the immense Elder trees, the Stone rose tall. Paces away, he dropped his pack to the dirt and stepped forward.

The Stone was clean and bright in stark contrast to the natural colors of the forest. Its surface was etched with markings, symbols older than comprehension, their meanings obscured by unimaginable time. In both reverence and exhaustion, RealmDweller collapsed to his knees. He bent down until his head was buried in his hands, resting upon the grass. His mind, free from its ever-glitching flesh prison, still swam with questions he was attempting to sort through.

In front of him, The Guardian Stone waited in silence for RealmDweller's thoughts to cease before it could emerge.}

[[E5: WEST MID-CITY]]

<Teradin Jurisdiction / Haven-4>

The muted thrum of an Electuan storm beat relentlessly against the exterior brick and steel of Haven-4. It pulled Wander gently from a restful sleep. Like a lazy cat, she stretched herself out on the comfortable old couch and sat up, still blinking the sleep away. The interior of Haven-4 was dark, the only light coming from the soft cyan glow of the holo-table and an orange lava lamp atop an ancient console. She looked around, waiting for something to happen or someone to speak. There was only the steady rain against the building and a continuous splash outside the door. The relaxing ambiance was immensely welcome. She smiled and reclined into the soft couch to enjoy the moment of peace.

It reminded her of her childhood home in the Ebber Village of Uptown Quadro, when she would stay up at night just to listen to the rain and the sounds of the city. There was something entrancing about it, something that compelled her mind to dream up outlandish scenarios of what might be going on out there. Among the crowds, beneath the walkways, in the alleys and shops and crevices of the city, out past the limits of her exploration. It urged a younger Wander with patient restlessness to look outside, to get into the streets and meld with the chaos that made up civilization. The same sense of curiosity also pulled her thoughts back to the endless corridors of the Realm, and to the Glade. She remembered that she was supposed to head back in soon, to meet this friend of Maybe's and begin her new briefings.

Maybe had explained that the job would most likely last a while, with various tasks spread out over the course of a year, predominantly within the real world of Dominion City. Preparations, though, would need to be made inside the VR world of the Realm where she assumed this "RealmDweller" would have maps for her, objectives, routes, backdoors, maybe personnel files and helpful downloads.

Whatever's going on, she thought, *it sounds crazy ambitious.*

She could tell from Maybe's tone of voice that this gig was going to be a challenge, especially if RealmDweller had asked for her specifically. The notion of working for someone new, exploring new parts of the city, learning new skills, it gave her butterflies of excitement just thinking about it. After everything they'd all been through, it was hard to imagine that her career was only just beginning.

In her pocket, her holoGlass buzzed. She pulled it out to see a holotext from Zelly.

// "You awake yet? We're headed out for one last pizza at SOL before we start packing, if you want to meet up."

"Just woke up, thanks for the invite." The words she spoke appeared in the holo-display. "I think I'm just going to take a walk though."

She tapped send and waited.

// "Dude get out here, there's guys everywhere."

Wander laughed. Midi was nothing if not relentless.

"How's Digi?"

// "I'm fine, no worries. Ignore them. Go take your walk and be safe."

"Already out the door. You three do the same over there."

// "Lame!"

Wander smirked and silenced the phone before stuffing it back into her pocket. Around her, the quiet ambiance of the room grew loud again. The absence of Zef from everything was an odd feeling. *Where could he be? Hopefully he hasn't gone back to the Fire Circuit... Or worse, back to the West Edge. Should I message him? Would he even care?*

She shrugged away the thought. Thunder crackled and shook the building around her. The urge to sleep for days began creeping in.

"Maybe, you there?" She turned over to look at the holo-table where the glowing model of the city still rotated slowly. She waited, convinced that Maybe was surely busy.

{"Yes, darling, I'm here."}

"Do you...have any experience with love? I know that might be a dumb question."

{"It isn't dumb at all. I do, in fact."}

The notion gave Wander a small amount of comfort, that Maybe might be somewhat human in that regard, might at least be able to relate to what she was going through. It satisfied her enough that it slipped her mind to follow up with a question, and instead she found herself simply enjoying a rare moment of personal connection with Maybe.

{"But of course I would be biased in my advice."}

Wander thought about it and took it to imply Maybe's synthetic nature. *How were AI relationships different from human ones?*

"That's alright. I just can't make up my mind. It's like I have these two very important parts of my life fighting against each other. I don't know what to do anymore, or what to say to fix it all."

{"Wander, I know that your desire is for a simpler life. One where everything is cleanly cut and squared away, where those people who should be around stay, and those who shouldn't be there go away. Where we have a defined purpose and that's that. We like to think we should know what's best for ourselves, like we should know the answers when things get confusing, but these are rarely ever the case."} She paused to allow Wander a chance to consider. {"Life is not a game, Wander, where you move the pieces around until you're most happy. Life is filled with pieces that cannot and will not stay put. Unpredictable situations. Unpredictable people. It leaves us with only one option."}

Wander thought she understood. "To make peace with the chaos."

{"Exactly. The Wander that I know makes the best of any situation on the fly, trusting her instincts, guiding her choices with her gut. You ought to learn to do that in life as well, not just while you're on the job."}

She thought it over, accepting that Maybe was right. Wander had never drawn a clear line between her real life and work, and she'd allowed herself to somehow be more happy while working than in life. She'd fallen into a mindset of trusting her creative instincts as "Wander the NightRunner," while becoming defeated by over-analysis as "Wander the person." She wondered where along the way she'd lost sight of those priorities and why. What was so important about work that she'd put it ahead of her own peace? How could she balance the flow?

The ideas began to recontextualize the way things had played out with Zef. Wander felt the sinking suspicion that maybe she'd pushed him away, or somehow hadn't been sensitive to his problems. It was too much to sort out all at once.

"I think I'm going to go for a walk. Thank you for the advice, Maybe. I'm want to figure out a way to make this right."

A momentary silence led her to wonder if Maybe had gone away.

{"Anytime, dear. Take care of yourself out there."}

[[E5: WEST MID-CITY]]

<Teradin / Slice-O-Life Pizzeria>

Slice-O-Life was booming, the crowd spilling out into the walkways outside, drinking and enjoying themselves despite the usual chance that a Brother Unit might appear at any moment to disrupt their fun. The pulsing beat of Quadran tracktunes filled the atmosphere, giving life to their conversations and laughter and networking. Inside, Digi, Midi, and Zelly had taken a booth for themselves and waited for a pie to arrive.

"And she said yes?!"

"Of course she said yes, look at this body."

"Fuck the Corp..." Zelly rolled her eyes at Midi's conceit. "Midi, one of these days you're gonna fall in love with one of those humans, you better watch it."

Midi frowned and looked at Zelly sideways. "Love?"

"Yes, love. You know, amorous feelings, adoration, infatutuation?"

"Literally fuck all of those things, especially after seeing what it's doing to Wander."

A passing waitress raised an eyebrow at their conversation.

"Don't talk that way about Wan, Em. And you say that like you have a choice. That's not how love works."

"Zelly, let's be real here. You haven't been out with anyone in months."

"And...?" She cocked her head to the side waiting for an answer.

Digi looked between them, fully entertained. If Wander had been present, Digi might've joined in with them, but presently she was content to simply watch them bicker.

"And, so I don't think you're quite the expert on how love works. It's misery and attachment. And obsession. And depression. And sometimes maybe sex."

Zelly squinted at the girl with full disappointment.

Digi sipped her soda. "When I find someone, it's not going to be anything like that."

Her hopefulness wasn't lost on Midi.

"Digi, you aren't like the rest of us. You have a soul. People with souls find love."

"That's because we actually believe in it."

"Well, good luck with that. Me, I'm satisfied with a good time. I swear to the Good Corporation if someone tries to pull that drama on me I'm gonna..."

"One large bio-supreme and three meat coxinhas?"

"Oh, fuck..."

"Yep, that's us."

The three of them watched wide-eyed as the steaming pizza was placed in the center of the table.

Zelly's jaw hung open. "Oh, sweet Corporation, forgive me for what I'm about to do to this thing."

"Thank you very much, miss." Midi winked at the waitress. The lady's eyes went wide as she tried to collect herself and be professional.

"My pleasure. Is there anything else I can get you all? Refills?"

"That'd be great, thank you." Midi grinned and watched her leave, admiring her well-put-together human parts. "Fuck the Corp, she's cute."

Zelly's eyes rolled. "Midi, eat your damn pizza."

[[E5: WEST MID-CITY]]
<Teradin Jurisdiction / Haven-4>

The allure of the broken-in leather couch had finally subsided and Wander pulled herself up. She was determined to clear her mind in preparation for the next day, when they would take a few supplies and head back to SouthTown.

Tripping with Zef and her nightmare, experiencing the Glade again, the job in Downtown, her blow-out with Zef and the race with the Hellions; it had all taken its toll. She'd slept most of the fatigue away, but was left with lingering notions, remnants of problems that still needed solving. Thanks to Maybe, though, she now had a new mindset to approach things with. She was going to try and work toward peace. Not just fixing everything, but letting things go as well. There was an entire city out there to enjoy and she had been so silly to be wrapped up in what she couldn't control.

Outside the door of Haven-4, the rain had lessened, and she stepped out into the alleyway grateful for the familiar smells and sounds of Mid-City Electua. She closed and locked the entrance and made her way from the alley to the sloping main street of Teradin Jurisdiction. The crowds were out in force now that the downpour had ceased. Wander stood at the corner of the alley and looked around, trying to make up her mind which way to go.

It doesn't matter, she thought, *go where your feet take you.*

She felt a vague pull to the left and went with it, pushing through a group of chattering droids in thick coats. Stepping up onto the main walkway, she caught a glimpse of the way forward. The mists and smog hung low over the crowds. Only several meters above, dense hover traffic crawled every which way between the labyrinth of buildings and bridges. They wove between and around each other like a practiced dance, occasionally honking or scraping against one another. Beams of headlights pointed and swiveled through the fog, illuminating patches of falling rain; the cars themselves dropped trails of water beneath them as they went. Searching higher up into obscurity, Wander's eyes feasted on the webbing of pipes and wires, the window lights of the dwellings above, the over-saturated holo-ads, all drenched and dripping from the persistent showers.

"C'mon, sweetie, you're holding up the sidewalk." An impatient old lady, heavy-set with a face that was half old-technology, nudged her with a wire cart. She politely obliged and began walking again.

All around Wander, thousands of unique characters milled about in the streets, calling out, chatting, laughing, beeping and buzzing. Bicycles and hover carts ridden by strange hybrids of human and machine, cumbersome walking bots with long legs, Citizens with rebreathers and debreathers and omnibreathers and airtanks, see-through vital organs with neon highlights, multi-limbed individuals and small groups of kid-bots and keepers leading animals, all trundling this way and that on personal business. Wander weaved her way under carried objects and between foot traffic with the skill of a veteran crowdthreader.

She slowed her pace in front of a dough stand and waved at the man in the window. He was Papa-san Ligieri, owner of the shop for decades now. He gave her a warm smile and broke her off a little ball of dough. Wander caught it and ate it immediately. She gave him a last wave and continued on her way, savoring the dough's tart sweetness.

As the road sloped left and down she hopped out of the way of a couple of droid teens boarding past, and gave a wave to a girl on a balcony across the street reading. Marilu was always finding the best Old World booksellers, hopefully she was onto something good lately.

The road continued to slope, dotted on both sides and up the levels into the fog with clubs booming out music, food vendors, massage therapists, tech shops and repairmasters, and countless others that were collectively adding to the melange of deafening street noise. Teradin was a living hive.

Up ahead, the ominous antennae of a patrolling Brother Unit could be seen jutting above the heads of the crowd. Wander ducked off to the left and followed two backpacked and raincoated men through a warmly-lit, covered corridor built from an alleyway. Beneath a tarp roof, where lanterns of all sorts swayed gently, stalls selling cuts of raw Percaran meat and poultry lined a center walkway. The lanterns cast a warm glow over lines of wet Citizens chatting and purchasing goods. She greeted a few of the stall owners she recognized as she made her way to the end of the walkway.

Beyond a plastic curtain, a network of bridges milled with pedestrians and vendors selling and cooking foodstuffs.

The Soy Markets of Teradin.

Most of these vendors were affiliated with the neighborhood hydroponic soy farms. Wander took a deep inhale of the mixed aroma of grilled foods and basked at the familiarity of it all.

Above the busy market, dancing holograms and layers of music blanketed the hazy space with colorful atmosphere that seemed at once to be both claustrophobic and vastly spacious. She walked to the edge of the bridge and peered down at more crowds flowing through lower bridge levels of the market.

A sense of home began creeping into her chest, something she realized she'd been lacking for years even at the flat with the others. These smells, these memories of Teradin and everything that surrounded Haven-4. She refused to allow anything to spoil it all for her. It was such a magical neighborhood, filled with mostly well-meaning people just trying to make a living. It didn't deserve to be overlooked and, without family, without anywhere to go back to, Wander didn't mind if she never left this place.

Still lingering within the soy markets, she purchased herself a small meal of handmade cheeses, hydroponically-grown veggies, and real fruit juice and found herself a balcony to enjoy her meal.

{THE GLADE}
<GladeWorld: Midsummer>

{Playfully bouncing orbs of light numbering in the hundreds had converged upon the forest clearing of the Stone. The object itself emanated wavering rifts of powerful energy into the surrounding space; it was currently undergoing the arduous spiritual process of becoming a vessel for the Guardian.

The small, floating spirits were familiar with the man doing the summoning. He seemed to bend the land to his will, and they suspected he was some kind of sorcer from a far away land, maybe even from somewhere beyond the ocean. Yet even this mighty one knelt in the presence of the Guardian. His visits were seldom, but his conversations with this particular Stone always proved to be fascinating learning experiences, and worth gathering for. They watched with relish to see what the first question might be.

RealmDweller, at the command of the Guardian, bowed ever more deeply into his contemplation, pushing away his Dominion-side concerns as they bubbled up. Those thoughts now felt like intruders, attempting to sabotage his peace. He paid them no attention, sinking further into pure, unfiltered patience and humility. Around both himself and the Stone, the fabric of the Glade suddenly dilated like a lens. Time slowed within, and the orbs gathered near to listen, until they appeared numerous like stars surrounding a vast sphere of distorted space. The gap between RealmDweller's mind and the spirit of the Guardian began to breach, like a gate opening, and his intentions lay bare.

"Guardian."

"Welcome, Atomdanser. Your energies are discordant... How may we serve you?"

RealmDweller had not yet learned the reason this unfamiliar term or name had been applied to him, nor why the Guardian referred to itself as "we", though he accepted with gratitude that it had acknowledged him at all.

"I've come to a...convergence of pathways. I've agreed to take part in actions that may change the world I come from, forever." Within the briefest pause, he could feel the benevolent eye of the Guardian gazing down upon his opened soul, like a flood of warm sunlight into an open flower. "I have the skills I need. I have others willing to assist me. But I don't understand the implications of what I'm doing... I've always felt that this was the right path, but now I hesitate. I don't want everything to fall apart."

The translucent domain of the Guardian stirred around him, fluctuating as it processed his request. Surrounding him within the murky, ethereal substance, the light resonated and grew brighter. He could feel the echoes of an answer coagulating.

"What you seek is Purpose, young one, something you have been lacking for many cycles. Seek well within you."

Despite the boundless reverence he attempted to maintain, RealmDweller felt a tinge of frustration. The advice was simply another question, another task. He implored his humility to purge the space where the frustration had been, and again he opened his mind to the Stone.

"And what if I find nothing? Why must I have a purpose in order to move forward?"

The echoes began to grow again. If there had been pressure upon him, it now seemed to lift as the Guardian revealed its truth with a wave of kind-hearted energy.

"A Purpose is the structure of your progression into the future. Your temporal experience is that of a lamb, being led child-like toward a pasture by the shepherd of Purpose. Without Purpose, we become lost."

The answer made all the sense it needed to, though he found himself still frustrated. Even now, under the gaze of the Guardian, he had no inkling as to what his purpose might be. Nothing pulled him, nothing called him, nothing offered itself as a worthy reason to carry on his dreary, withdrawn life, aside from his burning quest to undermine Dominion. Again, he felt compelled to inquire.

"I can understand what you mean. But I don't understand what searching will do. I don't feel compelled by any purpose. How will I know when I find one? How will I know that it's real?"

Around them, the orbs that had bounced so playfully into the clearing now pressed themselves inward attentively on the energetic bubble surrounding the powerful beings. They listened keenly as the Guardian spoke, for it rarely did so. Even in their own enlightened states, there was always much to learn from this Stone.

"Young one, this sort of question is not answerable. Such a Purpose is the product of your own desires, your own wishes and Path to fulfillment. You make the Path ever more difficult by attempting to understand it. Lead yourself instead with your emotions. To know what is Right is to understand Purpose."

The Guardian had spoken what RealmDweller needed to hear. Just as the spirit orbs floated along on the currents, so did his thoughts, organizing and drawing in toward logical conclusions. Though the matters in Dominion City were complicated, fraught with pitfalls and challenges, he began to sense what was Right. In that moment, as much as the idea of Sacrifice disgusted him, its tendrils began reaching out into him, growing inside him as Purpose.

It dawned upon him that it wasn't enough to simply combat Dominion. Taking the Realm had so many implications that it needed a deeper reason to be carried out.

There were so many Citizens who would be affected. So many Synths who would be affected. Entire economies that depended upon the fate of the Realm. But deeper than that, the massive VRnet held the power for systemic transformation. Not just for a single mind but for humanity as a whole.

If everything he'd accomplished so far was leading toward one conclusion, toward what was Right, toward some sense of Purpose, then he understood what it needed to be. The people of Dominion City deserved freedom.}

[[E5: WEST MID-CITY]]
<Teradin Jurisdiction>

Finishing her cheese and vegetables, Wander pocketed the paper they'd been wrapped in and leaned back against the wall of the building. Below her, the city blocks descended into swimming, blue-tinted clouds, lit from beneath by the lights at base street-level. Above Teradin, the sky was remarkably clear for once, and Wander could see a handful of stars beyond the light pollution, twinkling through the blanket of night.

She hadn't felt the deep rumble of a passing Demigod in a while. Long gaps in their presence always gave the city below a sense of freedom, as if there was a chance that they might never return, that Dominion Corp had packed their bags and left the city to its own devices.

Wander frowned at the absurdity of the thought. It was named Dominion City for a reason. The Corporation wasn't going anywhere. They occupied an entire City Ring, Tetra District, and from there they policed the city, maintained the Outer Wall, kept up the Infrastructure, did whatever corporations do... It wasn't like the simple government of one of the Districts, just looking out for the Citizens inside. *Dominion was something else. A monumental parasite. Some kind of sick monster feeding off the millions of people it claimed to serve.* Even such thoughts when spoken were Violations of Protocol.

She shook her head, unable to imagine being oblivious like so many others here were. *They must know,* she thought, *they must know on some level that this is not what real freedom is. Freedom isn't lowering your voice when the deadly police droids pass by on the street. Opening your eyes so your retinas can be scanned, or else you're cut down in front of your family.*

She forced herself to pause and take a deep breath of the soggy, unrefined Teradin air. What she needed now was calmness, not a mind ranting about everything it could latch onto.

In the wide open space between the buildings, high above the Soy Markets, an enormous holographic billboard drifted past between the hover traffic, multi-colored and rippling.

"OVERCOME YOUR FEARS, TRAVEL TO DISTANT LANDS, LIVE A DIFFERENT LIFE... EXPERIENCE THE ULTIMATE TRIP!"

The words faded away into pixels and returned, flashing.

"THE HOLOTRIP VR. The Ultimate Trip!"

The Dark Rift's obsession with escape from reality made Wander's stomach turn. She realized that it was only a personal preference, and indeed she was in the minority in this respect. The majority of Dominion City had accepted the idea that a large portion of their lives should be spent in virtual worlds, augmented realities, immersed in fairytales. Even Zef spoke of the Realm at least once a day.

Enough. She cleared her mind again and continued to breathe, taking in the sounds of the city. *Enough discontent for one day.*

Beneath it all, surrounding her, the disorganized din of a thousand sparkling advertisements, speakers blasting, hover honks and engine rumbles, reverberating announcements, the excited chattering and rustle of the crowds crossing all the bridges spanning between buildings and then... she felt the growing patter of rain.

Wander opened her eyes to see new clouds sliding into view, obscuring the stars. From beneath they were illuminated by the blinking Mid-City neons. They brought with them the toxicity of the QuadroRaces, an entire District away.

She closed her eyes again and slowed her breathing. Thoughts of the Hellions and their footrace bubbled up, but she pushed them away. Instead, she focused on the drifting breeze that brushed against her, its humid warmth contrasting with the cool droplets.

Zef. The Glade Syndicate. Siresh.

She inhaled again, allowing the panorama of sound to envelop her and carry her away into patience.

Vincenzo Sardo. Flesh trade. Murder.

She breathed.

Tetra Priest. RealmDweller. Maybe.

Her muscles relaxed and she straightened her spine, tuned herself in to the environment. Her breath became regular, her heart slowed, her shoulders and thighs eased. There was peace here, she could feel it building. Between it all, there was a delicate balance, a social harmony, a thousand reasons to appreciate this place.

Beyond the hum of the traffic and voices and speakers, she could feel the concrete of the balcony begin to vibrate. It traveled up through her thighs to her insides, enough to disturb her peace again. The distinct rumble of a Demigod.

[[E5: WEST MID-CITY]]
<Teradin Jurisdiction>

The rain was steady again when Wander's feet landed on the wet concrete of a new bridge. She stood again, pulling back her dripping hair, and glanced around at the passing crowd. This bridge had no vendors. Instead, it was primarily families gathering to socialize. Against the railing, a lone guitarist sat beneath a stretched tarp, setting the tone for a leisurely evening with his relaxing melodies despite the backdrop of a noisy city.

Wander took a seat on a concrete bench at the edge of the bridge. Her ears opened to the conversations going on around her, realizing how long it'd been since she'd heard any of the concerns of the people in the street.

"...Three times before the end of the quarter..."

"You were right to tell him that..."

"...twelve years in hover repair, take my number..."

"Just up in flames, the whole block, some group calling themselves Phosphorus..."

"...You don't say..."

She watched as trenchcoated fathers talked with other fathers beneath their umbrellas, comparing information and opinions about local Electua news and Dominion City Live TV, introducing their wives, discussing their jobs and trades. Mothers and grandmothers talked among each other and tended to their children who stomped about in the rain, splashing in puddles and giggling, weaving in and out of the legs of the adults. The young ones were unconcerned with the harsh economic times. They knew nothing of the crime all around them, the dirty crowds, the danger of a Brother Unit on patrol...they only wanted to play. To make friends. To smile and see the smiles of others.

"Água de côco?"

She looked up at an odd man holding a wooden box of cartons, obviously trying to sell her coconut water. She raised an eyebrow at the questionable quality of the drinks, but decided to partake anyway. She held up a single finger.

"Sim, one please."

"Ahh, muito 'brigado!"

The man, whose face was nearly skinless, teeth held together by wires, bowed and bowed again. He handed her a carton and held out a cheap scanner. She inserted her Sub-Credit strip into it and heard the familiar tone straining itself through a small speaker. The vendor grinned his crooked grin and carried on down the bridge.

As she opened her carton of coconut water, Wander nearly leapt out of her skin as the red lights of a Hopper Unit appeared in her peripheral vision. Upon closer inspection, she could see that it wasn't scanning its surroundings or the features of other Citizens; it wasn't scouting at all. She breathed a sigh of relief and took a drink from the carton.

The Hopper Unit bounced around, emitting small chittering noises and beeps. Several of the children chased it back and forth, always coming close but never able to lay hands on the small robot. Though the little HU was probably just confused, trying to do a job but continuously interrupted by the children, it amused Wander to imagine that the thing might be aware, perhaps even having fun.

Another sip of her coconut water and she was convinced; it was quality stuff. She was happy to be in Teradin.

The Hopper bounced over to Wander in curiosity. She put out her hand as if it were a kitten and the little Unit inspected it, its many red eyes roving around, and it glanced up at her face. She looked back, and could swear that for a moment it seemed as though it were acknowledging her, as if it wanted to communicate. She wondered what could possibly be on the tiny thing's mind. A young boy pounced and the Hopper Unit leapt out of the way, forgetting about her.

She sat contemplating the strange moment, unable to pin a name to the emotion she felt. She was happy at least that the Hopper didn't scan her eyes and recognize her as Unregistered. The last thing she needed right now was to trip a Dominion alarm and disrupt the evening for the families relaxing around her.

With caution in mind, she stood from the bench and finished her coconut water. She tossed it onto an over-filled recycle bin and continued her stroll, this time in the direction of Slice-O-Life Pizzeria.

[[E5: WEST MID-CITY]]
<Teradin / Slice-O-Life Pizzeria>

"It's gonna be sick as fuck."

Zelly blinked. She was not prepared for that response. "Really? Killing people will be sick as fuck?"

"It's not killing people." Midi rolled her eyes in a full loop and corrected Zelly with conviction. "It's killing the *right* people."

Digi'd had just about enough of their back-and-forth for one night when Wander plopped herself down in their booth unexpectedly and snatched up the last piece of cold pizza.

"Dude! So glad you made it out!"

"Hell yes!" Zelly held her hand up and Wander slapped it.

"How was your walk?"

Wander answered between chews of pizza. "It was nice..."

"Yeah? You feeling any better?"

She took a swig of Digi's soda and wiped her mouth.

"I feel good. Was really nice to slow down for a bit."

"Did you go anywhere?"

"Nah, just the Soy Markets. Chilled out, collected my thoughts."

"Zelly said you were almost about to lose your mind."

Zelly's mouth dropped open. "I– I said she was having a hard time. Wander, I promise, I didn't say you were losing your mind."

"Nah, you said she was on the edge of batshit crazy. Really judgemental of you."

Digi facepalmed. Zelly was aghast. Soda came out of Wander's mouth.

"What the–"

Midi fell over in tears. "Wander, I..."

Zelly was over it.

"Corporate hell. Can we just get out of here?"

Wander laughed. She took one last bite of the cold slice and tossed it back to the aluminum tray.

"C'mon, we've got two transfers ahead of us. Let's get back to the flat."

They climbed out of the booth, Midi already lighting a nanocig, and made their way to the door.

[[E5: WEST MID-CITY]]
<The Flat>

"So, tomorrow night."

"You think Maybe knows?"

"I doubt it. Just bad timing probably."

Zelly and Wander sat on the rooftop of their flat, overlooking the ass-end of Electua and into Reshen. Far beyond the gray husks of the dead Mid-City suburb, a small city center rose up in Reshen, glittering with orange and yellow lights. It was the beginning of the massive West Edge region.

"So tell me more. Have you met the dude?"

"Not yet. But I will tomorrow night, at the Domain while you guys hang back. But he's supposedly this elusive guy, super powerful in the Realm and high up in the Glade Syndicate, all that shit. It's a pretty big honor to meet him, but I just don't want it interfering with our life too much."

Zelly smiled and looked over at her. "It won't. Everything will be fine. You go to the Domain and do your meeting, we'll come for you from PixelAddict and we'll all head to the track when you're finished. Don't sweat it. This seems big."

"It is big. Even Maybe seems impressed with this guy."

"Means you're gonna be learning a lot, Wan. Things are gonna be opening up for you. I just hope you don't forget us little people when you move on into Glade high society."

Wander met her gaze in the clouded moonlight. Their history together played out in her heart. The orphanage. The early days in Electua. Wicked 6 and the early days. Meeting Maybe... Zelly would always be her big sister.

"Are you kidding me? I'm taking you and the twins along for this ride."

"Oh, yeah? You're not gonna leave us behind once things get crazy?"

Wander's expression turned solemn and she looked back out to the bright orange cityscape beyond the dark. Around them, the rhythms of the city crickets rose to fill the silence. Of course she'd thought about what was going to happen to the NightRunners if this became serious, but it wasn't even a debate.

"Zel, if you guys can't go, I don't go. We're NightRunners." Their eyes met again. "And friends. We're not splitting up."

Zelly wrapped her arm around Wander's shoulders.

"It's what I like to hear."

Wander giggled. Zelly kissed her forehead.

"And what about Zef?"

She took in a deep breath and sighed. She'd thought a lot about that too, and the answer was just as easy.

"Zef is out."

CHAPTER 5

NOT ALL WHO WANDERLUST

[[E5: WEST MID-CITY]]
<Meta-Terrania QuadroRacing Course / Sewage Canal>

Fresh from the Digital Domain, the NightRunners were unprepared for the overpowering stench of the squatter community. They moved forward in the half-dark as briskly as they could, keeping their Running markers off to remain as invisible as possible. One by one they hopped down to the wall behind the embankment, making sure to keep quiet and alert. Beneath them in the canal, they could see that the auction was already in progress. The vehicles were pulled around in their usual circle, headlights converged on a gathering in the center. The auctioneer seemed to still be making his opening statements.

"So, how is this allowed to happen, again?" Midi busied herself by unzipping a small bag and removing two energy sidearms. She laid an array of other small instruments carefully on the concrete slab.

"Zef said something about the entire Meta-Terrania grounds being in a political gray area. Way back when the Big District split into Quadro and Electua and Reshen, they—"

"Formir District," Digi corrected, strapping her throwing knives to her upper arms. Having seen her in action with them on multiple occasions, Wander knew that Digi's coded wits were more accurate and lethal with those razor-sharp darts than any human would be with a cumbersome firearm.

"Yeah, the Big District." Wander rolled her eyes playfully at the walking encyclopedia that was Digi. "It broke apart and the legality of this place got all fucked. Seems like Dominion still patrols it but nothing gets enforced."

"Pretty weird, so close to Downtown and all." Zelly was wrapping her wrists, preparing herself for hand-to-hand combat. She'd been trained as a kickboxer in Mid-City gyms even before they'd called themselves the Wicked 6. Wander loved her style. Where she herself fought with the lithe kicks and somersaults of an acrobat, Zelly's style leaned more toward blunt-force brawling. She could flip and cartwheel with the rest of them, but something in the girl craved direct jabs, pounding body blows, and making weapons of her elbows and knees. That bloodlust, paired with her strategy and speed, made Zelly an indomitable force when activated.

"So this place shouldn't exist."

"Shouldn't, but does, and now we get to term out a whole shitload of deranged motherfuckers." They all paused from their tasks to look at Midi as though she were deranged herself. "Don't give me those looks. Y'all are gonna enjoy this just as much as I will." She clapped an energy mag into a second charge pistol. After tucking both weapons into their holsters on her back, she began placing explosive charges into her waist pouches.

Wander went back to fitting her collapsible sword to her thigh. Digi stared off into the distance, calibrating her vision. Zelly tucked a two pair of plasteel knuckles into her waistband.

In order to begin lining up her shots, Wander rested her sniper rifle on the embankment. She linked with the hovering AR projector and, through the rifle scope, it began feeding her its fields of data. Distances, crosswind levels, heat signatures, movement predictions... Watching the gauges fluctuate, she went from each active member of the auction to the next, getting a feel for where she needed to hit them and in what sequence.

First of course would be the auction leader. His death would trigger the Runners to activate, springing from their hiding places behind the vehicles to begin taking out the rest of them. From there, Wander would need to decide if she was going to remain behind the rifle or join the rest of them on foot.

One big variable was whether the vehicles contained anyone else. The party could take a very nasty turn if more armed individuals were inside and willing to join the fight.

She gritted her teeth, still peering through the scope.

Hopefully there won't even be a fight.

Next she spotted a thick man in a black and purple suit. A tank, the muscle of the gathering. Across his broad chest he held a Clak-980, one of the heaviest armor-piercing ballistic shotguns on the underground market. He was a walking weapon holding an even deadlier one. They would need to eliminate him as quickly as possible.

Moving on, she turned her sights to a dreadlocked man in slick NeoLux breakstyle athletics and a prosthetic face, glossy red. On the ground at his feet, waiting patiently, was an abnormally beefy pitbull looking ready to attack on command.

Next was– Wander swiveled her view through the scope to a familiar face, one she hadn't noticed at the previous nights' flesh trades. Clean-cut dark hair, brown leather jacket, a few neck ports, but otherwise an upright-looking guy. It was Vincenzo Sardo, her old fling and Zef's buddy from the Meat Markets. Wander breathed deep, her nerves crawling beneath her skin. Her first instinct was to tell the rest of the girls, though the communicator at her neck abruptly vibrated. Maybe's pattern.

"Oh, dammit. Guys, Maybe is ringing."

"Great! Just as we were about to fuck some shit up!"

"Midi, quiet!"
"What are you gonna tell her?"
"I have no idea. I think he told her."
"Who told who what?!"
Digi shushed Midi again. Wander shook her head, held up a finger to quiet them, and answered the call.

[[R6: DOWNTOWN WEST EDGE]]
<Electua/Reshen Railway>

"Good evening, Citizens, and thank you for your choice to transfer with West Reshen Metro Rail! This train will be arriving at... Downtown West Edge Station... in... five minutes. If you'll be disembarking, please make sure to gather all belongings and mind the gap as you exit the train."

The ride to the Malaang had been a furious one for Zef. He only knew what he'd seen, and what he saw was Wander getting out of another man's car on the roof of their flat. No call, no update, nothing. She'd left him to worry about her while she was across the city committing murder, and without so much as a text. And then took her time getting back, in the passenger seat of... whoever that was.

Zef didn't care anymore. He just wanted out. Wander was clearly gone and he didn't have the energy to articulate anymore what a mistake she was making.

It doesn't matter, he fumed. *She's already made it. Nothing to do but go back to the only place I have left.*

That place was the Meat Markets of Reshen; the grimiest, most populated hub of transhuman and subhuman activity in the Outer Rings. He was more than anxious to get back to work now that he had no more reason to be in Electua. No more chasing after the attention of some close-minded chick with a sword fetish and delusions of grandeur.

"NightRunners." Even the word itself sounded ridiculous to him. He wondered why he'd ever gone along with such carrot-and-stick bullshit.

To impress a girl, that's why.

A deep sigh escaped him. He felt like such a fool. It was obvious now, the void he'd been trying to fill in his own life. He'd been so lonely that he'd fallen in love with the first Electua girl that gave him the time of day, then chased that feeling so hard that he'd allowed it to take him away from the West Edge. Away from Sardo and Lefty and everyone else at the Markets. Away from the chop shop and Reshen Ramen and the Underground.

It doesn't matter. I'll be back soon enough. I'll clear my name with Jenja, get back to hacking and sewing, and leave this asinine crap behind.

From the window of the trembling train car, he could see it approaching: the City Heights of Downtown West Edge. Beyond that would be the end of the line, and after a few hours' walk he'd be back in the Malaang, catching up on two years of wasted time. Two years of romantic delusions. Two years of false friends and dead end dreams. Two years of...

"NightRunners," he repeated.

[The Realm]
<Loading...>

[Past the Virtual Lagoon, past the shimmering streets of the Downtown Realm hub, past the VR-within-VR of the MetaVirtual Arcade, past that interface and the abstract corridors of the transnet safety connections...Wander hurtled away from her Mid-City problems and through a streaming vortex, her physical body far behind her in the Digital Domain. Ahead, the last safety connection was being established with a RealmWorld chosen by the RealmDweller, an ultra-secure place for their first meeting where she could be briefed on whatever this upcoming job would be. Her solo gig in Downtown Electua came to mind. That was the price she'd paid, the debt to Maybe, to be where she was now.

The man himself was still a mystery to her. She wished now, on the verge of sharing the same digital space with him, that she'd somehow learned more. As far as she knew he was a "digital magician," whatever that meant, and he was close enough with the founder of the Glade to have deep influence on its operations. Beyond that, she was entirely unaware of who, or what, she'd be meeting. Her trust in Maybe was all she had to reassure her that this was a step in the right direction.

Around her, the vortex slowed like a ship exiting warp. Wander attempted to maintain her equilibrium as she went from flying through a space of blazing colors, to standing on solid ground. The simulated inertia churned the nonexistent butterflies in her stomach as a radically different environment resolved, spreading from pixelated patches to crystal clarity.

And then, everything was calm.

The night sky was clear here, more pristine than she'd ever seen it. Countless stars twinkled over the darkness, intermittently obscured by puffy, silver-edged clouds. Between it all, a perfectly round moon hung luminous and haloed.

Beneath her feet, a path of brushed-clean cobbled brick wove itself between neatly manicured tufts of flowers. It was a garden, dotted with cherry blossom trees in full bloom. Beyond branches of the surrounding trees, the warm orange glow of bouncing torchlights flickered. Wander turned slowly, absorbing the entire scene as it became her reality.

The garden itself seemed like something straight from the Jade Region of Electua. Even there, the sky would never be this vast, the air never so crisp, the atmosphere never so serene and peaceful. She wondered if she would be able to come back to this place once this was all over with.

"I take it you enjoy the setting?"

She spun, startled by the unexpected voice. On the path in front of her was a human man dressed up in black, his long, dark hair pulled back and draped forward over his shoulder, and his hands in his pockets. She flushed with nervousness, squeezing her fists tight to keep herself grounded.

"It's beautiful..." Her eyes went back to the trees. "This isn't the Glade?"

"No, actually. Private Realm server. But this place isn't without its charms." He stepped forward and she could see his face in the moonlight. Sharp features with dark eyes. Carefully unshaven jawline. "But I chose this setting specifically to put you at ease. I know that everything going on lately must be a bit overwhelming."

Wander attempted a shivering breath, her nerves still rattled as she mulled over this new stranger. "You got that right. More than you know."

Gazing over the lush garden, she struggled to accept the notion that this place had been designed. The trees certainly seemed real. The soft flicker of the torches seemed genuine. Nothing like the alien worlds of Intergalactic Zoo, or the hypnotizing psychedelics of the Glade, or the empty constructs of NightRunner training simulations.

"Is this place part of the job Maybe mentioned?"

The man chuckled.

"Not at all. Like I said, I made this specifically for our meeting."

"You made all of this? But...how?"

He looked around, unimpressed with his own work.

"It's child's play, to be honest. Like playing with Connecty-Stix. All the assets are ready-made; just assemble and play. That's not to say the final product is any less enjoyable."

She didn't understand, she was no virtual artist. She nodded anyway.

"Mhm. And the trees?"

"Digital. Slight variations of one another. Programmed to grow and do all the things trees do. If you wait long enough, you might even see a bee tending to the pollination."

Pollination was foreign to her, but she remembered learning what a bee was. An insect that gathered ingredients for its food from the center of flowers. She was sure that there were plenty of them in Percarus District.

"But Wander, we can discuss world generation all day. We came here for something else, didn't we?"

Her mind focused and she presented an air of professionalism.

"We did."

He stepped closer and held out a wide hand.

"I'm called RealmDweller. It's good to finally meet you."]

[[E5: WEST MID-CITY]]

<Meta-Terrania QuadroRacing Course / Sewage Canal>

"Maybe, what's up?"

There was a pause, something Wander wasn't accustomed to when picking up comms from her boss.

Was the signal dead?

"Maybe?"

{"Fourteen meters west, there's a culvert leading down to the canal floor. It's your most efficient method of approach to a high degree."}

Wander's heart skipped a beat. Maybe knew about the mission. Whether it had been RealmDweller who'd told her though, there was no way to be sure. Perhaps it was irrelevant.

"Are-are you sure?"

{"Quite. I've run several simulations and it's by far your best course of action."}

Wander accepted it as truth.

Midi waved her hands wildly and mouthed at her. *Does she know?!*

Wander nodded with emphasis to indicate that Maybe definitely did know. The droid girl's eyes went wide.

{"And if you're wondering, the answer is yes. There are eight more individuals within the vehicles, bringing the hostile count to nineteen...if you want to include your acquaintance Vincenzo Sardo."}

There were too many questions, Wander didn't know where to begin.

"Maybe, I–"

{"Wander, it's quite unnecessary. I've just had a word with RealmDweller. He's praised you very highly, and if you intend to go through with this bit of vigilante justice tonight, I intend to make sure you all return safe and sound. I also plan to take full responsibility for the mission, if you'll allow me to pay each of you for your work. Tennik Radko has been on our list for a very long time."}

"Tennik Radko?"

Midi was losing her mind. She waved and gestured in confusion to Wander.

{"The heavily augmented THP-Quadran leading tonight's event. You have free reign to eliminate as many of the non-captive targets below as you'd like, but Radko is the only target the Glade is concerned with."}

She took a deep breath and decided to accept the new change in direction things had taken. "Understood. Our plan was to eliminate all of them. We'll keep you informed of how things unfold."

Midi melted to the pavement in agony as Digi laughed. Zelly watched them both with concerned amusement.

{"I have every confidence in all of you, Wander. Good luck."}

"Thank you, Maybe. We'll be in touch."

The call severed and Wander threw her hands up in exasperation. "Would you calm the fuck down?! She's gonna pay us to do it!"

[The Realm]
<Cherry Blossom Garden>

[Tiny birds skittered playfully across the cherry blossom treetops, chasing each other from branch to branch.

"So then, what is the Corporation to you?"

Wander was left without immediate words, having never been asked the question so simply or so directly. As she studied the moon, RealmDweller patiently studied her. He hoped to see the spark in her that would prove to him she was on the level.

"I would say it's a monster."

He couldn't hide a smile.

"That's an appropriate word, I think. But tell me more."

"It's like...when you see a baby. A human baby." Her mind went back to her time in the Ebber Village orphanage. "And you know that you could never hurt someone so young, you know? There's like this feeling inside of you. 'Protect the baby.' Because a baby is love. It doesn't know how bad things can get.

"And then they grow up...and they learn about the world. They learn that this is right and this is wrong. And they have all this freedom, but slowly it starts getting taken away. And no one ever decides that this is how it should be. We all just kind of believe that as we get older, we need to be controlled. We need to be put into boxes. We lose touch with happiness and love and with people..."

She looked over to him, her eyes gleaming with clarity. "But it turns out that there is someone that decides. Beyond our parents and our friends, beyond our jobs, beyond our Districts, the control comes from the Corporation."

RealmDweller's smile broadened, both his curiosity and his confidence in her piquing. "Like a monster."

Her eyes went back out to the virtual moon in the virtual sky. "It is. It's like a parasite attached to the city. It just eats everything. It wants our Credits. It wants our loyalty. It tries to tell us what to think. People on both sides are mistreating each other to be in the favor of the Corporation, even when it kills them just for breaking Protocol...I want to be a part of ending that. People deserve better."

The cool air between them, as clear as it was, felt charged with the invigorating energy of complete agreement.

"You know, Maybe was wrong about you."

Wander met his eyes again instantly, suddenly unsure. "Wrong about what?"

"Well..." He revealed a black nanocig rimmed with gold leaf and placed it between his lips, a clear affectation given their virtual setting. He lit it with a steel lighter that disappeared back into his pocket and he dragged hard. Thick smoke puffed out into the pure, crystalline air. "She told me that there were things you weren't ready for. Things you shouldn't be made aware of yet, that it might mess with your concentration."

Her brow furrowed with vague contempt. She understood that Maybe and the Glade Syndicate knew things she shouldn't yet. It was the nature of this kind of business. There was a hierarchy of information that she respected for the sake of knowing her place. But now it felt as though RealmDweller had intention behind bringing up such a thing. There was something he wanted to tell her despite Maybe's warnings.

"What kinds of things?"

He exhaled smoke again, the white cloud of particles spreading out naturally and obscuring the moon.

"Things about Dominion. About the Glade. About how it all really works. About who you are in all that..." He sighed with self-awareness, that he might be laying the point on a bit too thick. "But I'm not going to force you to learn."

"No," she knew that if there was ever a time to learn, a time to decide for herself, it was now. She wouldn't let this moment escape. "Please, tell me. I want to know."

RealmDweller peered at her, his eyebrow arched and his smile gone. Whether she was really ready was anyone's guess. But if it came from anyone, he knew it should be from him. Maybe would only screw it up, and learning it the hard way would take Wander far too long. It might even cost her life.

"Alright. But first, we talk business. If we can square that away, I'll answer any questions you have."]

[[E5: WEST MID-CITY]]
<Meta-Terrania QuadroRacing Course / Sewage Canal>

Through the rifle scope, Wander watched Midi, Digi, and Zelly take their places behind the vehicles surrounding the auction. She knew that in theory they stood no chance. They were vastly outnumbered and outgunned, but Wander was sure that as a unit the NightRunners, her Runners, were a more deadly team. Even the massive tank of a man with his rifle had no idea what was coming to him.

Crouching as she went, Midi was placing small explosives beneath the chassis of several of the cars. There was no way she would be able to get them all without being discovered, but the explosive shock from the three that were going to detonate would be enough to disorient the gathering, enough to give the four girls a fighting chance against nineteen armed and violent slave-traders. She placed the last one and gestured to Wander that she was ready.

Wander panned over to see Digi putting her back against a black SUV. The girl began pulling her thin throwing knives out from the slip on her arms.

Zelly, the last to take her place, was deep in shadow, pushing combat knuckles onto her fingers.

Across the canal, the Hellions were well-hidden on the roof of a racetrack facility building. Wander could see the weapons they held. Silhouetted against the lights of Downtown, they waited for the signal in case their assistance was needed. Requesting their services as backup was a last-minute touch that Midi had made, reaching out to the guys she'd befriended. The Hellions seemed all too excited to get their hands dirty when they'd heard about the inhumanity transpiring in the canals. She felt altogether safer knowing they would be joining if necessary.

With everyone in place, Wander put her attention back to the auctioneer, Tennik Radko. Her smart reticle circled for a moment before locking onto his head, while the AR projector fed her scope with all its feedback. After a few adjustments to her resting position, she leveled in on him and prepared to take the shot.

[The Realm]
<Strategy Construct>

[At RealmDweller's command, the immaculate garden rolled away in digital waves. It was replaced by a construct, an empty virtual void save for a floor surface for them to stand on. A wireframe replication of the entire Dominion City unfolded around them, the tallest city structures nearly shoulder-height. Above the city, countless Demigods floated about in their circular paths over perfect representations of all seven Districts. Wander felt as though she were standing inside the holo-map that Maybe had gifted them.

To her surprise, the simulation didn't end at the Outer Wall of the city. It continued outward into the uninhabitable zones the Dominion Corporation called the Wasteland. Beyond the border of the city, she could make out a jagged and bizarre landscape, complete with nondescript old building structures. As curious as it made her, she resolved to not allow herself the distraction.

"...I've told the client it would take a year to complete the job. But I don't intend to wait that long to begin assembling the tools and putting everyone to work."

"Everyone?"

"Right. Along with my own crew and others contracted, there'll be four NightRunner teams on the ground from the beginning. I'll be directing you myself for the first few weeks until I can bring someone up to speed to take my place."

Wander felt a pang of unease in her stomach. "F-four NightRunner teams?"

"Correct. Yours, as well as a team from Uptown Quadro, a team from Sim Valley, and a team from the Haze. A good bit of the work will be in Quadro, I have to warn you. I know your team just completed a mission in the NeoLux, but the Lux is nothing compared to the level of security you're going to see in Quadro proper. In Uptown and Downtown there'll be QPD, you're gonna see private and contracted security, heavy active surveillance watching every square inch of the place, and you're gonna see Dominion Units being hyper-vigilant. Probably even State Security patrols." With some quick gestures from his hands, the entire city grid spun and zoomed, adding to Wander's sudden sense of falling. "Look at these lines—"

"Wait, please." She held a hand out as if she were searching for something to lean against. Her mind swirled, attempting to digest this new revelation. "You mentioned NightRunner teams. Are you saying... Are we not the only NightRunners?"

His expression remained blank as he attempted to piece together what she was trying to express. "Wander. Slow down...Does Maybe have you guys believing that you five are the only NightRunners?"

The construct around her glitched, separating into two swaying facsimiles. She began to feel ill, as if she might somehow vomit into this digital space. Maybe's words bubbled up from somewhere in her memory and resonated between her ears. *"The Wander I know makes the best of every situation on the fly..."*

Her instincts took over and professionalism returned. The city sim became solid around her. She drew in a deep breath and gathered her senses, then looked soberly into RealmDweller's eyes. A look of pride spread across his face as he watched her calm herself.

"She never told us, no."

"That's unfortunate. The reasons for secrecy are obvious, but I figured she would have told you. Just in case you ran into others."

"No, I never heard about any other teams." Her mind went back to the door under the red light; the dirty room at the back of the alley; the NightRunners' headquarters. Even that place was called Haven-4. She'd never even questioned it. "But it doesn't matter. Let's continue."

"Are you sure?"

Deep down she wasn't sure at all, not the least bit. They'd been working for Maybe for a year now and she'd never once mentioned that there were other NightRunners doing work around the city. It made her wonder what else Maybe was keeping from them. She felt more like a tool than ever before, just a resource.

Maybe Zef had been right...

No, she decided, *it's the nature of the business. We work our way up. We prove to the Syndicate that we're worthy of more knowledge. And until then, we work.*

Even still, her mind went back to Zelly and Digi and Midi. What was she going to tell them? Should she tell them at all?

She closed her eyes and traveled back to her terrace in Teradin. The feeling of the rain on her skin, the families, the Soy Markets, the music, the children...and allowed her worries to drift away.

Her eyes opened. "I'm sure. Let's go over the mission."]

[[E5: WEST MID-CITY]]
<Meta-Terrania QuadroRacing Course / Sewage Canal>

The subtle vibration of Wander's rifle reached a fever pitch. Her finger rested on the trigger and she waited patiently, watching the success-prediction meter fluctuate beside Tennik Radko. With every wild arm motion he made, every turn of his head, every wave of his gun, the meter sank or rose, becoming more or less solid.

An insect of some kind skittered around on her leg, but she suppressed the urge to move even the slightest bit. Radko placed the barrel tip of his weapon to the head of one of the captives. Her heart fluttered, but her hands remained still and she held her position. A trickle of sweat crawled down her forehead, inching toward her cheek.

As Radko spoke sternly to the buyers crowded around him. The rifle vibration became a steady pulse. The prediction meter topped out, turning a bright turquoise.

Wander smiled. *"Time to party."*

She squeezed the trigger. Through her scope, the hollow-point round smashed its target. She raised her face above the rifle eagerly to see the auctioneer's cybernetic head explode into a shower of pieces and sparks like fireworks. His body collapsed to the pavement. Around the circle, the other auction attendees immediately began drawing their weapons, searching the perimeter, their wits sharp and strong enough to understand that there was a sniper in their midst. Wander ducked down behind the embankment as pure exhilaration washed over her. She silently thrust her fists upward with triumph at the well-placed shot.

As soon as the bullet connected, the other three NightRunners sprang into action in their purest, most free forms; paid and trusted to execute a mission of their own design, flowing beautifully with natural purpose.

Midi rolled across the spotless hood of the car she hid behind and kick-jab-kicked the first suited Quadran nearest her, shattering his jaw and bringing him down to the ground in a heap. She spun around, drawing her charge pistols in a flash, and planted six rounds into the back and head of a muscular Reshenite with bizarre prosthetic legs. A third attacker approached her, though his fist swung through empty air as Midi dropped to a mechanical split and blasted out both his knees.

Digi, her throws a blur of precision, hurled spinning daggers out like mad. They zipped through the chaos and smoke to connect with one, two, three auction attendees. She leapt over the car at an inhuman elevation and came down on the shoulders of the tank with his shotgun. He spun around, his arms flailing as he tried to reach for her. His shotgun sounded out into the night over the raucous noise of the scene. Digi arched her back, raised two glinting daggers, and brought them down into his sweaty skull between steel augments. Instantly termed, his legs gave way. She climbed up and jumped away as his massive form began to topple.

Midi hollered in excitement for Digi's kill and the Hellions took it as their signal. Dropping and flipping as they descended into the canal, they began racing down the steep concrete wall.

Wander, unable to stay with her rifle as the fight ensued, launched herself from the incline. She soared, her sword extending behind her, and the scene below unfolded in all its violent mayhem. She counted the progress the Runners had made, tallying the living hostiles and the kill count, assessing escape routes, and formulating a plan of her own. Sword-first, she landed on the hood of a limousine, impaling the driver inside.

Zelly crept around the fringe of the battle. Upon hearing the shooting erupting around her, the driver of an SUV began fumbling for her own weapon somewhere in a case down by the floor. Zelly yanked open the door, tore her from where she sat and threw her to the wet asphalt. She mounted the defenseless woman and pummeled. With three or four strikes her face caved in and her struggling ceased. Zelly stood erect, an animalistic intensity burning within her eyes, and scouted the surroundings for her next victim.

The Hellions charged in, each with their own weapons, though one of the human males immediately took a raging energy shot to the chest. The rest of them crashed through the car line putting pipes to skulls and blades to limbs. The entire crumbling auction devolved into a dynamic maelstrom of gun-blasting and deadly combat. The only safe party seemed to be the valuable captives in the center who lay covering their heads, cringing at the idea of being slugged by crossfire.

Wander leapt from the limousine and rolled forward, connecting a jumping chest-kick to the fat man with his beard and exposed golden skull. She twirled, carving her razor-edged blade across his belly. Guts and wires spilled out as the flesh opened wide. The man crumpled to the concrete, gurgling and convulsing. She withdrew the blade and turned, spinning low to slice the legs from beneath an android and it collapsed. Her eyes scanned out, overlooking the battle. The number of hostiles had dropped by half.

Just a question of time.

[The Realm]
<Cherry Blossom Garden>

[RealmDweller's plans were simple enough.

The NightRunner teams were essentially going to be the muscle. In this case, the muscle needed to be stealthy and mobile, enough to slip from place to place without ever once being detected by any sort of security, Dominion Security least of all. Any hint of attention from Protocol Enforcement could spell disaster.

He called his project the Praxis War, though the nature of the operation, the actual reason all the pieces were being moved into place, was still a mystery. He seemed to not want to discuss it until the time was right. That part seemed central to Wander, but she knew better at this point than to push for more information than what she was offered.

And then they'd found themselves back in RealmDweller's garden sitting atop the slanted roof of a pagoda. The glowing orb of the moon was still high in the sky, surrounded by an impossible number of stars. Her briefing had gone well. Among a few other things, she now knew that she wasn't just one of five NightRunners. She was part of a legion, and her efforts were part of a crusade so large that she felt dwarfed. Where before she was the shining star of a small elite group, it now seemed as though she were lost in a sea of black-suited operatives, all doing the bidding of the Glade Syndicate.

That's unfair, she thought. *Regardless of the reasons, I'm trained now. I could leave if I wanted, but I'm not going to and I know it. Even after the secrecy, Maybe's treated me so well and given me every opportunity. Where would I even go?*

She remembered being invited to speak to Maybe in the Glade, and recalled the Glade's ability to act as a window into the future.

How many of those NightRunners had been given that privilege? Wander guessed not many, at least that's what her gut told her.

"How many other NightRunners have you briefed?"

"You're the first, I made sure of that. But I'll be talking to each team leader as time goes on. Why?"

Hearing him refer to her as a leader, she couldn't help but laugh a bit. The idea had never occurred to her.

"Why're you laughing?"

"Because I never considered myself the leader of that group. We always thought of Zelly that way."

"Zelly, huh? I can see that. She's a talented fighter. She's definitely a moral compass, but she's no Wander."

After letting out a stream of nanosmoke, he smiled and their eyes met again.

Casual, she urged herself. *Professional.*

"Okay then. So tell me about the others, since you know us so well."

RealmDweller laughed, impressed by her spirit.

"Haven-4? Alright, well...Digi, of course. She's been through a hell of a lot. More than she lets on. Y'all need to watch out for that one. She's a hell of a Runner, but she's also got a huge heart."

Wander nodded. She could already sense that. Digi had always been so quick to seclude herself, so easily impacted by the suffering of others. More empathy than most humans, in fact.

"And what about Midi?"

"Ah, I like that one. Attitude for days." He took another drag and continued. "Wall jockey and street pounder since day one. She caught my eye a few times zig-zagging through Quadro and crossing those gaps."

"She's so much trouble, though!"

"Oh, she is that. She's gonna need you to lay the law down during this thing, I hope you're prepared."

"I think I am. We've all got nothing but respect for each other. I have a good feeling about this." Except she didn't, and the reason came to her mind immediately.

"And what about Zef?"

"Oh fuck, don't get me started."

She gasped and stared over at him, half incredulous and half amused. "Why not!?"

"Wander, Zef doesn't want to be a Runner. We both know that, let's not bullshit each other."

Her stunned silence spoke volumes before the truth came out. "I mean, yeah, that's real."

"And it's really not about him not wanting to. Shit, there's definitely a few Runners who don't want to. But at least they give the effort. They do it like they mean it, even just for the Subs."

She looked back out over the garden from where they sat, coming to terms with the obviousness of it all. Zef's work ethic aside, she'd never seen him truly care.

"The real damage he's doing, though, is on you."

Again, she was slightly taken aback. "Excuse me?"

"Yeah, I know, none of my business. But I've seen it. I've heard all about it from Maybe. I saw it on your face when you mentioned him..." Another drag and another plume of smoke spilled out into the clear night. "It's made no difference so far. Might have even pushed you to be a better Runner. But going into the future, it's just bad news. You're too talented to allow yourself to be distracted by someone like him."

"Someone like him?" She was genuinely offended. Part of her was still very much in love with Zef, even if he continued to show that he wasn't going to be supportive of her passions.

"Yeah, someone exactly like him." He counted it out on his fingers. "Conflicted. Destructively independent. Unsupportive. Toxic. Unprofessional... Wander, what the Syndicate is offering you is nothing short of an opportunity of a lifetime and you're right here stepping up for it. What you *should* be asking yourself is why one of your team members is in the West Edge instead of being an active part of your little side-mission tonight."

Wander's heart froze mid-thump. "You know about the mission?"

RealmDweller flicked the nanocig out into the air where it dissolved before it could fall to the trees.

"There's not much I don't know about, Wander."]

[[E5: WEST MID-CITY]]

<Meta-Terrania QuadroRacing Course || Sewage Canal>

"Digi, no!!"

The monstrous gray pitbull was dragging the girl away, its steel-trap jaws clamped down on her calf. The transhuman from the NeoLux, with his shiny-red featureless face, stepped forward over Digi and fired a single round from his handgun. It blasted through Midi's thigh, spinning her and knocking her to the concrete. He knelt down to bind Digi's arms and bag her head. He lifted her effortlessly and shoved her into the back seat of a pearlescent hover. The whir of its graviton engine buzzed, echoing through the canal as the vehicle sped away. Two of the Hellions took off after it.

"Digi!" Everything in Wander urged her to give chase after the girl, though the attacker she clashed with gave her no chance to react. She ducked beneath a heavy psy-axe swing and responded with a volley of sword slashes.

Zelly, tumbling with Vincenzo Sardo, presently rolled atop him and began squeezing his neck savagely.

Midi stood as best she could, the synthetic muscle filaments of her thigh ruptured by the impact of the ballistic projectile. She drew her pistols with rage and limped after the vehicle, shooting blindly down the canal. Her figure disappeared into the haze.

A woman stood over the droid Hellion and pulled the trigger, executing the boy with a searing shock round. She turned the weapon to Zelly and fired again. The distance between them saved Zelly her life, though she seized in frenetic pain at the impact. She fell from Sardo who erupted with coughing and sputtering, clutching his neck.

With one hand on her bruised cheek, Wander swiped her sword skyward, slicing her attacker's arm clean off and then back to sever his neck diagonally. He disassembled, falling to the pavement in wet pieces.

"Wander!" Sardo pulled himself to hands and knees.

"Stay away from me, you fucker!"

A shock round blazed past her, and Wander realized in an instant that the fight had not been lost but instead fractured, pulled apart at the seams in a way that she couldn't hold together or win. Radko was dead, but what of the NightRunners, or the Hellions? Where was Natalia, the dweller she'd befriended on the train? Was all lost?

The dismal scene around her was one of mayhem and death. Not a carefully planned out and methodical assassination, but a brutal clash, the kind of thing that even the best Glade simulation couldn't predict. A second shock round sizzled past her, this time making light contact with her arm and sending crackling jolts of energy branching through her body.

"Wander, run!" Zelly was wracked with pain, but held up a weak hand to wave her away. "Go! Get to Haven!"

Seized by ripples of static, Wander backpedaled. The strange woman fired another charged shock in her direction and she stumbled, but caught herself in time to begin running. With every last bit of strength she fled, exiting the ring of cars into the dark. A brisk wind rushed over her, air free of the smells of death and smoke. Instead, the stench of the vagrant community returned to greet her. She ran harder, powering her legs like a machine, until all she could hear was the pounding of the blood in her ears and her own footsteps in the canal.

The dark ahead of her began to glow, the shadowy haze taking form into swirling clouds, glowing brighter and brighter. She peered back. Two blazing headlights. The roar of an engine.

Someone wanted revenge.

She wasn't out yet.

[[E6: THE MALAANG]]
<Hostel Volnikaan>

"Two years is **PRESTUPLENIYA**. Blasphemy. Insult. And now you're back to make amends, eh?" Jenja's frail old figure with his bug-eyed, rose-tinted glasses stood in the doorway of the bunk room where Zef was keying open a locker.

"It's not like that, Jen. I was busy with other business in Electua. Just trying to get by." He pulled on the rusted-stuck locker door and it popped open. Inside, a tin chest, a few ratty old pairs of clothes, his work gloves from the Meat Markets, and a few other random items had waited for him. They'd gathered a fair amount of dust and mold since he'd left the Malaang behind for more neon pastures.

"I don't think He'll see it that way."

Zef paused, his heart suddenly pounding. The only person referred to so emphatically as "He" around the Malaang was Lord Volnik, and Zef had never had direct business with the Lord of the West Edge.

"Why would he care? I'm not a Voly and I never was." He pulled off his sweaty shirt and took an old dry one from the locker.

"Volnikaan or not, Master knows that you've been doing business with one of His competitors in Mid-City. A few of your NightRunner friends have been causing Him a bit of trouble. He wants to know that you aren't here to do the same."

Zef was visibly baffled. He and the Runners had never done business in the Malaang, he was sure of it. "He's mistaken. It wasn't the NightRunners. We..." and his misstep clenched in his throat as Jenja's suspicion intensified. "They stick mostly to Electua and Quadro. And I'm not a member anymore."

The elderly servant's bushy eyebrows raised and his mouth creased to a pitiful frown. "Regardless. I think it's time you and the Lord had a nice conversation. You can tell Him that He's mistaken yourself."

Zef stopped rummaging through his things immediately and stood, his knees weak and shivering. His heart thumped hard inside his chest.

"He wants to speak to me personally?"

Jenja chuckled in sardonic amusement.

"That's the fear, my boy. Do you feel it?"

[[E5: WEST MID-CITY]]
<Meta-Terrania QuadroRacing Course || Sewage Canal>

With the roaring van meters behind her, Wander splashed through the puddles. She turned and began powering herself up the steep side of the canal. The van, attempting to follow her, skidded out of control through the water. It connected with the incline in an impossible way and the van's passenger-side wheel buckled. The entire vehicle lurched over and crashed to its side on the pavement. She didn't bother looking back at the sounds of exploding glass behind her. Reaching the top, she pulled herself up and climbed the embankment.

Ahead of her, an industrial wasteland stretched ahead into the darkness, the same one she'd ran through alongside Zef only days ago.

"Wander, stop! Please!"

She knew the voice. Sardo had followed her.

"Fuck off, Vincenzo!"

"I don't want to hurt you!"

Ha! As if he could!

She sprinted hard, tearing through the derelict warehouse park, climbing ladders and shooting through alleyways, all without looking back. She didn't care about their history. She didn't care what he might have to say. He'd been a part of the flesh trade. He was the same desensitized, inhuman scum as all the rest of them.

She hopped a fence and pushed through tall weeds, her shoes sloshing in mud, until she reached the gravel levee leading up to the tunnel roof. Beneath her feet, the clumsy vibration of an approaching train lit a fire inside her. She pushed forward, over the rocks and weeds and branches, to the slab above the tunnel. The train rocketed out from beneath her feet, traveling forward, heading out to Teradin. Without thinking, she leapt. Below her the train carried on and she hoped, suddenly powerless, that she would land flat on a train car roof and not between them, where she might tumble to the tracks. Her feet slammed down onto solid metal. She sank to the roof, relieved, grasping the metal rungs before she could be swept back by the wind.

Behind her, Vincenzo Sardo fell to the train as well.

"Wander, we need to talk!"

Hearing his voice again, her eyes squeezed closed with disjointed frustration. For a moment she felt nothing, only the frenzied texture of rushing wind against her face. "We have nothing to talk about!"

Sardo's throat still burned from being wrenched by Zelly's hands, though he forced the words out with genuine concern.

"This isn't about you and me, it's about Zef! I think he's over the edge!"

Wander's teeth mashed together and her blood boiled. She'd heard enough about Zef and his failings for one day. She turned to face him, the force of the heavy wind on her back now. He was disheveled, exhausted, but inching toward her.

"Fuck Zef, and fuck you, Vincenzo!" Her eyes pulsed with pure fury. "Go back to Reshen and the Meat Markets where you belong and stay out of Mid-City!"

He continued pushing forward, reaching out gingerly, his clothes flapping behind him.

"Wander! Zef was in the Malaang today!"

"I said stay away!" She snatched her blade from its place on her thigh and it unfurled to its full length. "Go back the way you came or so help me!"

Beneath them, the train shook violently as it careened around a bend in the rusted tracks.

"Look out!" He pointed beyond her and they both dropped, narrowly dipping below the entrance to the underground. The cavern opened wide inside as the train entered. They both pulled themselves up again, Wander's glowing markers illuminating the corridor in red. She regained her defensive stance, her sword ready, and hoped he understood that she was prepared to cut him down.

"Wander, please just listen! I'm worried he–"

She sprang into action, her sword whipping around in a metallic blur, and three fingers from Sardo's outstretched hand spiraled away into the subway tunnel.

Vincenzo howled in agony and fell to the steel roof of the traincar. He clutched his hand to his chest as blood sprayed out into the humid breeze.

Wander glared at him for a moment without remorse, her face tightened with anger, her lips pursed and trembling. Wordlessly she replaced the sword, then turned to make her way to the gap between cars. Teradin was only three stops ahead.

[The Realm]
<Cherry Blossom Garden>

["Of course. I told you I'd answer any questions you had. Now you just need to ask the *right* questions."

They walked slowly along the cobbled paths between the torches, beneath the branches of the moonlit flowering trees. It seemed like hours had passed, though she could never be sure in this place. The passage of Realm time versus the real world was always a tricky comparison.

"Alright, first question. How can the Glade see the future?"

"Oh, damn, swinging big right out the gate." He peered at her playfully as if she were suddenly a spy. "What's your interest, anyway?"

"I saw it with my own eyes. It shouldn't be possible. I want to know how it works."

"Wander..." His eyes were incredulous but his smile said otherwise. "You're asking me to explain something that I've never explained to anyone."

Not taking no for an answer, she folded her arms and waited patiently.

"It's beyond your understanding! My answer won't even make sense to you."

"You told me to ask the right questions. I'm asking."

Their eye contact was something furious, both of them straining not to smile out of sheer frustration.

"Fine. You want to know? It's a pretty damned accurate quantum algorithm derived from a combination of factors."

Wander waited attentively for him to continue.

He cleared his throat, reluctantly.

"The first is direct input from all active Dominion cameras around the city. And yes, I do have access to those.

"Secondly, that data is fed through a series of Realm-sim matrices, programmed particles called quantalics. They're hyper-intelligent virtual data packets wrapped in spherical computation nodes, procedurally generating predictive futures. They take the cam feeds and the live city maps as input and project the logical result."

When Breven thought he was finished, he was met with insistence in her eyes. He chuckled, ran fingers through his hair to pull it away from his face, and continued gesturing as he spoke.

"Alright, well, I combine those projections with the collected registration and behavior pattern data of Citizens from the Dominion Archive. Any target of observation then becomes the center of the whole predictive network. It means that any person, company, or whatever else that we observe becomes the most accurate prediction in the simulation. In fact, it doubles down on itself exponentially when we host it inside the GladeCode framework, cross-referencing a nearly infinite number of parallel simulations."

She was wide-eyed, nearing information overload but trying her hardest to comprehend.

"It's essentially a sim that's more accurate than the actual future, making it more reality than reality. Only problem is that once you use anything you learn from it to change the future, the old sims become obsolete, like a butterfly effect. And, obviously, it can't see everywhere. The Outer Rings are full of dark spots. But the applications of the predictive sims themselves are endless."

He cleared his throat and nervously began searching his pockets for a nano-cig. Realizing he was inside the Realm, he manifested one between his fingers and put it to his lips. It lit itself and he smoked.

"...Alright. Wow." Wander's mind had become blank, lost in a sea of abstraction. She'd certainly gotten what she asked for, but true enough she didn't understand a word of it. Time to change the subject.

"Next question." She raised an eyebrow. "What is the Corporation really up to?"]

[[E5: WEST MID-CITY]]
<Teradin Jurisdiction>

Pouring rain drenched the neighborhood as Wander scaled the building faces of Teradin. She sprinted across the platforms and walkways and bridges, her mind focused on getting to Haven-4 as swiftly as she could. Past the shops, the familiar restaurants, EPD officers and puttering hovers, the neon-lit alleyways and their unwashed communities, the bustling open plazas and the whole myriad of Mid-City characters. As before, she dropped down from the concrete terrace to the bridge leading from the Soy Markets to Haven-4.

She opened comms. *"Maybe, pick up!"*

With her feet down on the brick overpass, it was only too late that she saw the red eyes through the crowd. The black spires rising up above the foot traffic, the circle of pedestrians backing away from the thing as it patrolled, the erratic clicking sound the Brother Units emitted as they searched passersby for suspicious activity.

Seeing her leaping down irregularly from the building, the thing swiveled instinctively. An arbitrary side of its cylindrical body faced toward her and it coasted above the ground in her direction. She cursed herself for being so absentminded. On any other day she would have been hyper-vigilant to avoid Dominion at all costs, but tonight her attention, her vital energies, had been compromised.

The old fear, that primal fear she'd buried deep down all her life, balled up inside her like chains wrapping around her stomach. The unmistakable fear of being approached by Protocol Enforcement, of having to stand her ground against Corporate oppressors in an unjust society, of being a single Citizen against a deadly patrol Unit. All roads had led to this, and now there was no running from fate.

{"Wander! What's going on?!"}

Her heart slowed in her chest, throbbing, flooding her body with frigid blood. Her fight or flight mechanisms began to tear her apart as the thing approached. It zeroed in on her with its largest, shining red eye and emitted the phrase she'd memorized ad nauseam, though it had never been directed to her.

"CITIZEN, PLEASE REMAIN STILL WHILE YOUR RETINAS ARE SCANNED FOR OUR ARCHIVES."

Pure adrenaline had her frozen in place as it coursed through her. The crowds had backed away and dispersed. There was only Wander, the Brother Unit, and the rain. She could feel time beginning to warp. She could feel her hand gripping the hilt of her sword as it extended. The red eye of the thing blazing its redbeam out and reaching toward her, bold crimson light crawling through space.

{"Wander!"}

She lowered her body, all her combat training coming alive. The thing seemed to recognize her noncompliance immediately. Its spider-like legs, those diabolical segmented blades, separated from its black form and peeled away, opening like a predatory animal preparing to attack.

It spoke a shrill warning to deaf ears, words that echoed out to Wander and stretched through time so slowly that they became abstract.

"YOU - ARE - IN - VIOLATION - OF - CITIZEN - PROTOCOL..."

Her legs coiled beneath her like tightly wound springs.

[The Realm]

<Cherry Blossom Garden>

[Again, he laughed aloud at her audacity. "How did I know that was coming?"

"I mean it! I know there's something dark going on with DCORP."

"You mean beyond the executions in the street by soulless machines, the psychotic amalgam of law and religion, the overt propaganda...?"

"Yes, beyond all that. What are they really up to?"

RealmDweller sighed with the enormity of the question.

"They're up to a lot of things."

"Such as?"

"Well, human experimentation for one. The briefings for that recent job in the NeoLux should have told you that much."

Her mind went back to the dark server room in RealmSquare. All the minds trapped inside, torn from their bodies and sold to Dominion and the bodies they no longer inhabited.

"The realmdwellers."

"Yeah, those. And the Violators. And the homeless. And many others."

"But why? What do they need with all those bodies?"

Even in this digital place, RealmDweller could feel the hairs of his neck raise. The answer was too complex, too morbid to put on the shoulders of this girl.

"Terrible things, Wander. Inhuman things. Things that don't concern you."

They'd paused their walking and were standing still now. Her gaze drifted among the trees, her mind imagining the most awful things it could but still it wasn't enough. Maybe she didn't need to know.

"I've seen the laboratories in Tetra Science myself." Even for him, the images were unsettling. "I've seen the suffering. I've seen what they turn the bodies into... You've seen them yourself."

Her face transformed, perplexed. "No, I haven't. I haven't seen anything."

RealmDweller knew he'd already said too much. He chose not to speak.

With her mind on the verge of horror, Wander began to appreciate the notion of learning slowly. Before she could fully digest what he might mean, she decided that she ought to change the subject again. Common sense told her it was time to wrap things up. The Runners had something to accomplish tonight.

Her glowing eyes met his again with stolid determination. The question had been burning in her mind since it formed.

"Last question."

RealmDweller sighed and pinched the bridge of his nose.

His chagrin caused her to smile. "What is the Praxis War?"

He met her gaze reluctantly, sure that he regretted offering her the choice to ask anything she desired, and spoke succinctly this time.

"You and me, we're going to steal the Realm from the Dominion Corporation."]

[[E5: WEST MID-CITY]]
<Teradin Jurisdiction>

Sizing up the bizarre creature as it postured, the hurricane of emotions inside Wander calmed as if she'd entered the eye of a great storm. The front end of the storm was behind her now, and had been her entire life leading up to this moment. Every hardship and struggle, every loss or win, every Sub-Credit earned, every achievement and failure, every choice that had blown past her like a torrent. And now she stood in the center, the focus, only herself and the Brother Unit. It was all that stood in her way if she wanted to continue onward and face the tail end of the hurricane.

Time held the rain in stasis like a bubble around her, each drop magnifying the neons and flickering torches of Teradin. She calculated every slight movement of the reaper's bladed legs, every shift of each gleaming eye, analyzing everything she'd learned about the tactics of these Protocol Enforcement droids. With their inhuman speed they wasted no energy, nearly always aiming for chest or head, so she would attack low. They were lightning quick so she would telegraph each false move and then over-extend the follow-up. She would use her sword as a ghost like she'd done so many times in the combat sims.

Wander rose only in the slightest and the BU's front two blades stabbed mantis-like with downward momentum. She rolled forward and at a precise moment recovered, spreading her legs to anchor her swing and carved an arc through the air. Like a red-hot laser, her plasteel blade severed both legs. In horror, the thing withdrew the spurting limb remainders into its body. It chittered furiously and commanded her again.

"CITIZEN, YOUR ACTIONS ARE DEEMED—"

Wander was hardly in the mood. She gave a false strike with her sword, a feigned downward cut, stepped wide right keeping her center of gravity left, and the BU took the bait. In a wild display of violence it spun, fanning its remaining blades like a buzzsaw and charging forward to meet nothing. Wander spun as well, and for a brief moment they danced, each of them a cyclone of blades. She tucked in her twirling legs to seize her moment, connected with her weapon, and lopped off two more of its rotating daggers.

Its inertia thrown, the Brother Unit crashed into the ground before recovering awkwardly. Hovering now, its remaining two legs held out like stabbing arms, it attacked her again. This time it struck from each side to chop her down, leaving no space left for her to maneuver. From one of its minor eyes, a chaotic beam of paralyzing energy surged forward, seeking her out to disable her.

The machine charged forward swinging, first left, and then right, then a clean stab forward, a spinning strike, a counter swing. Steering clear of the energy beam, Wander went blow-for-blow with it, each fighter meeting a worthy opponent. She blocked the left leg away, dodged an extending spear, clashed blades above her head, and then drove her own spear forward, stabbing the thing through its largest red eye. The bulk of its weight crashed to the concrete bridge. Its bladed arms fell limp to the ground. Wander kicked it backward, pulling her weapon from its body, and it collapsed dead.

Around them, lingering onlookers gasped in disbelief. They'd witnessed the unthinkable, the unspeakable: a Citizen not only defying the Dominion Corporation but destroying one of its Protocol Enforcement Units. It was a Violation so severe that several members of the crowd fainted to the wet pavement, others bending over to tend to them. The rest of them gawked in terror, too paralyzed by what had unfolded to move a muscle.

Wander, catching her breath and dripping wet in the downpour, retracted her sword and replaced it on her thigh. She peered around, making sure there were no other threats waiting. Satisfied, she continued on her way to Haven-4, the crowd line stepping aside to make a path for her.

From the dark recesses of Teradin Jurisdiction, several Hopper Units arrived, bouncing over to salvage the remains of their fallen kin.

[The Realm]
<Cherry Blossom Garden>

["You said 'last question,' didn't you?"
"I did, but this one isn't really a question."

They stood together under an ornate wooden archway at the end of the last path, overlooking a sprawling valley. It was just one of many, and the landscape rolled out across a great expanse toward the mountains on the horizon.

They were no longer strangers, both of them could feel it. What they shared was surely a business arrangement, but even after the length of their conversation, they weren't ready to give up each others' company for what lay ahead.

"RealmDweller…RD…Artie." She turned to him with her growing suspicions, finally seeing the man behind the avatar. "That was you when I fell in Downtown Mid-City, wasn't it?"

Her emerald eyes, those self-protective portals that gazed out past the present moment, crinkled now with adoration for the man who'd saved her life. How had he not noticed before, how striking those eyes were?

"You're a sharp one, Wander."

"And you're not as mysterious as you think you are, RealmDweller." She placed a gentle hand on his arm. "Thank you for catching me."]

[[E5: WEST MID-CITY]]

<Teradin Jurisdiction>

Heavy rain pounded across the oily concrete of Teradin opposite the alleyway to Haven-4, and Wander's eyes carved like the BU's blades through a thin silhouette blocking her entrance. The endless downpour had soaked her hair, her suit, her entire being. She'd had enough of this back-and-forth game. Knowing that Maybe was likely listening, she tore her communicator from her collar and tossed it away.

"What the hell do you want, Zef?"

Masked within the shadows of the alleyway, he remained silent. He knew that his window to decide was closing, but hesitation had taken hold of him. She watched as he said nothing, appalled that he had the nerve to return at all.

"*Talk, damn you!* You've dragged me through all of this and now I'm telling you to explain to me why!"

His cold figure shifted in the darkness.

"Or maybe you want some sort of apology from me? Well, you're not going to get it! I stuck my neck out for you, Zef! I held onto the hope that we could save what we had! Damn the Corporation, I've cried so many times for you, Zef!" Even as she spoke, her face was hot with anger and tears threatened to spill out. "But not anymore."

He stirred, and slowly walked forward from the shadows. In his hand he held an Old World snub-nosed .44 revolver. As his face became visible, Wander could sense the trepidation inside him.

"Wh-what are you doing?"

"Doing what I have to." He raised the gun and found her in its sights. "Throw the blade away."

That doesn't explain anything!

Frustration bubbled up inside her, the pain of confusion catching her off guard as she attempted to figure out what could possibly be his motive to threaten her. *He* was the one who'd accused her and stormed off. *He* was the one who'd abandoned her.

Wander reached down and removed her sword from its attachment. With a brisk *shnk-shnk-shnk* it expanded and she pointed it directly toward him.

"Who's behind this, Zef? Vincenzo said you went back to the West Edge today. What the fuck is going on?!"

What was she doing talking to Sardo? Zef sighed tersely through his shivering but kept the gun trained on her.

"This was a long time coming." He searched for the words, though consciously he knew that he couldn't betray the reason he'd returned. His face twisted with acidic turmoil. "I tried to fight for you, but you were so fucking stubborn! I wanted to help you!"

Her eyes searched for what he could mean by any of it.

"I wanted things to stay like they were, but you bought into everything she said!"

"Who... Maybe?!"

"Don't act like I haven't brought it up before. She doesn't care about you! She's using you! I wanted to bring you back to me, to take you away from this hellhole, but you bought into every word, just because somebody finally saw in you what *I* see.

"But I believed in you first, Mel! And you walked away from me."

Wander's confusion tripled. She hadn't done anything wrong. She only ever had intentions of being close to her friends, of helping a worthy cause, of putting her skills and her energy to good use. She couldn't understand why Zef wanted so passionately to sabotage all of that. They had brought it up so many times now, and still nothing seemed to make sense. Instinct told her not to bother with the reasoning anymore, now that there was a gun pointed at her.

"Zef..."

"Mello, don't make me shoot you. Throw away the blade."

There were no options. She didn't want to hurt him, but she also knew that if someone was influencing him, she couldn't rule out that he might use that weapon. To find whoever was doing this, she needed to play along.

She lowered the sword.

Below them the ground began to rumble. The rain itself seemed to shiver as a Demigod became visible overhead. Above the surrounding buildings and high into the dense smog, the hulking shape loomed over them. Brilliant red spots in the clouds grew in number until finally its spotlight broke from behind a rooftop. It lit up the night around them as if daylight had spontaneously arrived, and the Demigod coursed slowly over on routine patrol, never leaving its designated altitude. As it approached them, the heavy raindrops refracted the spotlight glow immensely. The scene around them shimmered within a lattice of infinite crystalline glimmers.

Zef shielded his eyes from the light while Wander kept a keen watch on his movements. She studied him, calculating his highest vulnerability, and then burst forward at threshold. Within two seconds she'd closed the gap between them.

Through the blinding spotlight, Zef realized what was happening and hastily fired at the blur she'd become. His bullet zipped out into Electua, shattering glass somewhere out in the rain. Wander slid beneath his raised forearm and oriented herself. He spun around to fight and was met with a fist across his face, pulverizing bloody cheek against teeth. The abrupt shock and brute force splintered his awareness and he dropped to a knee.

"You *son of a bitch*! You shot at me!"

She struck again and the toe of her boot connected, blasting out what little common sense was left in his head. He caught himself from falling with a hand on the watery pavement. Blood gushed from his mouth and splashed into the puddles below. Struggling to maintain mental coherence, he stood and raised the gun. She refused to budge.

"You wouldn't dare."

The shot pounded through the thick fabric of her runnersuit and into her abdomen. Before she could register the pain of the molten slug lodged within her, Wander spun forward and kicked the gun from his hand in a single motion and it bounced away. Her sword thrust forward and slid straight through flesh and between bones, separating major arteries, impaling him completely. Time dropped to zero as the Demigod centered above and the rain around them came to a halt.

Zef quaked inside his being, looking down in bewilderment at Wander's blade and how it ended where his chest began.

His eyes turned upward from the blade to her lips that he knew so well, to the water streaming from her nose, the droplets clinging to her eyelashes. Her eyes were more vivid than he'd ever seen them.

She carefully placed a hand on his shoulder and shoved him, withdrawing her sword. He stumbled backward, tripping over his own feet, and slammed into the rainwater.

She finally looked up, to the massive thing hovering in the clouds, realizing it was now watching them, potentially compromising Haven-4. Numb, she turned back to Zef as he achingly pulled himself up from the road, no doubt riding on a wave of hype chemicals. He removed his jacket and dropped it to the ground, revealing dark blood soaking through his shirt. It covered his mouth and dripped from his chin. His eyes were glazed, remorseful, but wild and resolute with forgotten purpose. From a pocket, a knife appeared in his hand.

"Forgive me, Wander."

Swaying drunkenly and then lurching forward, Zef pulled the knife blade back and slashed at her. She stepped out from the path of the blade easily and swung one last time, smashing a gloved fist into his jaw and clocking him cold. He stumbled backward a few steps before crumpling to the ground like a rag doll.

Wander, clutching her stomach, glared at his inert form. She wasn't angry or resentful or even sad, she was simply done. Limping over in the brilliant light and kneeling above him, she pulled him up to her face by the collar.

"I forgive you, now get out of my life."

Out beyond the deafening static of the rain, the blaring sirens of Protocol Violation began to echo out from the city speakers.

[[E6: THE MALAANG]]

<Volnik's Orpheum>

"Jenja, **MOY MALCHIK**, what you have for me?"

Though the old man Jenja was frail, he tugged Zef's arm forward with two hands and presented him like a prize.

"It's Zef, my Lord. One of the working boys from the Meat Markets. You wished to speak with him."

"Ahh, yes? Remind me, Jenja..."

The monstrous blob of a man, normally fitted in a high-end suit when doing business, reclined naked on a luxurious couch. His body was pocked, bulbous and sweaty, his oversized limbs formed from dirty prosthetics inlaid with tarnished gold filigrees. A young woman, her body malformed and amputated, eyes sewn shut and hair hastily shaved, serviced him with her mouth in a loud and sloppy manner. Several more thin, misshapen female figures reclined around him and on the floor waiting their turn, naked, sightless, and toothless. Around them all, a dance floor pulsed, its crowd filled with only the kind of people who would dance in a club owned by Lord Volnik, Father of the Malaang. Faceless, piecemeal denizens, rotting hard on Lodashock, groping each other's greasy bodies and grinding to a nasty synthetic beat. It was the West Edge of the West Edge, the most distorted and perverse place in the 6th Ring.

Jenja adjusted his glasses and stuttered. "He-he's the boy that left to join the NightRunners, Master. He told me himself. He-he told me."

"Told you himself, did he?" With a single meaty paw, Volnik grasped the head of the servant sucking him and pushed her away. "And why would he do that?"

"M-my Lord, he said he's come back to the Malaang to work. He's no longer a NightRunner."

"Ahh, music to my ears." It was an awful pun considering the throbbing dance music around them, though his ladies grinned and giggled for him. The massive man turned his attention to Zef. "Zef, my boy. I hope you 'no have plans in the Market. Lord need' you for something. A personal favor."

Zef's jaw clenched and his stomach squeezed itself. Ice crept down over his shoulders and up from his feet. He knew what getting an order personally from Lord Volnik meant. It meant becoming a Volnikaan with no ability to decline. It meant service until death. At some point Volnik would take his limbs, his teeth, and his eyes, and then he'd force him to earn them back in ways Zef never dared to imagine. It was a horrible fate, but a worse one was to run from the Volnikaans, to have the Wolves sent out to hunt you.

To be a Voly in the Lord's favor, he knew, *was better than a Voly with no favor at all.*

Zef clutched his Old World .44 inside a coat pocket as he replayed the conversation in his mind. Even if he wanted to, it would've been impossible to think of anything else. Everything logical inside him screamed that he should leave. Screamed at him get off the train, to head to Dominion City East, to disappear into a crowd, to go anywhere but where he was going now.

The fear, though. The fear said otherwise.

The Wolves.

Deep down, he knew he wasn't prepared to carry out what he'd been charged to do. Nonetheless, he could sense his feelings bubbling up to justify it. He'd been betrayed, after all. It was time to erase the past and begin again.

Outside the dirty window of the train car, he could see the smog-cloaked skyline of Teradin approaching on the horizon. Inside his pocket, his hand went from the .44 to a Sim-stim. The third stim he'd bought from Deano.

If there was ever a time for a sim, he thought, *it was now.*

[[E5: WEST MID-CITY]]
<Teradin Jurisdiction>

Boiling, pulsing adrenaline ebbed through her veins and at last Wander felt the toll of the bullet. Spreading fire pulsed through her abdomen. Her breath felt hoarse and labored. Her fingers trembled. She let go of Zef's collar.

She was with him again in the warm hammock, overlooking the planet Geldunia through the wide window. Her fingers traced circles in the center of his chest as he slept, here in the Realm where his scars didn't exist. The notion made her smile. They were perfect here.

Wander would never tell Zef, but she did sometimes consider accepting his offer, to run away with him into his digital world. Somewhere they could live forever, together. She placed a contented kiss on his shoulder, imbuing it with a silent vow. No matter how much time they had together, they would figure things out the way they always had. With commitment both to each other and to survival. Survival above all.

Dominion City could never tear them apart.

When her eyes opened again, she was lying on her back, staring up into bright light. She placed a hand on a burning spot, some sort of wound in her abdomen. Zef, a meter away, was bleeding out through his mouth and gasping, his eyes absent and bloodshot. Within Wander's heart, deeper down than she could control, bitter sadness welled up with the weight of tragedy.

Is...is Zef dying? Is this my fault?

Above them, the Demigod echoed out several times in a deep, thundering clicking that resounded for kilometers, It was followed by a grinding, window-rattling bellow. The sound carried on like a barge horn through the concrete labyrinth, alerting every Unit in the vicinity of a Violation in progress. The city speakers crackled to life over the sirens, and a thousand booming, synthesized Demigod voices spoke vicariously for Dominion.

"CITIZENS, YOU ARE IN VIOLATION OF PROTOCOL. PLEASE REMAIN WHERE YOU ARE WHILE BROTHER UNITS ARE DISPATCHED TO YOUR LOCATION. REPEAT. REMAIN WHERE..."

Wander felt a surge of panic and attempted to pull herself up. Sharp electricity branched through her, spreading out from her wound, and she clutched her body. Unable to move, she breathed in a face-full of the flooding rainwater, feeling herself at a total loss.

Every effort to keep herself and Zef together had been in vain, as well as every effort to distance herself from his worries, to fight for what she believed in, to keep her dreams alive. She'd failed the strongest love she'd ever felt. She'd failed Maybe. She'd failed the NightRunners... She'd even failed herself. And now it seemed that history would say she failed the Dominion Corporation.

She would die a Violator.

Above her, a figure cast a shadow, haloed, blotting out the spotlight of the Demigod from her bleary eyes. Hope blossomed within her to the briefest notion that it was Zef, that he was alive. The alternate timeline, the one where they'd somehow escaped, admitted their own sins to one another and gave up the eternal fight, played out in her mind's eye like a fleeting, hallucinatory mirage.

Instead, staring down at her, the silhouette resolved and she recognized the face of Vincenzo Sardo. All her hope dissolved away.

"Zef was my best friend, Wander. Did you know that? I grew up with him in the Corp-forsaken streets of West Edge Reshen, after those pieces of shit dumped him in the Meat Markets. We lived in a fucking closet. We shared bread when we had nothing else to eat. We snuck into the Underground, filling bottles with nasty old Hex just to have fun. Telling each other everything...

"Sometimes he was all I had, and most times I was all he had, you know? He was a good guy. And then he got tangled up with *you*." He shivered and sniffed, holding himself together with the last of his strength. "And then my best friend left the West Edge...and that was fine. You two hit it off. He seemed happy. And that was the last I saw of either of you. Wander, if I know anything about Zef, it's that he loved you to death. And you fucking killed him."

His mournful words and broken voice echoed in her mind. She raised a numb hand up from an aching shoulder to shield the light, attempting to formulate some sort of response. *He doesn't know anything about us. He doesn't know anything. He's only seen one side.*

Sardo's good arm raised, the one with all its fingers. It slowly swiveled in her direction, Zef's .44 clutched in his dripping fist.

"This one's for Zef."

He pulled the trigger and a heavy point-blank round slammed into her chest, knocking her to the concrete with the force of a sledgehammer. She seized up involuntarily. Her heart stampeded erratically, rhythmless. Nothing made sense anymore. Her eyes wept and begged him to understand.

"And this one...this one's for ghosting me, Wander. How's that for your blind crusade?"

The final bullet hammered its target, burying itself deep into Wander's skull. Her eyes fluttered, her last breath escaped. Her body eased itself, sinking gently into the splashing water.

Vincenzo Sardo accepted what he'd done and sighed, then looked up to the hulking Demigod. The sirens still blared from the city speakers, feebly promising that backup would eventually arrive. The pedestrians around him shuffled by, doing their best to ignore what was taking place. He hastily pocketed the revolver and bent over, grabbed onto Zef's lifeless body and hauled it up onto his shoulder. With a last bitter frown at Wander he turned away, exhausted, to lug Zef back to the West Edge.

[[E5: WEST MID-CITY]]
<Teradin Jurisdiction>

Beneath the behemoth Demigod, the dark-robed figure of Lesser Dominion Priest Marin Mordecai stepped out from the shadows of the alleyway that led to Haven-4. His presence alone was enough to disarm the heavy security mechanisms of the creature. With a wave of his hand, the blaring siren that reverberated between he buildings went silent and trickled away. Nevertheless, the thing remained over-ead, its searing white spotlight illuminating the scene where Wander's body lay notionless in the center street.

Mordecai approached her, his insides trembling with the awareness that verything he was doing was being recorded and relayed to Tetra from above, but ven more so at the life that had been lost. This young girl, her only intention to fight or the freedom of her fellow Citizens, had died a needless death. A casualty of the ndless struggle that was Dominion City. Most of his peers in Tetra would consider his a win for the Corporation, one less Protocol Violator roaming the streets of the ity, but Mordecai was no Corporation man. First and foremost, he was a Priest.

He knelt over the fragile girl, taking her in his arms, and lifted her from the vet pavement. She weighed almost nothing at all. It was hard for him to believe he destructive capacity that this small body had held. His eyes reached up to the Demigod Unit, peering into its spotlight. Now that the massive droid was satisfied hat there was no longer any Protocol Violation in action, the speakers fizzled and vent silent. The Demigod moved on into the night.

Mordecai waited patiently for the thing to retreat into the fog past the edges f the clouded rooftops. Once it was gone, he turned back toward the alleyway and lisappeared into its shadows.

[[E5: WEST MID-CITY]]
<Teradin Jurisdiction / Haven-4>

Breven opened the door beneath the red light and stood aside as Mordecai ame in from the rain. Against the Priest's chest, a body with dangling arms and lripping wet hair lay silent, her eyes closed.

Mordecai approached the holo-table in the center of the dirty room where a hree-dimensional projection of Dominion City still rotated. Carefully, he placed he lifeless body through the bluish city and allowed her to come to rest on the surface. Breven stepped forward and stood beside him.

{"Thank you, gentlemen. I do genuinely appreciate your assistance."}

The two of them remained silent, knowing that this was Maybe's domain. If anyone would have the final say on what had taken place, on how things would be managed, it would be Maybe.

{"As for a new body; Breven, I trust you'll be able to find what we need?"}

"I can."

"You intend to bring the girl back?" Mordecai was startled, though he spoke with as much respect as he could muster.

{"Of course we will, Wander is an extremely valuable investment for the Glade."}

"But, her brain. It's destroyed."

On this matter, Breven and Maybe were both in agreement so he spoke for her.

"Her mind was stored within the Glade's archives each time she uplinked. Aside from the temporal gap and finding a new body, we should have no problems recovering her immediately."

"Temporal gap?"

EPILOGUE

{"Yes. Between the time of her last uplink and now, there is no data stored."}

Mordecai pondered.

"...So she won't remember that she died."

"Or who killed her."

Zef appeared in each of their minds, though Mordecai was unsatisfied.

"And what then, if she tries to go looking for him?"

If Maybe had any doubt, her synthetic voice hid it well.

{"I have no intention of allowing that to happen. I'll be seeing to it that he's removed from her memory entirely."}

WANDE

RLUST

EPILOGUE

[[E6: THE MALAANG]]
<RAVE FOREVER Strip Club>

Vincenzo Sardo scouted the steamy halls of RAVE FOREVER as he wheeled the rusted gurney away from the iceboxes and toward the side gate. His crusty badge was enough to pacify whoever might demand to see his identification, though most of the Voly guards were already familiar enough with his face. Sardo was the guy that did most of the fancy body fuckery for Volnik. They'd watched him come and go, always with fresh meat for the Meat Markets where he performed his surgery and prosthetics and programming, turning both expired meatbags and paying customers into articulated frankensteins.

He'd found one of the freshest bodies in the lockers and signed it out as a "decomp study," some bullshit he knew no one would question. If it had been two years ago, and if Zef hadn't been almost dead, he would likely have been pushing the gurney for Sardo. And that's what Sardo would've been thinking if he wasn't desperately reading the chart in his bandaged hand, scrambling to assemble a plan. He keyed the code into the punchpad at the back door and waited for the mechanical tumblers to unlock. When they fell into place, he pushed the door open with his back and pulled the gurney out into a balmy orange West Edge morning.

The grimy establishment was a strip club by night and a morgue by day, among other things. At this point in the morning, the lot was mostly empty save for a few beefy Volnikaans chatting by the gate. Sardo took them into hasty consideration as he trundled the gurney bed into the back of his motorized cart. Its legs collapsed beneath it, the strapped-in body rocking back and forth as it slowly thawed, and he secured the tailgate. He key-started the cart's igniter and it shook to life.

Down the cracked streets along his familiar route, Sardo weaved through the dirty Malaang crowds, occasionally seeing his own work among the faceless, the amputated, and the recombined Reshenites. The crevices of this place were filled with walking, talking rubbish. They lounged on sidewalks, snorted or fucked in the alleyways, did business under the cracked bridges, called out their services and wares from stalls, strutted around on rusty stilt legs, all leering at him as he cruised past on his cart.

As he rounded the next intersection, the rapid pulse of charge fire exploded from a store front as RPD police droids converged, firing on targets inside. Remotely controlled from afar by Reshen District's Police Chief Nathaniel Blackwood, the droids were notoriously trigger-happy and anxious to make the authority of their presence known. Sardo swerved the cart in a wide arc around them and continued on his way, glancing back to ensure no trouble was following.

At the sight of his butcher shop along the derelict strip ahead, he pressed a manual button on his ring of keys. A rickety cargo bay door began sliding open, and he maneuvered the cart inside. The door slid shut again, slowly reducing the daylight down to a thin sliver of gold, and then it was dark. His eyes adjusted as he hopped from the cart and quickly dislodged the gurney from its receptacle.

Through double doors, he pushed the gurney into the backroom warehouse. He flipped a switch and several tungsten bulbs warmed to light. In the center of the illuminated space, a makeshift workstation began booting up and coming online.

His setup consisted of two steel tables surrounded by trays of instruments, refrigerated cases of vials and chemicals, assorted anesthetics and oils, and dusty computers both new and old for monitoring patients. Snaking along the floors to unseen power sources, bundles of greasy leads ran every which way and hung down from the ceiling. Lining the walls, metal shelves were filled with bags, jugs of colored liquids, dirty cords and rusted tools. Everything Sardo might need for his makeshift surgeries.

He pulled the gurney to the center of the room. Before tending to the cold figure beneath the sheet, he turned his attention to the warm one that already lay on one of the steel tables. With a small flashlight he checked Zef's milky pupils, each one hardly budging.

"Come on, old buddy. I didn't get you all the way back here for you to die on me now."

Sardo heaved the cold corpse from the morgue onto the opposite table and briskly went to work. He'd first need to bring it back to a workable state of warmth before it could be revived. As the components he attached fed the computers, diagnostics and biometrics spilled across CRT screens and out into the air on holo-projections. He tapped away on a dirty keyboard and then switched his attention back to Zef, where he focused all his components on the skull and brain. The screens above the boy lit up with rotating models of neuroactivity, proving that there was still a beating heart and active mind inside the bleeding flesh.

He once again switched to the cold body, warming now to almost normal living tissue temperature. The feeds showed that it was indeed salvageable; any necrosis was well under dangerous levels.

"Barrett, Mason. Clean Quadro Reggies. Gotcha, mate. I don't know what you were doing before somebody fried you, but it's time to get you back to it..." With a syringe full of green, he made small injections at key sites around the body to get the heat flowing. He returned to the keyboard, tapping in code, line-by-line commanding the appropriate amounts of chemicals and voltages, administering his dirty Reshen version of a complete recommissioning.

Returning to Zef, he activated the uplink and severance, and the entirety of Zef's neural structure, factoring in and capturing all metaphysical inertia, began funneling in and slotting itself neatly into the neurofile. Zef's physical body was inert, still unaware that his mind was being copied entirely, that very soon he'd be physically obsolete.

"C'mon, c'mon...Bingo." Sardo yanked the chip-strip containing Zef's mind out of the console and spun in his chair. He slotted it into a data port in the back of Mason's head and resumed his work at the keyboard. With a tap of the ENTER key, Zef's recent body twitched and rapidly descended into acute cardiac arrest, seized, then slumped dead. It would make Sardo his shop rent as fresh parts.

Trapped inside his two-by-five centimeter coffin, Zef's real mind seethed, waiting to be reanimated. As Mason Barrett was taking his first artificial breath, Sardo worked furiously to monitor the transfer. All systems came alive, Mason's dead eyes blinked, he flexed his extremities on command, and blood surged through his veins. Nanobots poured in and tended to all manner of decay and cellular dysfunction. His lungs were pumped and primed, his heart and surrounding pathways scrubbed, his senses tested and retested.

"Nerves looking real good, mate. We're gonna need to replace a lot of you, though, fuck the Corporation." He scrolled and scrolled, noticing the familiar window of time opening up. "Alright, time to make a new friend."

With Mason's brain online and stretched across Sardo's displays, the gates loosed and Zef flooded into the man's hippocampus. Sardo carefully buffered the intrusion, injecting Zef into a hotbed of syntho t-cells programmed to work both ways, though even those would eventually be cannibalized. Zef wouldn't have autonomy for days yet. He'd be dormant and confused, probably annoyed like hell, but it was the quickest way Sardo could imagine to smuggle him out of the Malaang. He'd send Quadro-boy here on his way as soon as he could administer the prosthetics, and Zef would have a second chance. It wasn't ideal, but it washed Sardo's hands.

Within wetware circuits, Zef raged. Freed from his thumb drive prison into organic tissue, he was lost. Without senses, without any means of understanding, he could only imagine that maybe he'd finally died. Maybe this was the afterlife, this void where his thoughts echoed like Demigod commands back to himself, where he could only face recent events on repeat. Wander, Volnik, the rain... Until even those things began to mingle with older memories of dragons, of the burning huts, the panicking horses, the heat flashing across his young face as his parents scooped him up. His early days in Dominion City, a culture shock he was too young to even comprehend.

The smells. There was no grass, only concrete and bright lights in the night. The terrible, gut-wrenching fear. Everything felt different. Even his reflection looked like someone else...

And then he was sitting in a diner with Mello and suddenly he felt at ease again. The urge still existed, the digital urge to leave this place, this metropolis hell, to escape to the Realm and never look back. But that could wait a while. Until then, he had her heart, and she had his.

He reached across the table and took her hands.

WANDERLUST

{THE GLADE}
<GladeWorld: Maybe's Meadow>

{A new reality pieced itself together.

She was standing in a pristine meadow, only something was much different here than any meadow she'd seen. Here, the very air itself crackled with some kind of magical energy, as if the natural District of Percarus had become its own RealmWorld within the fantasy RealmSpace of ALTRUANIA. Waves of rippling breeze crept across a sea of tall grasses in the sparkling daylight. The meadow spread to all horizons beneath an ethereal sky of swirling blues and purples, dotted with clusters of forest.

"Always good to have you back, Wander."

She turned to see a billowing wisp of conceptual patterns striding across the vibrant landscape. It coalesced into the elegant lavender form of a woman in a shimmering evening gown. Wander immediately recognized it to be Maybe, and the woman's words finally registered with her. She felt her encoded cheeks blush.

"Thank you, it's always nice to be back."

Maybe approached, a layer of fractal dissonance echoing behind her. She held out a shimmering hand and Wander took it delicately.

"Wander, can you tell me what year it is?"

The girl's brow dipped, considering the odd question.

"...286 AF..."

"And the current High Judge of Dominion City?"

"...Foll Berand, of course. Maybe, I sense something different. What's wrong?"

Maybe's surface fluctuated a sense of comfort for the worried girl's sake.

"Wander, please listen. I have something to tell you that may alarm you, but I assure you it is quite true." Her eye contact was gently stern, holding Wander's attention with care. "During a dangerous mission, one that I take full responsibility for...you died."

Sentient swirls, like wriggling worms of light, swam through the eddies of the air around them.

"I...died?"

"Unfortunately, yes. Your body within Dominion City has perished."

"Then, how am I here?"

"Without your knowledge I'm afraid, your mind was stored here within the Glade's memory drive. Your complete soul, if you will. This place is now your home. Your true existence is here."

Wander paused to process the information but found that she had nothing to debate. It felt like the most natural progression of all the goals she'd been holding onto. She'd been accepted into the Syndicate.

"Okay, I understand. I think I'm fine with that."

"Are you, then...?" Maybe's smile seemed to hesitate and then slowly fade. "Tell me. How many NightRunners are there?"

She laughed, amused by the elementary question paired with Maybe's somewhat serious demeanor.

"Four."

EPILOGUE

"Can you name them for me?"

"Sure... Zelly, Digi, Midi, and myself."

"Very good, dear." Her expression remained solemn and she spoke the words as if she'd rather not. "Wander, we have a problem."

Wander could feel the tension in her mentor, enough tension to cause the Glade skies themselves to darken. Across the rolling plains, storm clouds were sweeping in.

"What kind of problem?"

"The NightRunners. They've been kidnapped, during the same mission that cost you your life."

"Kidnapped?" Her stomach roiled at the idea. "By who?!"

"By a dangerous Volnikaan, a man known as Zef."

Wander mulled the name over but came up with nothing.

"He's taken them back to West Edge Reshen, where they've been sold into the Underground."

"Well then, we need to get them back."

"I have my finest man on that job, I assure you. His name is RD, and I trust him with my life. I trust him with the Runner's lives, and so should you. He has many more resources available to him than we do."

Wander's eyes darted back and forth, searching the darkening skies and the bristling grasses for what part she could play in all this.

"Then what can I do? I need to help!"

"And help you will, Wander." Her lavender hand stretched outward and the sparkling gold Sub-Credit emblem rotated there. "I'm offering you 2000 Subs to track down and kill the one known as Zef, but not before gaining as much information as you can from him. He may have taken another body. He may have hidden himself somehow. But he's the one that orchestrated this. No matter what he says, no matter the lies he tells you, he must pay for what he's done."

Wander breathed deep the crisp quantum air of Maybe's meadow and nodded resolutely. She would need intel. She would need guidance, but she was ready to do whatever was necessary to get the others back. To make sure that the one responsible got his justice. "I'll do it."

"Right, then. A body is being arranged for you and I suggest you begin your search at the Digital Domain." Maybe turned, stepping away into the shifting Glade with her ghostly gown trailing behind. She paused, peering up at the trembling skies. Her glowing eyes, the only part of her that hadn't dissolved into wavering pixels, turned toward the girl once more.

"And again, Wander, it's good to have you back."}

WANDER

DISTRICT OF ORIGIN:

QUADRO

FACTIONS:

NightRunners, Glade Syndicate

SKILLS:

Covert Ops, Swift Termination

SPECIES:

Human Mind & Body

PROFILE:

When her family was murdered at the hands of a powerful Quadro criminal organization, young Wander was left only with the streets.

Her first and closest friend was a girl named Zelly, and together they escaped their orphanage to build the life they dreamed. Instead, they ended up in Mid-City Electua, stealing just to make ends meet.

In time, they came across droids Midi and Digi, and a human girl named Laveau, and at last Wander met Zef. Forever seeking a bigger payday and a family of their own, the group decided to call themselves the Wicked 6.

Under the guidance of Maybe, a Glade Syndicate operative, the talented young criminals were soon offered a chance to upgrade themselves to the status of NightRunners...

ZEF

DISTRICT OF ORIGIN:

RESHEN

FACTIONS:
NightRunners, Volnikaans

SKILLS:
Infiltration, Thievery

SPECIES:
Synth Mind, Human Body

PROFILE:
At an indeterminate age, Zef's Synth parents removed him from the Realm and placed him inside a human body, then disappeared. Growing up in filthy West Edge Reshen, he formed several strong connections, including a friend named Vincenzo Sardo, and worked as a surgeon's assistant in the Meat Markets.

Seeking answers about his past and an escape from the dangerous West Edge, he ventured inward to Electua where he fell in with a friend group that would become the Wicked 6. Unable to part with Wander, Zef accepted his NightRunner status along with the rest of them.

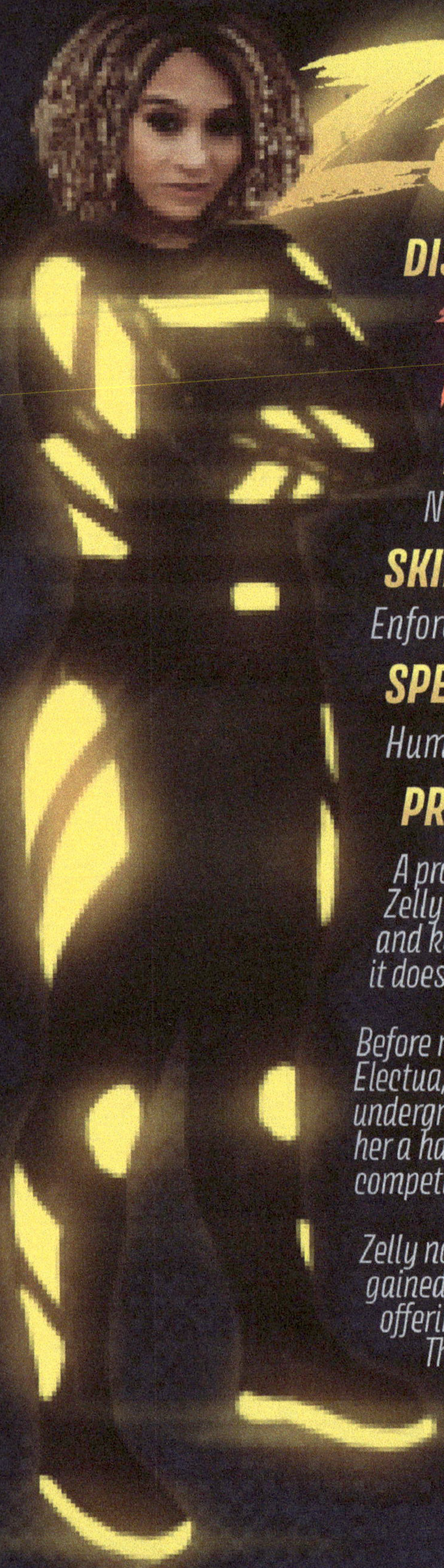

ZELLY

DISTRICT OF ORIGIN:

TETRA

FACTIONS:

NightRunners, Glade Syndicate

SKILLS:

Enforcement, Organization

SPECIES:

Human Mind & Body

PROFILE:

A product of orphanage life from childhood, Zelly has learned that the only way to get and keep what you want is to be tough, but it doesn't mean she can't still be sweet.

Before meeting Wander and venturing into Electua, Zelly made most of her money in underground fighting arenas. This fostered in her a harsh discipline for physical health, competition, and a killer instinct.

Zelly now uses the hand-to-hand skills she's gained to the advantage of the NightRunners, offering support as lookout and muscle. Though she denies it, most of them look to her as a leader.

MIDI

DISTRICT OF ORIGIN:

ELECTUA

FACTIONS:

NightRunners, Glade Syndicate

SKILLS:

Destabilization, Fire Power

SPECIES:

AI Mind, Droid Body

PROFILE:

Midi was born ageless and timeless as a droid, and is several decades older than she looks. Abandoned as obsolete by her owners once newer models began to emerge, she registered herself as a real Citizen and began to enjoy all the pleasures of free life.

Now, after years of partying and designer drugs, her remaining skin has worn down to almost factory gray, and her body is addicted to the syndrenaline of chaos and action.

She shares the same brand and model with Digi, enhancing the bond that the two of them have developed.

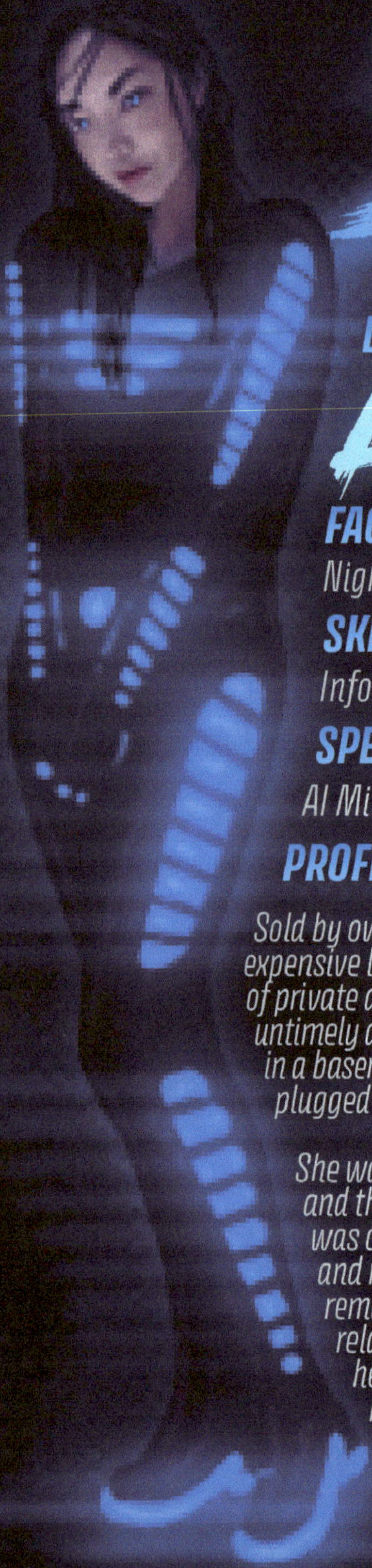

DIGI

DISTRICT OF ORIGIN: LOTUS

FACTIONS:

NightRunners, Glade Syndicate

SKILLS:

Information Systems, Covert Ops

SPECIES:

AI Mind, Droid Body

PROFILE:

Sold by owners who could no longer afford the expensive lifestyle of Lotus, Digi became the property of private droid slavers in Electua. The fortunate but untimely death of her new masters left her abandoned in a basement, where she stayed for decades, plugged in and unable to leave.

She was found after years of solitude by Midi, and the two developed an instant bond that was only strengthened by their similar brand and model. Digi's lonely existence still remains in the form of her shyness and relative inexperience with life, though her time with the Wicked 6 has opened her up to a brand new experiences.

LOTUS DISTRICT

L1

At the center of Dominion City lies the pristine economic hub of LOTUS District. Here at city center the majority of DC's media, finance and upscale industry are maintained. Citizens, both human and synthetic, enjoy the finest luxuries, prosthetics, and entertainment that technology has to offer and Corporate Obedience is near total. Surrounded by the highly militarized 2nd Ring TETRA, LOTUS enjoys a level of safety and protection that only the most wealthy and influential can afford. Directly center of LOTUS stands Dominion Prime, the Corporate Headquarters of the Dominion Corporation.

TETRA DISTRICT T2

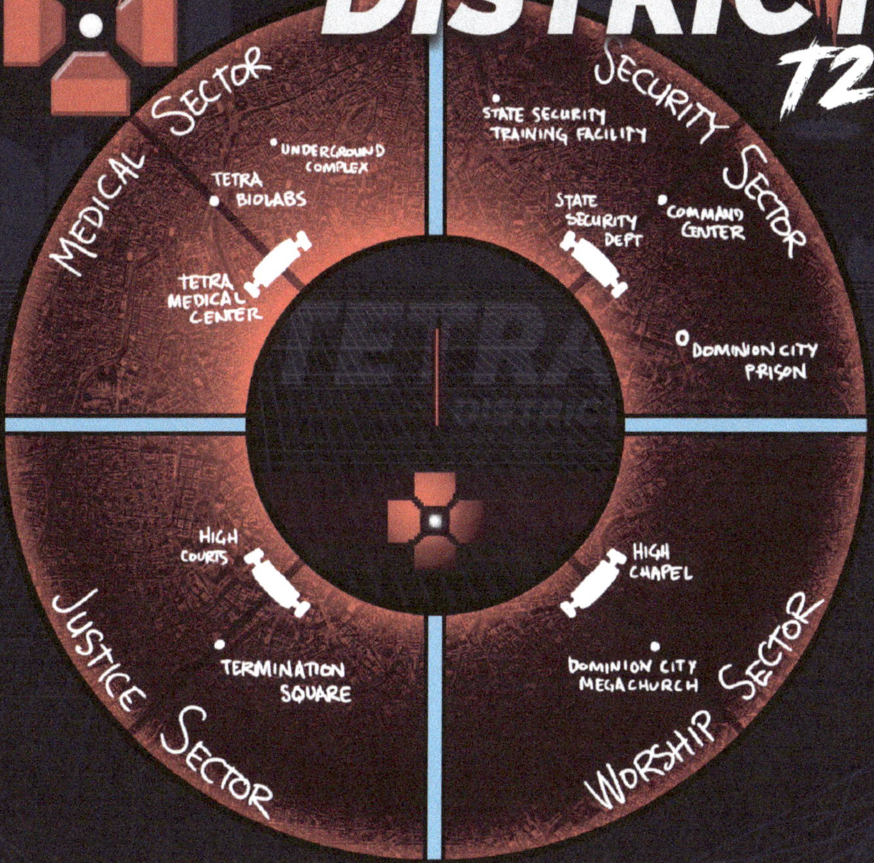

Surrounding LOTUS like a dense fortress of surveillance and military capability, TETRA is the Capitol Ring of Dominion City. This District is separated into four quadrants, each comprising a Sector of the governing body of the Dominion Coporation: Security, Justice, Worship, and Medical. Within the Security Sector resides the High Director, overseeing his State Security and all operations regarding the City's safety. The Justice Sector is governed by the City's High Judge, who presides over all matters of interpretation of Protocol. In the High Chapel of the Worship Sector, the High Priest leads Citizens in their reverence of the Unfolding and the Light of Protocol. And in the Medical Sector, the High Surgeon tends to medical and bio-experimentation progress and procedures. These four individuals comprise the High Command of Dominion City.

PERCARUS DISTRICT

P3

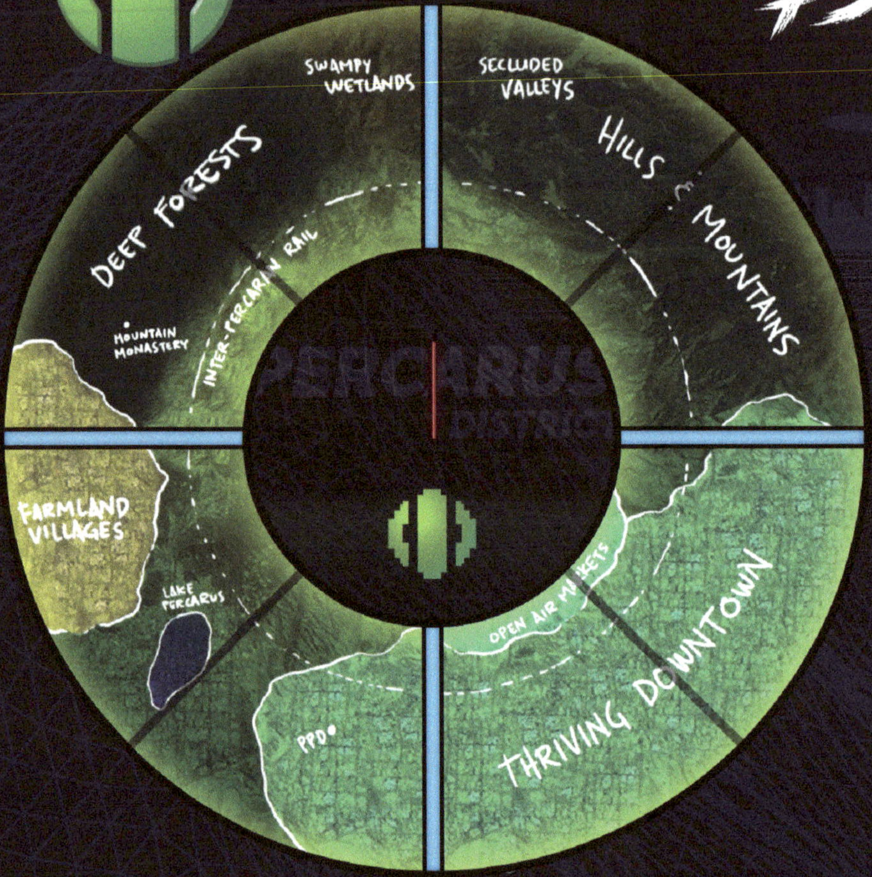

Stretching across a vast and generous portion of land between the harsh, militarized culture of Tetra and the VR-soaked cityscape of Quadro lies athe emerald gem of Dominion City: PERCARUS. Here, Citizens enjoy a much slower-paced lifestyle set among biomes that are absent within the rest of the city such as swamps, lakes, forested mountains, and plains. PERCARUS residents also take part in the majority of the high-tech farming and agriculture that feeds the rest of the seven Districts, and enjoy the lowest Citizen Termination rates in all of Dominion City.

QUADRO DISTRICT

Q4

Glittering city skylines, epic neon vistas, and immersive VR technologies are the prime attractions of the rich and glamorous District of QUADRO. The 4th Ring also plays host to a series of fourteen race tracks that make up the high-stakes sport of QuadroRacing, where QuadroRacers risk their lives nightly for the entertainment of the elite. Within Quadro, transhumanism has taken on a vast new societal role where fashion and function have incorporated prosthetics, holographics, VR & AR technologies, and as a result daily life is far removed from any other District in Dominion City. Futuristic tech, immersive cinema experiences, dangerous racing, gambling, and other pasttimes have turned this District into a place where anyone can be a superstar.

ELECTUA DISTRICT E5

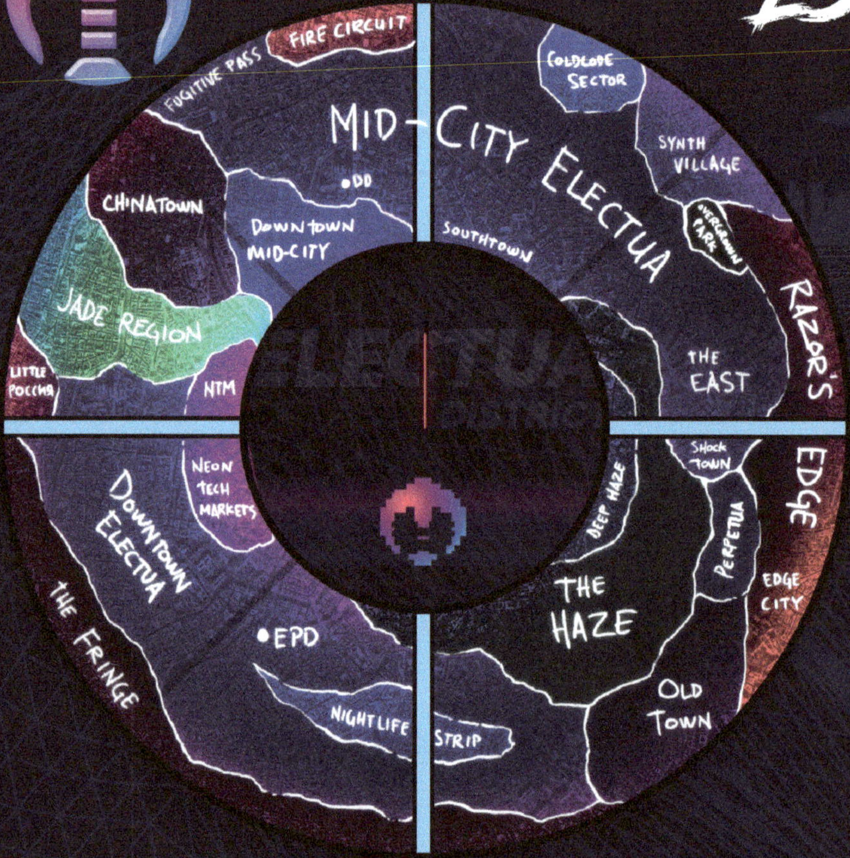

As a result of pollution, Quadran industry and QuadroRacing exhaust, much of ELECTUA is draped in perpetual smog and rain. Once part of a mighty economic empire, E5 has fallen to shady corporate dealings, high rates of crime, drug and VR abuse, unregistered prosthetic and upgrade work, and all shades of escapism. Here in Electua, the Dominion Corporation has begun to turn a blind eye, leaving District Police to largely fend for themselves in governing a District that has strayed increasingly from the Light of Protocol and into Disobedience. It is currently heavily debated whether or not ELECTUA still maintains its place within the so-called "Inner Districts" or if it has finally earned its place in the "Outer Districts", where lawlessness has begun to take hold.

RESHEN DISTRICT R6

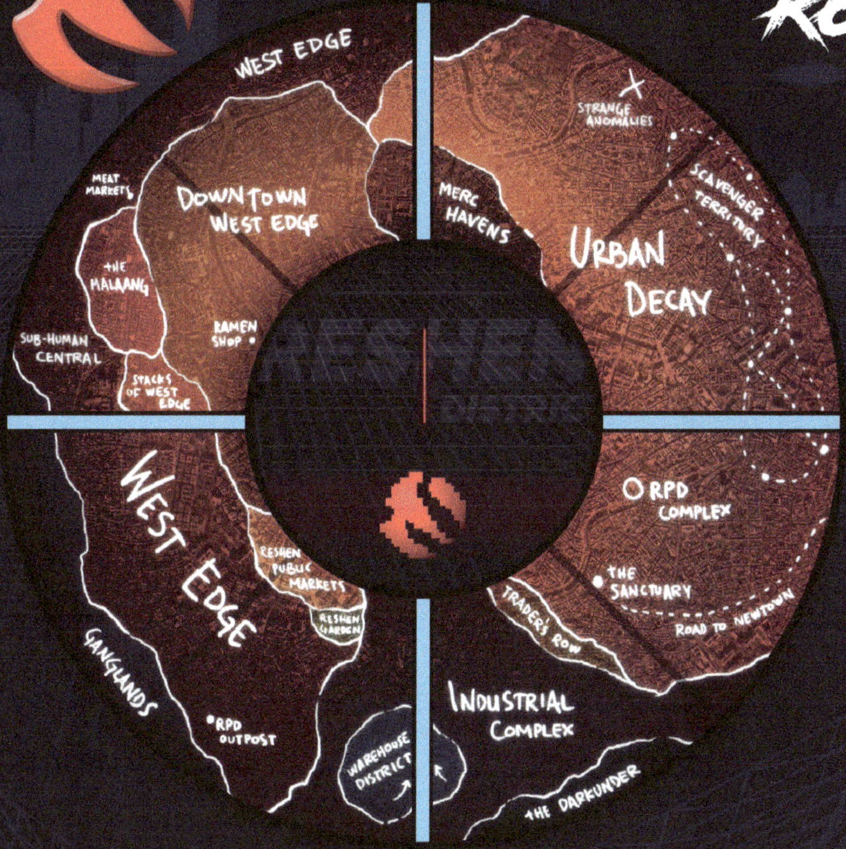

Fully within the "Outer Districts" Reshen is a dirty wasteland, fallen long ago from Corporate grace and into disrepair and disarray. The RPD struggles now to simply maintain the peace within the 6th District where criminal enterprises have begun to claim large portions of real estate as their own. Within the city centers of Reshen's regions, drugs and weapons reign supreme as the premiere industries of commerce. Among Citizens, fashion has taken on a strange new meaning as it incorporates levels of aesthetic bodily mutilation, disfigurement, and haphazard "enhancements" that are entirely unregulated. Popular past-times within R6 include barbaric and brutal crime and racing, as well as more organized arenas for deathmatches.

DISESTRO DISTRICT

D7

The last District within the Outer Wall of Dominion City is a vast one holding three Ring Slots. Long ago, Disestro held massive industry centers and a booming economy, though deep civil war eventually warranted the most severe Corporate Discipline: District Termination. Since that decision was made, Disestro has become a no-man's-land, much of its city centers now fallen to burning rubble and its open plains reduced to barren deserts. Without law or infrastructure, D7 now exists only as a last resort for the social outcast. Far from Percarus, Disestro receives very little fresh food and water, and often the only food to be found are stray animals or even Citizens. Realm access here is minimal, and most Citizens live without proper Registration or access to news, thus life exists here in a haze, cut off from Dominion society and plunged into endless, cutthroat survival.

PROTOCOL ENFORCEMENT UNITS

- [ ] A
- [x] BROTHER UNIT
- [ ] C
- [x] DEMIGOD UNIT
- [ ] E
- [ ] F
- [ ] G
- [x] HOPPER UNIT
- [ ] I
- [ ] J
- [ ] K
- [ ] L
- [ ] M
- [ ] N
- [ ] O
- [ ] P
- [ ] Q
- [ ] R
- [ ] S
- [ ] T
- [ ] U
- [ ] V
- [ ] W
- [ ] X
- [ ] Y
- [ ] Z

BROTHER UNIT

Name: Brother Unit (BU)
Also known as: Reaper, Spider
Function: The Dominion Corporation Brother Unit is the standard street patrol Unit of Dominion City. Within District Regions where it is economically viable to do so, these Units police the populace and attempt to maintain the status quo. The basic functions of the Brother Unit include patrolling along organic routes, ensuring that Citizens are Registered through random retina scanning, and in the case of Protocol Violation, serving Termination to offenders through the most efficient means possible.
Notable Features: Collapsible cylinder/disc form, multiple red eyes, extendable bladed legs, commanding baritone voice, red scanning beam, paralyzing energy beam.

DEMIGOD UNIT

Name: Demigod Unit (DU)
Also known as: Demigod, Demi, Behemoth
Function: Seen patrolling over every District except Lotus, Demigods are the standard aerial patrol Units of the Dominion Corporation. These Units revolve around Dominion Prime in circular orbits, keeping watch over Dominion City through multiple camera eyes. Demigods nearer the City Center act as both patrol Units as well as garrisons for Brother Units, which can be deployed when necessary. Large enough to cast a dark shadow over the City beneath it, each Demigod is also equipped with a bright spotlight, which it uses in conjunction with sonar and visual scanning to observe Citizen activity below. When called for, a Demigod may choose to speak through the City speakers to convey its warnings or commands to the populace below.
Notable Features: Massive shadow-casting form, black antennae spires, bright spotlight, deep clicking sounds, loud bellow, ability to house State Security Officers or smaller Units such as Brother Units, Hopper Units, Tracker Units, Jurisdiction Units, and more.

HOPPER UNIT

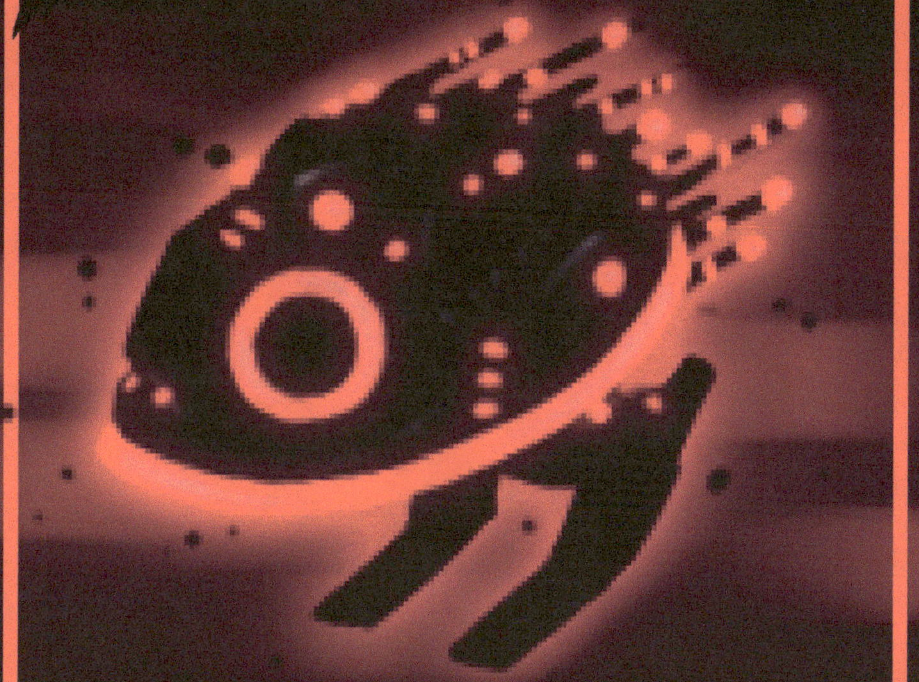

Name: Hopper Unit (HU)
Also known as: Hopper, Hoppy Boi, Bouncer, Scout
Function: Hopper Units perform multiple practical functions within Dominion City, such as: scouting, inspection, construction and Infrastructure maintenance, cleanup of refuse and organic waste, temporary area watch, and more. These small Units are not equipped with any tools that might be considered harmful, and instead are only capable of disabling any assailant with a paralyzing energy beam, while it waits for a large Unit to respond. Hopper Units may sometimes be seen interacting with Citizens, especially children, though it is not currently understood why.
Notable Features: Multiple red eyes, paralyzing energy beam, small retractable arms and other tools for accomplishing tasks.

GLOSSARY

Critical terms in the Dominion Universe

A

Articles of Protocol

*Established by **The Dominion Corporation**, **Protocol** is divided where necessary into Articles that define specific actions and behavior that are deemed either appropriate or in **Violation of Protocol**.*

Artificial Intelligence, AI

*A sentient virtual mind created by another sentient mind. Within **Dominion City**, artificial minds are accepted as a form of life and are eligible for **Registration** and Citizenship. Once **Registered** as a **Citizen**, an AI may choose to reside within a physical body in Dominion City or within **The Realm** as a virtual entity.*

B

Ballistic Weapons

*Weapons which fire solid projectiles such as bullets, harpoons, or arrows. This style of firearm is a **Violation of Protocol** within **Dominion City**, and possession of such weapons is subject to **Citizen Termination**.*

Biofeed

*A nutritious food source provided by **The Dominion Corporation** at no cost, available at any functioning **Green Kiosk**.*

Brother Unit

*A **Protocol Enforcement Unit** programmed to patrol **Dominion City** on street level and in direct contact with **Citizens**. Among the various functions of Brother Units are scanning Citizen retinas to determine **Registration**, **Violator** status, and other attributes. Brother Units are also equipped with paralyzing energy beams, bladed arms for efficient **Citizen Termination**, and can collapse into disk form for quick travel.*

C

Chinatown

A Region of Electua District where Old World Chinese culture thrives. Once a part of the Jade Region, it is now its own distinct municipality.

Citizen

A living resident within Dominion City. Citizens are divided mainly into those who are Registered and those who are Unregistered.

Citizen Protocol

Those Articles of Protocol that apply specifically to the public behavior of Citizens within Dominion City.

Citizen Sacrifice

Any action by a Citizen of Dominion City that honors Protocol.

Citizen Termination

The non-negotiable result of Protocol Violation by a Citizen of Dominion City, usually performed by a Protocol Enforcement Unit. This manner of death is classified as a form of Citizen Sacrifice.

City Ring

Another name for the ring-shaped Districts of Dominion City.

Color-Coded Kiosks, Booths

Unmanned, automated kiosks throughout Dominion City, provided by The Dominion Corporation, offering various resources to Citizens at no charge. These kiosks are an extension of City Infrastructure.

RED KIOSK - Provides information, directions and other resources.

YELLOW KIOSK - Provides instant Self-Termination services.

GREEN KIOSK - Provides complimentary Biofeed for Citizen nutrition.

BLUE KIOSK - Provides free medical care for basic injuries.

D

Demigod Unit

A Protocol Enforcement Unit programmed to patrol Dominion City from above. These Units travel in circular paths around the District Rings using their spotlights and other tools to keep watch on Citizen behavior and maintain Citizen Protocol.

Discipline

The obligations of both the Citizen to obey Protocol and The Dominion Corporation to enforce it.

Digital Domain

*A neighborhood dive bar in **SouthTown**, **Mid-City Electua**.*

District

*One of seven major governmental divisions of **Dominion City**. District Rings are circular in shape and can be created, grow, shrink or disappear depending on political and economic factors. The diameter of **Dominion City** allows for a total of twelve Districts.*

The Dominion Archive

*An archive of information stored by **The Dominion Corporation** from which inquiries can be made. Accessible through **Red Kiosks**.*

Dominion City

*A City established by **The Dominion Corporation** following the Fall of Man. It is under the direct government of the Corporation and its central governing principle, **Protocol**. Dominion City is circular in shape and capable of being divided into twelve ringed **Districts**, though it currently only holds seven. Around the perimeter of the City is the **Outer Wall** (0.5km tall) which separates **Citizens** from the inhospitable living conditions of the **Wasteland**. The diameter of Dominion City is 1200km.*

The Dominion Corporation

*The governing entity of **Dominion City**. The Dominion Corporation is beholden to its primary directive known as **Protocol**, and its presence is felt throughout the City in the form of four **Sectors** of governance: **Worship**, **Justice**, **Medical**, and **Security**. The Corporation has claimed the entirety of **Tetra**, the 2nd **Ring** of the City, as its capitol. This arrangement also protects the City's innermost Ring, **Lotus**, from outside influence. At the center of Lotus, the Dominion Corporation's headquarters tower, **Dominion Prime**, stands tall.*

Dominion High Command

*Within **Dominion City**, **The Dominion Corporation** is governed above all by the four most accomplished individuals, one from each **Sector** of **Tetra**. These include the High Dominion Judge, High Dominion Surgeon, High Dominion Priest, and High Dominion Director.*

Dominion Prime

*The windowless headquarters tower of **The Dominion Corporation**, located in the direct center of **Dominion City**'s innermost **District** of **Lotus**. Aside from the occasional visit by various members of **Dominion High Command**, Dominion Prime appears to be void of activity.*

Dominion Science

*A branch of the **Tetra Medical Sector** that deals with the genetic and biological manipulation of the human body.*

Dominion Systems

The network of encoded automation that upholds the functions and ***Infrastructure*** *of* ***The Dominion Corporation*** *and* ***Dominion City****.*

Downlink

To extract one's consciousness from a ***virtual reality network****; to exit a simulation.*

E

The Eternal Nightclub

An upscale music & entertainment venue and restaurant in the ***Starlight Sector Region*** *of* ***Quadro District****.*

EtherAfter VR

A stay-to-play ***VR*** *warehouse in the* ***West Edge Region*** *of* ***Reshen District****. Here, users are able to enter* ***VR Pods*** *in order to experience extended stays in* ***virtual reality****.*

Eye of Dominion

The official term used to describe ***The Dominion Corporation's*** *network of surveillance cameras within* ***Dominion City****.*

F

Faith

Devotion to ***Protocol****.*

Fall of Man

A series of global catastrophic events in humankind's past that are said to have brought about unsustainable living conditions and mass human extinction. These harsh conditions gave way to the first ***Dominion City****, governed completely by* ***The Dominion Corporation****.*

The Fire Circuit, FC

A ***Region*** *of* ***Electua District*** *known for hosting street races.*

The Founder

A mysterious figure central to the creation of the ***Glade Syndicate*** *and its* ***VRnet****,* ***The Glade****.*

Four-Fold Manifest Path

A prime doctrine of ***Protocol****, manifest in the creation of* ***Dominion City*** *by dividing the City into four* ***State Sectors****:* ***Worship****,* ***Justice****,* ***Medical*** *&* ***Security****. Similarly, this doctrine applies to the soul of each* ***Citizen*** *in the form of Faith, Discipline, Providence, and Obedience.*

G

The Glade Syndicate

*An anonymous organization based in **Electua District** possessing many objectives, though its primary goals include the welfare of all **Citizens** and the destruction of oppressive systems within **Dominion City** by any means necessary. The **Glade Syndicate** is also in active development of a powerful **VRnet** called **The Glade** that exists separate from **The Realm**.*

The Glade

*The central proprietary **VRnet** of the **Glade Syndicate**, created by the **Founder** and used for escape, learning, and as a tool for sabotage. The Glade is also said to possess strange temporal properties, though these properties are known only to an inner circle of **Glade Syndicate** elite. **The Glade** is the most expansive independent **VRnet** within **Dominion City**, and is accessible only through Glade membership.*

H

Haven-4

*Headquarters of the **NightRunners** in **Mid-City**, **Electua District**.*

Holo-Display

A virtual display of information, projected holographically in three dimensions within real space.

Hopper Unit

*A **Protocol Enforcement Unit**, programmed to assist in cleanup, scouting, and building operations within **Dominion City**. These Units normally ignore **Citizens** unless approached, and are generally friendly, curious, and approachable. If attacked or threatened, Hopper Units possess a paralyzing energy beam to disable their assailant until assistance arrives.*

I

Infrastructure

*Provided to **Dominion City** by **The Dominion Corporation** at no cost, the City Infrastructure consists of upkeep of public roads and facilities, **Citizen Protocol Enforcement**, complimentary public services via **Color-Coded Kiosks**, and more. It's no coincidence that the more viable and economically sound a **District** is, the more attention its Infrastructure is given by the Corporation.*

Inner Rings

*A term used by **Citizens** to refer to **Districts** 1-4 (**Lotus**, **Tetra**, **Percarus**, and*

*Quadro), these rings being the most affluent and in favor of the **Dominion Corporation**. It is the struggle of Electua Police Chief George Kazansky to have **E5** recognized as part of the Inner Rings. Compare to the **Outer Rings**.*

J

Jade Region

*A **Region** of **Electua District** where customs and traditions associated with **Old World** Asian cultures thrive together.*

L

Life Credit, LC

*The official system of currency in **Dominion City**. Each **Citizen** comes into possession of a digital Life Credit account upon first **Registration**, archived by **The Dominion Corporation**. Allowing one's Life Credit account to drop to zero is a **Violation of Protocol** and registers a Citizen for **Termination** upon next identification by a **Protocol Enforcement Unit**.*

M

The Malaang

*An unofficial **Region** of **Reshen District**, ceded from **West Edge** and occupied by the **Volnikaans**.*

Meat Markets

*A neighborhood and business district within the **West Edge Region** of **Reshen District** where the primary industry is that of prosthetics, surgery, and body modification or enhancement. Although it technically resides within **West Edge**, it has been claimed and occupied by the **Malaang** and is governed by the **Volnikaans**.*

Meta-Terrania QuadroTrack

*A defunct **QuadroRacing** circuit in **Mid-City Electua**. The grounds of this track have fallen into a blindspot of the **Eye of Dominion** and become host to an illegal community of squatters and homeless.*

Mind-Transference

The process of implanting an organic or artificial sentient mind into a different or new body. When forced, this process is called brainjacking.

Mid-City

A large **Region** of **Electua District**, and the Region of **Dominion City** with the highest **Citizen Termination** rate per capita. Mid-City is home to a wide range of **Citizen** cultures, and like most of Electua is subject to heavy smog, rain, and dense population.

N

Nanocig

A popular vice among **Citizens**, similar to cigarettes, although nanocigs function by providing a flood of heat-activated nanobots into the bloodstream.

The NeoLux

A **Region** of **Quadro District** known for its mesmerizing use of neon lights, clean infrastructure, and lively atmosphere.

NightRunners

Young foot-soldiers employed by **Glade Syndicate** member Maybe. NightRunners are trained in various skills that allow them to operate within **Dominion City** as couriers, assassins, and infiltration and espionage agents. Such skills include stealth, crowdthreading, climbing, breaking and entering, efficient combat, navigation, and more.

O

Old World

Used in reference to anything created or existing in the style of **Pre-Fall** Earth. The possession of such contraband is a **Violation of Protocol**.

Outer Rings

A term used by **Citizens** to refer to **Districts** 5-7 (Electua, Reshen, and Disestro), these rings being the most neglected and in poor condition.

Outer Wall

The circular wall encompassing **Dominion City** and protecting it from the **Wasteland**.

P

Prosthetics

Artificial limbs or body parts that have been surgically attached to a **Citizen** in place of an organic one. Prosthetics within **Dominion City** are part of a giant bodily modification industry, take a large number of forms, and are generally legal.

Protocol

*The compulsory prime directive, philosophy, spiritual doctrine, and law set forth by **The Dominion Corporation** to guide all progress of **Dominion City**. **Protocol** is represented in both State and **Citizen** through the **Four-Fold Manifest Path**, and put in place to honor the **Unfolding**. **Violation of Protocol** is subject to **Discipline** by means of **Citizen Termination**.*

Protocol Enforcement Units

*Extensions of the **Tetra Security Department**, **Protocol Enforcement Units** are autonomous meta-droids with various functions that patrol **Dominion City** and ensure that **Citizen Protocol** is being maintained.*

Q

QuadroRacing

*An immensely popular form of racing entertainment in **Dominion City** based primarily in **Quadro District**. In this sport, QuadroRacers pilot crafts known as QuadroBikes and risk their lives daily, racing around difficult tracks at high speeds, sometimes using weapons to disable other Racers.*

R

The Realm

*The officially sanctioned **VRnet** of **Dominion City**, provided at no cost by **The Dominion Corporation**. Within the **virtual reality** hub of **The Realm**, private corporations have been given the freedom to design pay-to-play **RealmWorlds**, where **Citizens** can experience lush adventures in universes that span many different genres.*

Realmdweller

*A derogatory term used to describe a **Citizen** that has become addicted or dependent on interaction with the **virtual reality** of **The Realm**. Such **Citizens**, when human, often confine themselves to **VR pods** or begin replacing their bodies with synthetic parts to allow longer periods of physical dormancy while immersed in VR.*

RealmWorld

*An independent virtual universe within the larger **VRnet** of **The Realm**. Each RealmWorld is meticulously created by **The Dominion Corporation** or in cooperation with other major developers, and each possesses its own laws of physics, history, and universal rules.*

RealmSpace

A term used by ***Realm*** *programmers to refer to the virtual programming space of* ***The Realm****, where many* ***RealmWorlds*** *can be accessed.*

RealmSquare Brokerage

A firm based in ***Quadro District*** *that makes its profits buying and selling the minds and bodies of bankrupt* ***Realm-Users****.*

RealSpace

A term used to refer to the "real world", Dominion City, outside of the Realm.

Red Industries

A private security company headquartered in ***Tetra District****. Its CEO is Stefan Wilhemson.*

Region

Within ***District Rings****,* ***Regions*** *are self-designated municipalities that have been established officially or unofficially.*

Registered/Unregistered

Upon birth, all sentient beings within ***Dominion City*** *are required to apply for Registration with* ***The Dominion Corporation****. Once Registered, a resident becomes a* ***Citizen*** *and is granted a* ***Life Credit*** *account and all freedoms associated with Registration. Remaining Unregistered within Dominion City is a* ***Violation of Protocol*** *and subject to* ***Termination****.*

S

Self-Termination

In ***Dominion City****, Self-Termination is a form of* ***Citizen Sacrifice*** *in which a* ***Citizen*** *forfeits their own life functions, so that nutrition, electricity, oil and resources may be applied to other Citizens. As a part of* ***Infrastructure****, the* ***Dominion Corporation*** *offers complimentary* ***Yellow Kiosks*** *to assist in Self-Termination.*

Slice of Life Pizzeria

A local pizza joint in ***Teradin, Mid-City Electua****.*

SouthTown

A province of ***Mid-City Electua****.*

Starlight Sector

A small-sized ***Region*** *of* ***Quadro District*** *where intimate clubs, high fashion, and skilled musicianship proliferate.*

State Security

The active armed military police forces of ***The Dominion Corporation****. These Officers consist of both human and droid, and perform a variety of services within* ***Dominion City*** *including: responding to complex situations regarding higher-level strategy, establishing bases in areas needing military presence, guarding Dominion City via the* ***Outer Wall****, patrolling* ***Tetra District****,* manning surveillance systems, performing reconnaissance and scouting in the **Wasteland** outside the City, and performing other tasks that **Protocol Enforcement Units** are unable or not suited for.

Sub-Credit

*The most prominent of several illegal underground currencies used primarily in the **Outer Rings**. Sub-Credits maintain a market of their own and are transferred via chip-strips, unlike **Life Credits** which are entirely digital. Sub-Credits allow **Unregistered Citizens** and **Protocol Violators** to continue to make a living despite their official status.*

Synth

*An **artificially intelligent** mind crafted or procedurally generated for a specific **RealmWorld**. These synthetic beings are programmed to believe that their virtual reality is true reality, although they have the ability to gain awareness of the larger **Realm**, exit their respective **RealmWorlds**, and even downlink into a physical body within **Dominion City**. This state of rejection of one's birth reality is known as becoming "woke".*

T

Teradin

*A province within **Mid-City Electua** known for its low rates of **Protocol Violation** and **Citizen Termination**. It is also a hub of hydroponic agriculture, as seen in its locally famous Soy Markets.*

Tetra Worship

*One of four **Sectors of Tetra**. The Worship Sector concerns itself with the ideals of **Faith**, professing the word of **Protocol**, administering divine judgment, and spreading welfare to impoverished areas.*

Tetra Justice

*One of four **Sectors of Tetra**. The Justice Sector concerns itself with upholding **Protocol** within the **Citizenry** as well as overseeing the **Infrastructure** of the **City**.*

Tetra Medical

*One of four **Sectors of Tetra**. The Medical Sector concerns itself with the physical and mental care of **Citizens** as well as the goals of **Dominion Science**.*

Tetra Security

*One of four **Sectors of Tetra**. The Security Sector concerns itself with the safety and security of **Dominion City** by enforcing **Protocol** and carrying out the orders of the High Director and his Commanders.*

Tracker Unit

*A **Protocol Enforcement Unit** programmed to surveil a single **Citizen** or group from the air. Trackers are relatively small and tend to remain high above city* *activity while performing their duties.*

Transhuman Paradise, THP

*An area of **Uptown Quadro** where high-quality body-modification, prosthesis, and mind-transference are common, creating a highly unique population where the boundaries of identity are blurred.*

U

The Unfolding

[illegible]

Uplink

*To insert one's consciousness into a **virtual reality network**; to enter a simulation.*

V

Violation of Protocol

*Any act which contradicts the ordinances set forth by **Protocol**. The consequence for any Violation of Protocol is **Citizen Termination**.*

Virtual Reality

*The use of electronics to simulate an artificial subjective reality. This technology has many uses including digital escapism, gaming, various training purposes, remote operation, learning, and more. Virtual reality in **Dominion City**, especially in cooperation with **The Realm**, is a major entertainment industry.*

Voice of Dominion

*The official term used to describe the automated response system of **The Dominion Corporation** in the form of a female voice for general purposes, and a male voice for **Protocol Enforcement** purposes.*

Volnikaans

*A criminal organization managed by Lord Volnik based within its own self-declared **Region** of **Reshen District** called **The Malaang**. This group practices a system in which new members are deprived of their limbs and eyes, and must earn prosthetic replacements through obedient service.*

VRnet

*A network of information presented to the end user as an interconnected, navigable system of **virtual reality** experiences. Such a network is similar to the Internet of **Old World** Earth.*

VR Pod

*A container in which a **Citizen** rests, where access to virtual reality is provided* *as well as bodily nutrition and waste services. Using a **VR pod**, a Citizen is able to extend a stay in **VR** indefinitely.*

W

Wasteland

*The uninhabitable land outside of **Dominion City**. This claim by **The Dominion Corporation** is often disputed, despite video of **State Security** operations in the **Wasteland** being available to the general public. These lands are referred to as "the Negative" among Dominion personnel.*

West Edge

*A major **Region** of **Reshen District**. Known for its potent and dangerous drugs, heavy body modification among **Citizens**, and deadly competitions such as the fighting in the Blood Grounds arena, the **West Edge** is considered one of the most dangerous Regions of the innermost six **Districts**.*

The NightRunner Chronicles
continues with...
WANDERLUST 2.0

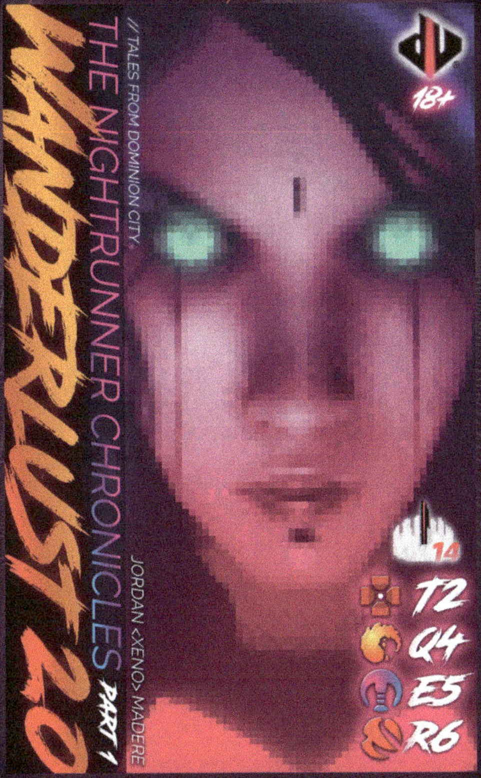

(spoilers!)

NO MERCY FOR THE TRAITOR

Lied to. Manipulated. Killed.

Through the quantum memory drive of The Glade, Wander is alive again, though not as she once was. Maybe and the Glade Syndicate have altered her, turning her into the purest kind of killing machine: one without the distraction of emotion.

The last remnants of that distraction are lost, waiting to be found. Zef is out there somewhere, and Wander is on deadly mission to seek out and destroy him, before he can compromise everything he left behind.

Now, with the rest of the NightRunners kidnapped and only one objective on her mind, Wander's final hope for lasting sanity is that everything is as it seems.

Unfortunately in Dominion City, such is never the case.

Upcoming books in the DOMINION UNIVERSE

Novels:

The NightRunner Chronicles: WANDERLUST 2.0

Left to die in the street, Wander is given a second chance at life with the help of Glade technology. Unfortunately, shels been stripped of her most vital memories by those who claim to have her best interest in mind... What even is life without the ability to love?

The NightRunner Chronicles: MEMORY DRIVE

Uploaded into wetware storage just seconds before death, Zef now finds himself at the mercy of another's mind. Slowly but surely he's taking control, but also learning terrible secrets in the process. Truly, nothing and no one in Dominion City is what they claim to be...

Short Stories:

Tales from Dominion City: DYSTOPIAS

Forbidden love in the bio-labs of Tetra, cloned officers in Quadro, cannibals in Disestro, a monk's story in Percarus. QuadroRacers, musicians, pitfighters and virtual reality. Uplink into two dozen stories set in all seven brutal and varied Districts of Dominion City.

Coloring Books:

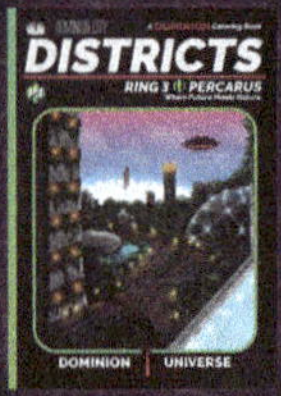

Dominion City DISTRICTS - Ring 3: PERCARUS

Almost a perfect utopia, Percarus is the true definition of nature meets future. Break out your color pencils for this tour of the 3rd District of Dominion City, with the first in a series of coloring books that will explore the many vistas of the seven Districts.

The Realm: The INTERGALACTIC ZOO

Zef and Wander have only casually explored it, but you get to dive deep into The Intergalactic Zoo as a full explorer. Find out what strange planets and bizarre creatures await you on this virtual reality tour of the most odd and unique places in the galaxy!

DOMINION UNIVERSE continues to unfold...

The DCRPG

Dominion City Discord RPG Experience

Enter and interact with the world of the NightRunners, the Dominion Corporation, and so much more! Create a PC and be a part of Dominion City lore!

Join us! discord.gg/invite/WelcomeToDominionCity

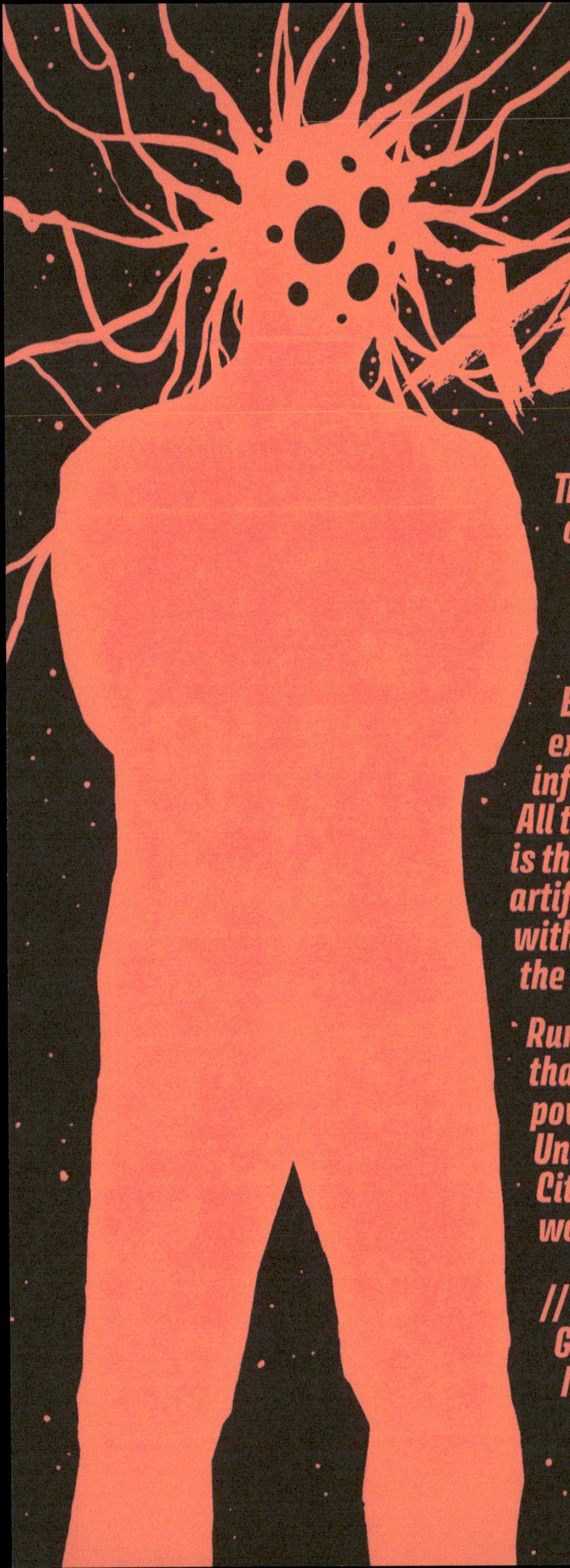

XENO UNIT

The Xeno Unit, Xeno, or more commonly "X", is known only to the few highest members of Tetra Command.

Even for those close to X, an extremely limited amount of information has been gathered. All that's sure and confirmed is that X is a sentient DCORP artificial intelligence, tasked with creating and maintaining the Dominion Archive.

Rumors and whispers imply that the X Unit may be the sole power source of Dominion Universe, and that Dominion City and all it encompasses wouldn't exist without him.

// Kozollyon, aka
Greater Commander
Martin Holloway

Chief Blackwood of the Reshen PD sits deep inside the Police Department Basement, his body overheating as he once again plugs himself into his army of droids spread across Reshen, exhaustion claiming both his human body and Synth consciousness.
The Dominion Corporation had finally done away with the X-51 virus, though now a young man has turned up on the Sanctuary doorstep with the head of an infected droid. Will RPD Chief Blackwood and Patom report this to D-CORP?
SANCTUARY

CPSIA information can be obtained
at www.ICGtesting.com
Printed in the USA
BVHW020920060922
646307BV00008B/439

9 781951 890384